1961

A NOVEL

PETER DANN

ISBN-13: 978-0-6455429-0-5 (Paperback edition)

ISBN-13: 978-0-6455429-1-2 (Ebook edition)

10 9 8 7 6 5 4 3 2

For Marilyn, light of my life

CHAPTER ONE

H is mother says his father is staying at the sawmill office, but he doesn't quite believe her. There's no office at the sawmill. There's a shed where Gint McCreedy sits at his sloping table making cigarettes all day, poking loose bits of tobacco with a matchstick. Sometimes Gint answers the phone, or screws up bits of paper and throws them in the bin. This shed is not an office, though. And why would his father need to keep his eye on Gint McCreedy's pencils and ash tray anyway? There isn't even a bed in Gint McCreedy's shed. His father must be staying somewhere else.

"It doesn't matter where he's staying, Ralph," his mother says. "The point is, he's not here."

"But why?"

"There's twenty-six letters in our alphabet, and so help me, if I hear this one again, I'll scream."

"It's not a letter. It's a word."

She never listens though.

When she finally makes her great announcement, Grandpa Doc throws back his head and snorts. He can see the plastic thing his grandpa's teeth are glued to.

"I take it that's your considered opinion then," his mother says.

"You try your luck, girlie. You just try your luck. You don't know a good thing when you see it."

She gives him half an hour to run across the paddock and tell Stevie Bell, and then he has to help. They gather up his father's things and dump them in the little room behind the garage, on the concrete floor. His father's saddle. All his father's clothes. His hats and boots. His pool cue.

"He can come and get it when he's good and ready," his mother says. "Grandpa Doc won't have to be here. And you remember, Ralph, we're both your parents. You can't have favourites, you know."

It's just another thing she has completely wrong.

———

THE DAY THEY LEAVE KARNOOK, Grandpa Doc is supposed to come back home to see them off.

"I'll ring the surgery," she tells him over breakfast. "You can leave your patients for half an hour, I'm sure."

These certainties his mother invents, they seem like iron rules to her. She's rung the surgery, though, and Grandpa Doc has not come home.

The Consul is parked in the drive by the verandah steps. His mother bustles in and out, carrying the last bags and boxes. Between the rose beds, Mr Vernon is bent over his Victa, pulling on the cord, cursing the bloody thing. It's only half past nine, but it's going to be a stinker by the forecast.

Already sweat is staining Mr Vernon's old man's navy singlet. Mr Vernon wants to get the doctor's lawns done early so he can get his hands around the long brown bottle Grandpa Doc has left him in the fridge.

He leans back in the wicker chair and stretches out his legs. The only part of him the sun can reach now is his sandals. The verandah shades all else.

He gazes down the long pale drive between the pines to where his grandpa's Jag may soon appear, or not appear, depending on the actual state of things right now. Up in the pine tops, the crows caw and flap. Mr Vernon walks across the lawn towards his ute, shaking out his hand. The crows rise up and swirl, encircling each other, then flutter down and perch again not far from where they started.

His mother looms above him, her eyes hooded just like always when she makes this pretence of speaking to him. She never actually speaks to him, in fact. She speaks to his chest. Just half an hour ago, she called his chest a little narkypants.

"What are you planning for your tadpoles, Ralph?"

"Take them," he says.

He addresses her ankles.

"They'll only cook in the car. That's not what you want, is it?"

"I'll put ice blocks in."

"Grandpa Doc isn't going to look after them, Ralph. You should take them down the creek. That's what you'd want, isn't it, if you were a tadpole?"

"They're not the creeky kind of tadpoles."

"It'd be the kindest thing, Ralph."

The kindest thing. As if she cares. The kindest thing would be to stay right where they are. Get his father back.

Tell him she's sorry. But she never will say that. Not to Grandpa Doc, not to himself, and never to his father. She is not a sorry-saying kind of person.

His tadpole tank is by the tap under the study window. The kindest thing. He raises the glass box. Water spills onto the garden bed. He drags out the slippery weed in handfuls and tosses it aside, then upends the tank entirely. The flapping bodies leap and skitter even as his heel descends on them.

By ten fifteen, their car is packed, its tyres are crunching gravel in the driveway. Only Mr Vernon is there to offer a farewell, a severed carburettor raised in his left hand.

———

THEY DRIVE IN HEAT, his mother behind clip-on sunshades, stiff-armed at the wheel. He holds the map across his thighs as a sunshield, refolding the concertina each time they cross another crease. From time to time, he counts out miles elapsed and miles to go, trying to punish her, but she ignores him.

They cross the Murray River, and now the roads are marked in white instead of yellow. A new state. Is this their brand new life? It doesn't look too different to him.

They take their rest breaks trampling down long grass beside the road. His mother will not stop at shops because they are economising. In Karnook main street, though, she stopped at Cantwells, and Stuka Williams came out, carrying a blue jug and a handbag thing. Now it turns out this handbag thing is called a water bag, fixed onto their bumper bar. Lovely cool water, his mother tells him. Like the swagmen used to drink. Like water soaked in carpet, actually. His father never would have drunk such stuff, he's sure, and his father is a proper countryman. She doesn't know a thing, his mother. To eat, she's brought tomato sandwiches and fruit, her usual yucky stuff. This is her religion, what is good for you. The bread is sodden, and the pepper sets him coughing.

By afternoon, the sun is on his mother's neck and shoulders and it's his turn in the shade. The paddocks pass like sliding doormats. Haysheds slant under the sun, their stuffing spilling out. Sheep cluster in pitted shallows that once were dams, while shimmering roofs float on the horizon. Occasionally he glimpses a thread of steel, but never a wagon or locomotive. He has tired of counting out accusatory miles. Conversation in the car has long since ceased.

The steel towers are the first sign that they are getting close. The pylons stride like scarecrows over the paddocks, looped together with skipping ropes of wire that lose themselves in a distant smudge of mountains.

He will not forget this day. He will not forget, and he will not forgive.

———

THEY CRAWL ALONG A NARROW LANE. His mother hugs the steering wheel and peers up through the windscreen. Weeds pass on either side. Fragments of jutting brick poke at the Consul's tyres. They scrape by a stack of discarded pine branches, browning needles threaded with Christmas glitter.

Beyond paling fences on their right, a long expanse of brickwork, red and angry, rises up two stories high, reflecting back the heat of the declining sun. Wooden staircases zig-zag up to protruding porches.

"You said it would be good," he says. "You said apartment."

"We will have an apartment, Ralph."

"I'm going home."

The car lurches to a halt.

"You said apartment," he says. "Like in America. These are just upstairs shop places."

"I never said America."

"You said apartment."

"Apartment just means place, Ralph. That's all it means."

"I'm not staying here. It's crap."

"What are you going to do? Walk home?"

"I'll get the train. Grandpa Doc can get me at the station."

"And I'm going to buy a ticket, am I? You really think Grandpa Doc can be bothered looking after you?"

"Grandpa Doc and Dad."

"That isn't going to happen, Ralph. This is our home now."

"We have a home."

"We don't, Ralph, actually. Grandpa Doc's has never been our home. Grandpa Doc's was only ever temporary."

"We've always lived there."

"It was never our intention."

"We still lived there."

"Yes, and now we're going to live here."

"So why can't Dad be with us too?"

"We're not getting into that again."

"Because he has to think about things."

"He does. And thinking is not your father's strong suit."

"It's just a car."

"The car is the least of it, Ralph. There's other things."

"Barney Hill."

"You really are our Little Mr Big Ears, aren't you. I'm not discussing Barney Hill, Ralph. We've come all this way. You haven't even seen our apartment yet."

"Have you?"

"I don't need to, Ralph. I've talked to Mrs Green. It's furnished. It has two bedrooms. And it's near enough to Dr Schlimmicht's. Plus there's the shops."

"It's a dump."

"Ralph, I know you've heard things. Grandpa Doc, I don't know what he fills your head with, but I do know this. You can't believe a single word he says. You seem to think I'm the most awful mother a boy ever had. Well let me tell you this. There's a lot worse could have happened to you than having me for a mother. Now go and make yourself useful and find Mrs Green while I find us the gate. It's Zelda's. Zelda's Gowns."

He gets out, bangs the door.

Gates and paling fences stretch out on his right. Squeezed behind are narrow yards, dominated by the high brick wall. On his left are single-story factories and work-shops, shabby affairs of brick and fibro with flattish roofs. Somewhere above, a vent is squeaking as it turns. A trickling sound escapes a louvre window covered by iron bars.

He leaves the lane and walks round to the shops, where he finds Zelda's Gowns.

As he enters the shop, the fluorescents are going off one after another. He is left standing in a musty gloom, surrounded by gaping mannequins. A smell of fabric hangs in the air.

"You must be the boy."

A bulbous figure looms out of the shadows.

"I've been waiting for you."

The speaker is an oversized parcel, her wrapping near to coming adrift. Under a sweaty brow, her eyes are small and grey, while her cheeks are like river deltas of capillaries.

"My mum says you should let us in."

"So what's the story? There going to be the three of you, or just the two?"

"Two what?"

"It's not a test, tuppence. Is your father with you or not? That's all I want to know."

"He's coming later. He has to think about some things."

"Is there a lot for him to think about?"

"I don't know."

The bulbous figure leans in close and pokes his breastbone.

"I'll tell you this for nothing, sonny Jim. A man who has to think about things, he isn't worth the paper he's written on. There's a word for the wise from Mrs Green. Now you run along. I'll be out directly."

"Can I go through the back?"

"Don't you even think of it. I could have my ladies back there, taking off their clothes."

"They're not there now."

"They might be in the dark, for all you know. Go on. You run along."

He returns the way he came. As he turns into the lane, the dumpy tub is there before him, waving after the retreating Consul.

"A little!" shouts Mrs Green. "Back up a little, woman!"

The Consul brakes.

He comes up to Mrs Green as she flaps her bodice against the heat, her jelly arms aquiver. By the full light of day, the violets that enwrap her are iridescent.

"What a ning-nong, honestly!" says Mrs Green. Back up a little, I said! You brings her back here and I'll move my car, seeing she insists so. She could have fitted in quite easily."

Mrs Green hobbles towards a pale blue Humber, parked in the middle of a gravelled space behind her shop. She lurches from side to side with the grace of a vaulting horse. He waves to his mother to bring her car nearer.

Mrs Green flings open the Humber door, executes an awkward pivot, then throws herself back into the driver's seat with so much gusto her elephantine legs are left projecting through the open doorway. After much groaning, her ship is righted. A fleshy arm appears, grabs the handle of the door and pulls it shut. Puffs of smoke billow from the Humber's exhaust.

Back and forth the vehicle moves, with much heaving on the car's enormous steering wheel from Mrs Green, much braking and clutching as their landlady-to-be pursues her goal of surrendering the least possible ground with the greatest possible show of effort.

The Humber lurches in jolts and starts until a tiny morsel of territory is finally conceded and the Humber's burbling ceases. The driver's door swings open and the human vaulting horse begins to extricate herself, wisps of wrapping displaced and repositioned as circumstance and modesty require, until at last Mrs Green is vertical and more or less in functioning order.

"There!" says Mrs Green. "All quite unnecessary. Still, a welcome is a welcome, I suppose."

His mother pulls in, squeezing the Consul into the narrow space Mrs Green has given up. Moments later, the women greet each other formally under the stairs, then start in with that huff and blather his mother and women like her seem to find essential while summing up a new adversary.

At last Mrs Green produces a set of keys and they start up the stairs.

When they reach the upper landing, Mrs Green's poor heavy bones demand she pause to catch her breath. He takes the opportunity to look out over the lane towards the declining sun.

They are at the top of a long rise, much higher than he realised. Beyond the workshops and factories, the land dips out of sight, then comes into view again a mile or so away. He can make out a patchwork of streets and houses there, and beyond that built-up area, a smear of bushland, grey and olive. Past this wilderness, an escarpment rises up, along whose ridge he recognises the silhouettes of tiny roof tops. Above these, a glint of something airborne — a tiny, silent aircraft, drifting towards the horizon.

He turns to find himself alone on the empty landing, the porch door ajar.

———

IT TAKES ONLY the briefest glance into five ill-smelling rooms to confirm his worst suspicions. Shouting and tears follow this, then promises of non-specific compensations somewhere over the horizon. After all this needless upset, there is fish and chips from the local shop, a banana split with caramel sauce, and the making up of beds. He declines his mother's offer of a bath in the yucky pink tub jammed against the yucky pink toilet, and lies at last in a stranger's bed, his dressing gown and shirts hanging in a stranger's wardrobe. His bedlamp, flannel sheets and bedspread, these are all familiar, but his real treasures — his crystal set, his aero engine, his encyclopedias and Meccano — these are packed, still, in the cardboard box that lies unopened on bare boards in the corner of the long, narrow room.

There is no point in opening this box. His father must and will appear. He will show up and tell his mother, once and for all, You cannot go on doing this. You cannot go on spoiling all our lives. Now pack up everything, because we're going home.

He lies in bed, eyes open, and he waits.

CHAPTER TWO

She aims to break him down, but won't do anything too suddenly. She's cleverer than that. Probably she will stop arguing back. She will say she understands. Above all, she will make out everything is normal. He will not let that be, however. Normal is the way things were before.

It's not the car, she says. But it is the car, it must be. It's all about the car. Then under that, it's how they tricked his mother into coming back from Queensland with her baby, which was him, and then it turned out Grandma wasn't even ill, or if she was ill, wasn't dying, or if she was dying, in the end, she was taking so long about it she may as well not have bothered. His mum and Grandpa Doc, the whole time screaming, fighting. It wasn't his dad in all those arguments. His mum and Grandpa Doc, at each other like cats on heat, and she calls him Little Mr Big Ears. You'd have to have been deaf in Grandpa's house not to have heard the shouting.

It's not the car. Of course it's the car. The little Hillman all smashed up in Grandpa Doc's garage right now, it's headlight hanging out, its bumper twisted and front corner all stoved in. That little Hillman — Grandpa's stupid, pointless offering when his wife really was finally dying, when there was no chance at all she'd ever get to drive it. But Grandpa Doc had to give his wife this lady's car with its two-tone duco and leather seats, its walnut dashboard and its silver dashboard clock. Hand delivered, all the way from Albury. They came out on the verandah to greet the service driver with his white gloves — and three weeks later Grandma was dead.

At least his mother got to drive the Minx. She was allowed to drive it into Karnook on the afternoons she helped out at the surgery. Other days as well, if Mrs Rogers was indisposed. She could take it shopping, too, but that was it. Grandpa Doc didn't want the Minx getting all clapped out. Scuffed. Dirtied. Taken for granted. Mr Vernon had to brush the Hillman's carpets every fortnight, and then a shade wash in the garage with suds and sponge, and then a rinse with just the hose. It was like the mousey little woman Grandpa Doc had dominated half a lifetime had become this little Hillman Minx, sidled up to his long black Jag in gleaming deference. That his own father could not drive the Minx went without saying.

So many things about his father went without saying. They had a set against him, basically. Grandpa Doc was forthright in his scepticism. Grandma was cooler, but even so she never said too much about the whole business, which was their way of referencing his own arrival in the world. His father was disappointing — he didn't need big ears to work that out. Wouldn't work in an iron lung. He heard that one long, rainy afternoon when Grandpa Doc and Johnnie Walker had spent a bit too much time in each other's company.

This beef was always there, just beneath the surface.

Got anything coming up, Ray?

Hear there's another road contract going out past Brigalong, Ray.

It wasn't like his dad never got work. Fencing. Raising a shed. Digging out rabbit burrows. The odd shift at the Carter's Arms. He wasn't a total slackarse. He just didn't like certain kinds of work, that's all, the kinds the McGillycuddys regarded as a proper job. Serving in some shop. Sitting in some office. And what would have been the point? His father couldn't type. He couldn't spell. He worked with his hands. They were ashamed of him, that's what it all boiled down to.

His mother, too — they were ashamed of her. Ashamed of her rank stupidity. In their hearts, they must have known their Rose hadn't been taken advantage of. The whole mess in that outback hospital, she got herself into that all of her own free will, and if Ray Halliday chose her, then she just as surely chose him. The man had a broken pelvis, for God's sake! her father used to rant. Meaning what? She had fallen for her cowboy. It was pretty simple, wasn't it?

Or was it simple? Did Rose want Ray, or did she really want to stick one up her parents, prove to the whole of northwest Queensland she didn't give a damn what Dr and Mrs McGillycuddy were thinking a thousand miles away?

If so, she certainly made her point. Made it in spades when they brought in Rockin' Ray in the back of a poddy truck, straight from the rodeo. Saw her chance then, Rose.

Hadn't even used the portable x-ray machine before. Only been in the hospital six weeks, green as they come, but the duty doctor wouldn't lay a finger on Rockin' Ray till they had some pictures, so Rose had to learn fast. She did learn fast, too. Ten months later, he was born.

All of this, Little Mr Big Ears has put together from a scrap here, a scrap there. What he has never worked out, though, is what can be the glue that holds this family together where no-one likes each other in the least. What is he missing? And still there is the mystery of the car, the broken little Minx in Grandpa Doc's garage.

His father never should have taken her, he understands that much. It's hardly stealing, though, when your own wife drives a car three days a week. And it's not like anyone ever said out loud he couldn't drive it. There was this under-standing, that was all. But what if his dad never had this understanding? Did they ever think of that?

Every Friday night, they all went down the Carter's Arms and drank — Barney Hill and Boysie, all that lot. The useless tools, his mother called them.

This Friday night, his dad and all the useless tools decide they'll go to Boysie's after closing time — out to Seven Mile Creek, where Boysie's had his tent up ever since his missus threw him out. They can hardly walk that far, not with a carton, so his dad shoots home and sneaks inside and gets the car keys. And it isn't like he takes the Jag. He takes the Minx, that's all. Then him and all the useless tools go out to Boysie's and they sit in the bottom of the creek and drink the carton.

This isn't the problem, though. The problem is what happens next. Boysie and the other useless tools decide they want to have a sleep down in the creek bed, but his dad and Barney Hill don't want to lie down in the creek. They want to get in the Hillman Minx. They want to go on back to Karnook. Which they do, except they go a funny way. They go a really funny way. They go along the Wooruk Road, and the Wooruk Road doesn't go anywhere near Karnook. It just goes out to this bunch of ironbarks they call the Wooruk Forest. His dad and Barney Hill, they're driving down this Wooruk Road in the dark, and suddenly this tree jumps out and smashes up his grandma's Minx.

His mother is that mad when she finds out. Barney Hill! she wails out. Of all the people in this world, Ray! Barney Hill!

Is it really not the car? If they're not here because of Grandma's Hillman Minx, then why on earth are they here at all?

———

IN THE PETER STUYVESANT ADVERTISEMENTS, the tall blonde skinny lady lives in an apartment. All her walls are pale, and all her rooms are high and filled with light. Through her open windows, she can see the other skyscrapers where all the other tall and skinny people live who smoke their cigarettes. Across the water, there's a lady statue with a torch that you can climb right up inside. That's an apartment.

Mrs Green's place is no apartment. It's a hole. In the central passageway, the only daylight leaks from other rooms or sneaks in from the porch. In their TV room, a lichen-spotted skylight admits a dreary greyness and there's no other window. Their bathroom is the same. In his own long, skinny bedroom, the only window is a little square of louvres high up at the end. In the kitchen, there's a window over the sink, but it won't open easily, and everything looks greenish from the lime gloss walls.

Only his mother's room has any decent windows. There are two of them, looking over Blessington Street. Immediately below these windows is the long verandah of the shops and the back face of the Zelda's Gowns sign, two bits of tin nailed on a wooden frame. Behind this sign are lumps of moss, a tennis racket handle, bits of flower pot and a plastic globe no bigger than a golf ball, drilled with holes.

His mother says the smell in their apartment is from must. She says This place just needs somebody living in it. One day she lugs a mop and bucket up the stairs and mops the lino in the kitchen and the bathroom and the passageways, then props the kitchen window open with a milk bottle. She jams the back door open with a suitcase.

"You close up any place for long enough, you're bound to get a little odour," she tells him. "It's not anything."

Standing one day at his mother's window, he notices a woman at a second story window across the way. She is about his mother's age. She appears behind a flywire screen, blowing her smoke out through the mesh. His mother does not smoke because it is not good for you, but this woman is a different type. Most likely she is cynical and hard, just like he hopes to be himself one day, once he has worked out the trick of it, how to ensure no-one takes him lightly ever again.

To achieve an end like that, who would not be willing to do something that is not good for you occasionally?

———

He thinks a lot about his father. He wonders where he could be staying, how he's going with his thinking about things. His mother won't be drawn on any of this. As far as she's concerned, they're getting on with things.

"I'll tell you one thing," she says. "Your father isn't going to come and get you. You can give that one the kybosh. He hasn't the imagination."

She tries to make out everything is fine. She'll be starting her new job soon, and that will be wonderful. And in a few weeks, he'll be starting school.

She slips up, though, one afternoon when he's complaining yet again about this dump she's brought them to. She really lashes out.

"You think I'm such a dummy I can't find a proper place for us to live, don't you. You haven't heard yet how I crunched Mrs Green about our rent."

This is leading to some trap, he's sure. Another tale of how his mother got the better of some shopkeeper. Got in the last word.

"How?" he says.

This should have been her cue, but suddenly she falters.

"You're going to get all thing," she says. "I know you are."

"All thing about what?"

"We never can have a mature, sensible conversation."

"I aren't going to get all thing."

"You promise?"

He promises.

"OK. Well, you remember the day I came down to Melbourne on the train for my interview with Dr Schlimmicht? You probably didn't even notice, you're so off in your own little world. Anyway I did, and once my interview went off so well, I thought, well, now I'm going to have to find us somewhere to live, and I had the advertisement for this place in my purse, you see. So then I came round here and looked in through the window, but that didn't tell me much, because we weren't going to live in the dress shop, were we? I could have asked for a look through upstairs, obviously — but then I thought how can I get the lowdown on this place before I talk to Mrs Green? I mean, what if there are awful neighbours or something like that? So then it occurred to me about the milk bar."

"Is this a long story?"

"Do you want to know all this or not?"

"All the other stuff I don't."

"It only takes so long because you keep on interrupting."

"Go on," he says.

"So anyway, young-man-who-knows-everything-already, you can't just go barging into a milk bar and say Give me all the lowdown on so-and-so. You have to be a bit subtler than that. You have to understand the way to talk to people — and your mother, believe it or not, just has that knack, on account of I've dealt with so many difficult people in my life. People like your grandfather. You'll say I'm boasting, but I can tell you within five minutes I had that milk bar woman eating out of the palm of my hand. Showing me photos of her grandchildren, she was. Postcards from her trip to Ayers Rock. So then I mentioned how I was interested in this apartment, and she just blurted out about the... well, there was this heat wave, you remember, and the old fellow, it took so long to find him."

"What old fellow?" he says. "What do you mean?"

"Well, he was dead. That's obvious, isn't it?"

"Dead how?"

"Ralph, there must be a million ways to die. The human body, it's just like an old clock sometimes. It winds down. And we all have to die sometime. It's nothing to be afraid of."

"But how did he die? What happened?"

"Ralph, that is not the point of this story. The whole point is your mother is not the complete idiot you take her for. Once I found out no-one would take this place on account of ... Well, it's all gone now, obviously, but for quite some time, apparently, there was a..."

"Was a what?"

"It's a perfectly natural process, Ralph. Just think about the pumpkins from Grandpa Doc's veggie garden, how we used to store them in the second laundry, and then sometimes... When a body dies, it just becomes a part of nature, Ralph. There are these chemicals, we call them enzymes..."

"Where did he die?"

"I don't know all the details, Ralph."

"Was it in my room?"

"Ralph, you said you wouldn't do this."

"You said there wasn't a smell! You said it was must!"

"And you said we would have a sensible conversation!"

"Did he die in my room?"

"Ralph, all I know for sure is that it couldn't possibly have been in your room. I distinctly remember asking Mrs Green if the gentleman happened to be found in the back bedroom."

"And?"

"Well, you've met Mrs Green, Ralph. She's not exactly a picture of clarity on all points."

"So he could have died in my room."

"Ralph, it doesn't matter where a person dies. The point

we should be focusing on is now we have a place we can afford. That is a good thing, and no small achievement on my part. I really think you owe me some kind of gratitude for this."

Gratitude? For all this bullcrap about must, and how she's always liked fresh air and windows open? They've still got the milk bottle propping up the kitchen window.

Grandpa's pumpkins, he remembers those. Pumpkins and more pumpkins, stacked up in the second laundry in case a war with atom bombs broke out. He'd rather die than eat a pumpkin, but Grandma liked to roast one now and then, and it would be his job to go and lift one from the stack. Oozing from the bottom of the stack, more often than not, was a brownish puddle. All those old clock pumpkins, winding down.

There are many stains at Mrs Green's not properly accounted for. The floorboards in his bedroom. The lino in the kitchen and passageways and bathroom. The carpet in the TV room. All bear stains of dubious origin. He works his way on hands and knees, stooping and inhaling under the kitchen table, beside his mother's bed, in the narrow gap between the toilet and the bath. So many of his sniffs suggest the worst, but none is quite decisive.

Could the milk bar lady tell him more? He pays a visit. There's a woman behind the counter, but he cannot see a single postcard of Ayers Rock, and this woman is too young for grandchildren. She might know something all the same, but how is he supposed to ask? In the end, it is the woman who speaks first. He points to cobblers and milk bottles, snakes and aniseed squares, then pays his shilling.

Later, in the lime green kitchen, he chews on emerald

snakes and gazes at the lino's darkest streaks, quietly grateful for the milk bottle still propping up the window.

———

HIS MOTHER, chooser of all things, has chosen him a school. He'll like it, she has declared. He's going to the tech.

"You're just not one of these boys who wants to learn French and trigonometry, are you Ralph?" she says. "Engines and airguns, that's the kind of thing you like. Things that go bang. Things you can touch. That's what tech school's all about. You'll be able to drill things and bang things all day long, and there'll be lots of kids who'll be real strugglers. You could be a star."

"I don't want to be a star."

"If you and Mr Boyd had got on better in grade five, it might be a different story."

"Mr Boyd was horrible."

"All the other boys and girls still learned their decimals, Ralph. Their parents weren't called in for a little talk."

"It doesn't matter about decimals."

She says they have to take a journey. It will be an adventure. They will go and see his school, then she wants to show him Dr Schlimmicht's clinic, where she'll soon be working.

They drive to Glendale Tech and pull up opposite the entrance. His mother asks if he would like to have a look around.

"It's a dump," he says.

A waist high chainmesh fence marks out a boundary. Behind the fence, a line of straggly bushes softens the facades of low flat buildings clad in concrete blocks. An elevated sawdust trap marks what must be the woodwork building.

"It'll look much better when there's people around," his mother says.

"Like our place."

"If you bring this nyah, nyah attitude to everything, Ralph, of course you're going to be disappointed. You want to get out, have a look at the playground?"

"I've seen it. It's all crap."

"You'll make lots of friends here, Ralph. You'll probably make friends you'll have for life."

"Can't wait," he says.

From here, they go to see the famous clinic where his mother will be taking all her x-rays. This clinic, it turns out, is just a house with concrete where the garden used to be. A red sign out the front says Schlimmicht Radiography.

"Is this it?" he says. "A house?"

"It's not a house inside, Ralph, it's a brand new clinic. This could be a whole new opportunity for us. People around here, they have to go to Ascot Vale to get an x-ray, or Broadmeadows. I'm going to be the public face of this new practice, Ralph. Dr Schlimmicht, he'll be relying on me. I'm the one who'll be seeing the patients. Dr Schlimmicht, he'll just be in the background. The patients will never see him in the least — and just as well, most likely."

"How come?"

"Well, he's a bit of a cold fish," she says. "I'm sure we can manage a professional relationship, though."

"Is he a Nazi?"

"What on earth would give you that idea?"

"Dr Schlimmicht."

"He's not a Nazi, Ralph. You can hardly hear an accent at all."

"Great."

"You don't sound the least enthusiastic."

He cannot stand how she is always making out like he is such a grump and she is such a positive personality. He always seems to lose this game where she's the umpire and declares herself the winner every time.

They go on home.

———

His resistances are crumbling, he can tell. In spite of everything, he's getting used to it. The dinginess. The Air-o-Pine to hide the smell. The having to go downstairs then up the lane to get to anywhere at all.

It's still a crummy dump, though, really. If Stevie Bell came on the train — if anyone would let him, if his mum could find a place for Stevie Bell to sleep — then Stevie wouldn't mince his words. It's shithouse, Spook, he'd say. Then Stevie could go home. He can't go anywhere, however. He's stuck.

He's had a look around the shops and they're pathetic. All the usual mum shops. There's a hardware shop, so that's OK. A pet shop, too, three puppies in the window. No model shop, though. No shop that's just for kids, unless you count the milk bar. It's so near the shops, his mother says. It's so convenient. Big bloody deal. There's shops in Karnook. They have shops everywhere.

He can't even find a way to get an aerial. In Karnook, he would lie in bed at night and listen to the quiz shows on his crystal set that Grandpa Doc had made for him. Bob Dyer and Jack Davey. All those questions about who wrote this book or that book where the answer was always Somerset Maugham. That religious nut with his mesmerising rrrrs, Garner Ted Armstrong. Arrrrmageddon. At the second carrrrming. And that warrrrter became wine.

In Karnook, he put his aerial up himself. A few weeks after Sputnik, climbed the old wisteria with the wire between his teeth. Grandpa Doc out in the driveway, supervising, till his mum came out and had hysterics. Just ignored her, kept on climbing anyway. A crystal set without an aerial is nothing. Tied the wire up to the chimney pot, and his crystal set worked perfectly.

At Mrs Green's there's no wisteria, and the roof is twice as high. An aerial's impossible, so his crystal set and headphones lie in the bottom of his wardrobe, and the worrrrkings of the Lorrrrd must go unheard.

One day he notices a pole. It's just a glimpse, a tiny tip of aluminium, and he has to step right back against the border of the lane to see that much, but this tip of aluminium is worth investigating. Once he gets around to Blessington Street and looks up from the far footpath, it's obvious what he must do.

There will be no hysterics this time. His mother is out. As he steps down from her bedroom window onto the verandah, his main concern is shoppers down below. If someone happens to look up and shouts, that could be difficult — but people rarely do look up, he knows. Even he didn't notice all the TV antennas on the roof before today.

Quiet and swift, that will be his method. Eyes down, coil of wire in one hand, string and scissors in the other, he makes his way, anxious to avoid the places where the metal might squeak.

On near inspection, the wooden ladder fixed to the wall turns out to be a flimsier affair than he had hoped, attached by mortar plugs that dribble sand when he gives the frame a shake. He climbs up anyway, his eyes fixed on the brickwork inches from his nose.

It takes forever, but at last he's peering over a balustrade at terracotta tiles and several poles and guys. He pulls himself over the top and tumbles into a box gutter. He lies here half a minute, breathing heavily, then gets up on his haunches. The balustrade is high enough to hide him, he thinks, so long as he is careful.

Hunching over, he pays out wire along the tiles, then takes a banana from his pocket and ties one end of wire around the fruit. Breaking cover, he strides up to the high point of the roof, whirls the banana around his head, then lets it fly in the direction of his own back yard. The slack wire whips and tautens, its other end wrapped around his fist.

He works fast. He ties a length of string onto his wire — the string's a crummy insulator, he knows, but it's all he's got — then ties that string onto the tallest of the aluminium poles, as high as he can get it.

Minutes later, he is climbing through his mother's window. He hurries down the stairs and has just reached the bottom when his mother drives in beside the fat blue Humber. He glances back to see his banana swinging in an arc halfway between the roof and ground.

His mother doesn't notice anything, apparently. He helps her carry up her shopping bags, then goes into his bedroom. He has just hoisted his chair onto his bed when he hears someone knocking on their porch door. After a few moments, his mother calls.

Two women are at the door. One is Mrs Green, still puffing on account of her heavy bones. The other woman — blonde, in pink, her hair tied back in a French roll — he's seen before behind a flywire screen.

Mrs Green gets to the point. This lady, she says, has just now seen a boy doing the most extraordinary things up on the roof. This lady felt she had a responsibility to make enquiries, and quite right. Someone could have been in danger. Someone could have been putting someone else in danger, too.

"It was something like that," the lady in the twinset says.

All eyes are on himself.

"Well?" his mother says.

It is perhaps not his finest hour. He starts off with the Sputnik, because that is where it all began, in fact. A satellite no bigger than a basketball, he tells the ladies, then how a rocket flies in stages, each one falling off as it ascends. This brings him to the thermionic valve, how there are five of these in his Grandpa's radiogram where they heard the Sputnik. He is just getting to the filaments when Mrs Green cuts him off.

"Do you have any idea the damage you could cause?" she says. "One tiny drop of water, that's all it takes. That drop gets in, then we have frost, they all go pop, and next thing we've got water pouring in. Then the wiring, that goes soft, and next thing after that we've got a fire. Have you begun to think about all this?"

His mother suggests he may not have. Mrs Green, though, is just getting started.

"It's all very well for me," she says. "My premiums are all paid up. It's a condition of my mortgage, as Mrs Bexley would know. This is Mrs Bexley, by the way. Mrs Bexley is our neighbour over the way, and you, young man, owe Mrs Bexley a debt of gratitude. This lady has possibly saved your life, if only we could be sure you'll never do a stupid thing like this again. I have my doubts, sadly, because young boys get up to all sorts when their fathers aren't around. I simply make that comment. A comment in the public interest. So come on now, young Edmund Hillary. What you got to say for yourself?"

He suggests there may not be any cracked tiles.

"But Mrs Bexley saw you!" says Mrs Green. "Saw you with her own eyes! You have been up there on our roof, haven't you?"

"A little bit," he says.

"A little bit? How can you be on a roof a little bit? You're either up on a roof or you're not. Do you even understand what tiles are made of? Terracotta. You know what terracotta is? It's not much more than mud! A bit of clay, that's all. Clay, that's all that stands between you and me and the elements, and I would have you remember that next time there's lightning up there and the rain is pelting down!"

His mother agrees it is a most serious situation. She will talk to him. It will never happen again.

The twinset lady says she felt she must say something.

"In case you're not aware," says Mrs Green, "Mrs Bexley's husband is manager of the ES&A across the way. A very fine bank, too!"

His mother finally drives the delegation from her door. She takes him into the kitchen.

"Well?" she says.

"I climbed on Grandpa's roof."

"And wasn't that idiotic enough? I could have throttled

your grandfather, encouraging that nonsense. What if you'd fallen off?"

"You haven't even been up there," he says. There's a proper ladder thing. There's a wall along the roof edge."

"What were you even doing up there? Trying to see a satellite?"

"I have to fix my aerial."

"My God! You and that flaming crystal set! Because your grandpa made it — that's what this is all about, isn't it?"

"I like it. I like listening to it."

"I'll get you a proper radio," she says. "Once I've been working for a bit. You won't even need an aerial then."

"I like my crystal set."

"Ralph, you listen to me, and listen good. All your grandfather has ever wanted, from the minute you were born, was to drive a wedge between you and me. Can you not see that? This isn't about you in the least. It's him. All he's ever wanted is to show the world what a useless, incompetent human being I am. That's why he egged you on with all that nonsense, Ralph, to get at me. It never was about you."

"He still made my crystal set," he says.

"I'm going to take that blessed crystal set and throw it in the bin, I swear! Can you not understand how much we love you?"

"Who?"

"Oh you are one ungrateful child, you really are. One day you'll look back, and I just hope you'll see how utterly ungrateful you have been. I only hope I live to see the day. You can ring me up and tell me I'm sorry, Mum."

"It wasn't my idea to come here."

"Don't you start on that again!"

He goes to his room and slams his door. He throws himself on his bed.

He cannot stand her. The way she speaks to him. The way she always has to get in how he is ungrateful. That, or else it's pubic hair. His Grandpa Doc, he had it right exactly. The Tearful Earful — that is just exactly what she is.

He sets the chair up on his bed against the wall and mounts. The chair legs press into his bedspread and its back scrapes on the wall, so it's not exactly stable. He wraps a hanky round his hand. He reaches up and pulls a glass plate from the louvre clamps, then stoops and lets it drop onto his bedspread.

Four times he repeats this process, and it isn't easy. The window's lower edge is inches above his head. At last the window frame is empty, though. Standing on tiptoes, he works his arm out through the gap and flails about. He touches the aerial wire outside, but can't quite grasp it.

Then he falls.

It's not a straight out fall. The chair back slides across the wall, and as his weight meets the glass panes on his bedspread, there's a horrible crunching sound.

His mother calls out from the kitchen. He scrambles to his feet.

"I'm fine," he calls.

He checks himself in his wardrobe mirror. He isn't bleeding, but there's glass all over his clothing and shards across his bedspread. Only two of the panes remain intact.

He slips the undamaged panes of glass under his bed, then lifts the corners of his bedspread, gathering up the broken fragments. He folds the cover and dumps the bundle in the bottom of his wardrobe. He shakes his clothing, kicks a last few slivers under his bed.

His mother enters.

"You're supposed to knock," he says.

"What's all this commotion?"

"I was doing somersaults."

"You ought to get outside for that," she says. "You ought to find some park."

It takes a while, but eventually she goes out in her car again.

He tips the broken glass into a bucket, then goes down to the lane. He wants to find some place to dump it where it can't be linked to him. All the neighbours, though, have taken in their bins.

A gate a few doors down is open and he takes a closer look. Within, he spies a large industrial bin, its lid thrown back, clouds of flies about its opening. Of course — the butcher's shop. Why not?

Flies dart against his cheeks as he draws closer. One bold wriggler crawls right up his nostril. As he snorts, he heaves the bucket up, and the sound of tinkling glass that follows is of slivers landing on something sodden.

As he steps back, spluttering in disgust, a remark of his father's comes to mind. He will never eat another frankfurter again.

———

Aunty Pearl, who reappears now in their lives, is not a real relation. All those years ago before his birth she studied x-rays with his mother, but she had an allergy to lead, so couldn't wear the apron. She never liked the uniform much anyway. Instead of taking x-rays, she married Uncle Paul, who worked in Metering at the Gas and Fuel.

He stayed at Aunty Pearl's in Brighton with his mother once, some years ago. Every night, Uncle Paul and Aunty Pearl walked Mitzy on the beach, but Mitzy could not go into the water. She would get wet. It wasn't allowed. Aunty Pearl would call out Come here, Mitzy! every time she went down to the water's edge. Uncle Paul would call out Mitzy! Mitzy! Come here, girl! Every time another dog came near and tried to sniff their Mitzy, Aunty Pearl would shoo the dog away.

Aunty Pearl has trouble with her eggs. His mother told him this. She wanted to have a little boy, but she couldn't because her eggs were wrong.

"You'd better watch out," his mother told him. "Aunty Pearl might try to kidnap you."

The day Aunty Pearl comes for lunch, they have salad because it's hot. Salad means lettuce, tomato, beetroot, cheese in silver paper, mayonnaise and bread and butter. Because it's Aunty Pearl, they have dessert as well. Real pineapple, in circles from the tin, with ice-cream.

After dessert, his mother tells him he can run along.

"Are you going to get a dog, Spook?" Aunty Pearl asks.

"We've rather finished with that Spook nonsense," his mother says.

"Spook?" says Aunty Pearl. "I think Spook's a fine nickname. It has real character."

"Ralph and I, we had a good long talk about it all. We decided we would drop it."

"You decided," he says.

"We did talk about it, Ralph. And now we're making a fresh start. It's time we left all that behind us."

"It's sort of cute though," says Aunty Pearl. "It really rolls off the tongue. It's cheeky, too. I like it. I mean Ralph's a fine name. It will always be your real name, darling, but Spook does have a bit of spunk to it. I wish someone had called me something a bit more interesting than Pearl. Mandy, that would have been good. Or Sparkles."

"You run along," his mother says. "Later, you can show Aunty Pearl your engine."

They want to be rid of him so they can talk about his father. When they stayed at Brighton, it was like that all the time. The moment he was out of earshot — or they thought he was — Aunty Pearl would start about his mother's bucking bronco.

Now their talk won't be like that. The subject will have changed. How his dad smashed up his grandma's car. How he had to go and steal it. How it's going to cost so much to get it fixed.

They haven't even started when his mother finds him in the hallway.

"Come on now," she says. "You need fresh air."

You need. This is another of her favourite tricks. Fresh air. He could write a book. His mother and her tricks, they drive him mad.

He goes down to the laundry, where his space is meant to be.

The end of Mrs Green's laundry bench — were ever so many edicts issued over so tiny a territory? Twenty-four inches, and not an inch more. The least hint of any fuel spill, and he'll be banned. If his engine can be got to go, then it can run five minutes in a week, and never on a Sunday. Mrs Green calls this arrangement generous.

The moment he sets foot in the laundry, he can see his territory has been invaded. Reckitts blue bombs and a Persil carton have encroached, and there's been a kind of carpet bombing of cleaning rags, with the result that his little aero engine, nailed onto its piece of wood, has tumbled onto the concrete floor.

He picks it up. The propeller looks OK, but he isn't sure about the engine body. He examines the delicate fins. He cannot see a crack — but then, he's heard his father talking about engines that have hairline cracks and water in the crankcase. What a crankcase is, he isn't sure, but he knows an engine shouldn't be dropped.

He blows off dust and grit, and sets his little engine back up on the bench.

It will never start, he knows. There's simply something wrong with it, or wrong with him — some fundamental failure that can't be repaired.

Ever since he got this engine, he's been trying to make it go. He has the proper fuel. He got this from the model shop in Karnook, the exact same shop the engine came from, he is sure. He saw it in the window before Christmas, then it disappeared.

Since Christmas Day, he's tried every possible setting for the needle valve. He's tried waiting between spins of the propeller. He's tried waiting and not waiting, spinning just the once then waiting, spinning and spinning again.

Is his engine flooding? He can never tell. How is he supposed to know? He has walked away and gone and had a Milo and come back, and any flooding, surely, would be gone by then, but it seems the Milo makes no difference. Every time he spins the prop, it's just the same old phutt. Never any smoke. He has a callus on his finger from the spinning, but his engine never fires. He'd ask his father, but he can't. His father never even showed on Christmas Day.

He takes the little fuel tank and clears it, blowing air. He runs a length of plastic tubing from his fuel bottle to the tank, then inverts the bottle till fuel dribbles out. He sets the little tank up on two blocks of Velvet, then re-routes the tubing to the engine inlet.

Will today be the day his engine finally snarls to life?

Flick. He drags his finger down the propeller blade. It spins with the usual dull phutt, but not a hint of a crackle or a pop. Flick, and flick again. Another flick. He fiddles with the needle valve. On and on he goes like this, flicking, altering the valve setting. Is it flooded? He counts to sixty. Well, forty. Flick, and then another flick. He removes a cake of soap beneath the fuel tank and tries again. No difference. He adds a cake. The fuel tank should be elevated, the instructions say. But what is elevated? Elevated how? How far? On the points that really matter, the instructions are useless. Flick and flick. Another needle setting. Flick. Flick. His engine's answer is always the same. I cannot start. I will not start. I don't know how to start.

He tips a heap of Persil powder on the floor, empties his engine's fuel tank over that and lights a match. Flames flare up with a sudden whoomph, singeing the hairs on his shins.

He stomps on the burning mess, but can't put out the flames entirely. His soles get hot. He rips his sandals off. The flames die down at last. Soon there's just a twirl of smoke spiralling up from the chary residue. He fills a bucket and sluices away the evidence of his misdemeanour.

He is sitting on the back stairs chucking stones at the cat when Aunty Pearl comes out on the landing and announces they are going to the pictures. His mother has things to do, she says. They're going on their own.

Kidnapped by Sparkles. Well, worse things have

happened. Aunty Pearl has always seemed more like a girl than his mother. He can't imagine his mother ever giggling.

They drive to Moonee Ponds in Aunty Pearl's blue Volkswagen. Once they get inside the Hoyts, who turns up but Uncle Paul. Aunty Pearl doesn't seem at all surprised. She tells Uncle Paul to get them dixie cups and Jaffas while she buys the tickets. Once they've everything they need, they head towards the stairs.

He's seen a film before, in the Institute at Karnook, but never in a theatre with an upstairs and a downstairs, and gilded banisters and thick red carpet.

Once they get upstairs, more wonders are in store. A golden dome arches overhead, carved with grapes and vines. Two giant chandeliers hang down, dripping with electric lights shaped just like candles. Plush velvet seats range in wide arcs, each seat fixed onto the floor so it can't move. Where the screen should be, a scarlet velvet curtain hangs in heavy folds, illuminated by hidden footlights.

They're so early, there's hardly another soul in sight.

"Best seats in the house," says Uncle Paul. "Where you want to sit?"

He gestures to a long, curved balcony that promises an exciting view of the seats downstairs.

"We can chuck down Jaffas," says Uncle Paul.

Aunty Pearl says Uncle Paul should stop it. They head down to the front row and take their seats, right in the middle. Aunty Pearl sits on one side of him, Uncle Paul the other.

If this is kidnapping, it's not too bad so far. He can remember, though, the walks on Brighton beach with Mitzy, and how each time they saw a freighter in the bay — and there were lots of these — Uncle Paul would explain about the plimsoll line, the paint that was a different colour on the bottom of the ship, and all about displacement, and how salt water was heavier than fresh, or else it was the other way around, and how Lord Plimsoll had discovered ships could sink. Does Uncle Paul just want a little boy to tell this stuff to every night? He isn't altogether sure he wants to be that little boy.

"I was just telling Uncle Paul about your father," says Aunty Pearl. "Having such a long, hard think about things, isn't he? It must be difficult, with all the different points of view to be considered."

"I suppose," he says.

They're going to see The Time Machine. He's looking forward to seeing how it works. He hopes they show it properly, close up, so he can see the parts it's made of.

Downstairs, people are entering the stalls.

"It can't be easy for your father," says Aunty Pearl. "All the same, I can't help wondering who's considering your own position in all this."

"Like Mum, you mean?" he says.

"Well, possibly. But then your mum, she's not exactly an objective party, is she? She might not really understand your point of view."

"What point of view?"

"Your father too," says Uncle Paul. "He might like to know where you stand."

"Paul!" says Aunty Pearl.

She says this in her sharpish, Mitzy-heading-for-the-water voice. Her voice she uses for the sniffy dogs.

"Paulie, darling, I was wondering if you could pop downstairs and get us a copy of next month's program. I'd love to know what else is coming on. Spook, he'd probably like to know as well."

"You can forget Anne Frank," says Uncle Paul. "Slit your wrists for that one."

"I wasn't thinking of Anne Frank specifically," says Aunty Pearl. "Come on Paulie, be a sweetheart. See what you can rustle up."

"OK, OK," says Uncle Paul. "I get the picture."

Uncle Paul stands up. He edges along the row, bounds up the carpeted steps and disappears.

"Men aren't always good at talking about these things," says Aunty Pearl.

He's almost sure Aunty Pearl's hand just brushed his knee.

"He'll be back any minute," she says.

"I don't really care what's on," he says. "I just like all the pictures."

"Spook, I don't want you to think I'm being an awful busybody. I can't stand that type of person myself. All the same, we do need to understand how you might be feeling about all these goings on. Feeling deep down, that's what I mean."

"About the accident, you mean?"

Aunty Pearl brings her face up close. He can smell her perfume really strong. Is this how a lady goes to kiss a man?

"It isn't just the silly accident, Spook. It's all the time before. When you were living in Karnook, did anyone ever say anything about your dad? Anything that wasn't completely proper, that's what I mean."

"You mean like Grandpa Doc?"

"What did Grandpa Doc say?"

"He said my dad's a no-good slack-arse."

"Goodness," says Aunty Pearl. "He must have been very cross when he said that."

"He was drunk."

"That's not exactly what I was meaning, Spook. I was meaning did you ever hear anything about your dad that might have been a bit embarrassing? I'm not asking what they said. I'm just wondering if anyone said a thing like that, that's all."

"Like how come he was working at the saw mill?"

"What I'm getting at, Spook, is whether there was any — I don't know quite how to put this — whether there was any secret thing people might have been saying about your dad behind his back?"

"Is Uncle Paul going to be long?" he asks.

"I just hope you haven't been carrying around some awful burden, Spook — some horrible... I don't know... some horrible thing, and who knows, one day it could all blow up, this thing, and it could all come spilling out, and then the consequences — the consequences for everyone, Spook — they could be dreadful."

"I have to go to the toilet," he says.

"All anyone wants is what is best," says Aunty Pearl. "But what is best, you see? That's our problem. Those of us who care for you, we worry about all this. From what you say, though — and you are telling me this, aren't you, darling — there's been nothing, absolutely nothing. That's what you're telling me, right?"

He nearly crushes her feet. He certainly bangs his shins against the armrests, getting out. Climbing the steps to the stairwell, he almost collides with a family coming down. He descends into the foyer, sees the silhouette man doffing his silhouette hat, and rushes through the door into a white-tiled expanse. Uncle Paul is at the urinal. He goes into a stall and shuts the door.

So what now? He hadn't thought of Uncle Paul being here. He pulls his pants down and sits. If Uncle Paul should turn around and look under the stall door, at least he has a plausible story — but what he really needs is for Uncle Paul to go upstairs and for the film to start. Then when he comes back and joins them, Aunty Pearl will have to shush.

He hears the urinal flush. He's almost sure he's in these toilets with Uncle Paul alone. If anyone else came in, he'd have heard the squeaky door. So has Uncle Paul turned round? Has he recognised his sandals? If so, has Uncle Paul realised he hasn't done a poo?

He doesn't want to do a poo. But what if Uncle Paul and Aunty Pearl swap notes?

He said he had to go. He stomped all over my feet.

He was in the dunny, but I didn't hear him do a poo.

Would they talk like that? Would grown-ups ever say such things?

He hears the sound of water running in a basin. Should he call out? To say what? I'll be a minute? As if his poo is still in progress. You don't have to wait. I know the way.

What if Uncle Paul does wait? Then he'll have to make a poo come, and he can't. Uncle Paul will realise he's a faker.

He was in the dunny. He said he was going to do a poo, but he didn't. He's such a faker.

He stood right on my toes.

He should have been more careful with her feet. She was nearly going to kiss him.

He hears the towel machine's kerchunk kerchunk.

"That you, Spookus?" says a voice like Uncle Paul's.

"Just be a minute."

"No hurry, mate."

"I don't know if I can do it or not."

"Don't worry, mate. It happens to the best of us."

The gents door squeaks, then bangs. Is Uncle Paul still out there, or do they have extra company now?

Two brown shoes come into view near the bottom of his stall door.

"All this stuff your aunty's asking, mate — you don't have to say a thing if you don't want to."

"It's OK," he says.

"It's just the way she is, mate. Never die wondering, your Aunty Pearl."

"I just thought I had to go," he says.

The brown shoes shift a little, but don't back away completely.

"Have you seen him?" he asks.

"Who's that, old son?"

"My dad."

He hears a urinal flush. So they are not alone.

"Putting a bloke in a bit of a predicament there, old feller," says the voice of Uncle Paul.

"So have you?"

He hears a deep, fruity cough. A smoker's cough. That's not Uncle Paul. Water running in a basin.

The brown shoes draw a little closer.

"Listen, mate," the owner of the brown shoes says. "Sometimes we have to make a promise we don't like, OK? Then we have to keep it, see? I don't like this any more than you do. Thing we've got to remember, mate, is none of this is your fault. And we never had this conversation, either, OK? Just count up to a hundred and I'll see you up there."

The shoes move off. Kerchunk kerchunk. The door

bangs shut, and then a moment later the door bangs shut again.

By the time he reaches the top of the stairs, the cinema is in darkness. He descends to the front row and resumes his place between the kidnappers. Together they watch Bugs Bunny and Great Castles of the Highlands and then The Time Machine — details of whose workings prove to be frustratingly elusive. In between, there is no mention of his poo, or his parents, or this horrible thing that someone may, or may not, once have said in Karnook.

The next morning, his dad turns up at Mrs Green's.

CHAPTER THREE

Or is this in fact his dad at all?

This man who shows up unannounced looks like his dad, and yet there's something missing. His father never had a swagger, but he had an ease of movement, a gliding grace remarkable for a man whose recovery from a broken pelvis was so slow. This grace is gone. His father has gone stiff, somehow. It's like he is on edge. Afraid.

One brown, battered suitcase is all he's brought.

Can it be for real, this suddenly-I'm-here performance, or do they stage it just for him, too old for wise men and frankincense, but maybe good for one last fairy tale? Have they been talking on the phone? Working through Aunty Pearl? Something has been going on behind the scenes — but if this is a show they're putting on for him, why does his father barely seem to know his lines?

His father goes through all the motions, anyway. Sticks his head in every room. Flicks the switches on and off. Nods and sniffs the air a little — but not too much. Has he been coached? Forewarned?

"Home is where the heart is," his father says at last, and tosses his suitcase on the double bed.

Once his father has unpacked, there's a quiz show in the kitchen. His mother plays Jack Davey, and his father is the sole contestant. He himself must play the audience, not listening on their radios at home, but in the studio live, observing each quiver of a lip, each intake of breath.

"So what about your pelvis?" his mother asks. "Do they know about all that? If you had to carry a woman from a burning building, could you do it? Could you carry me?"

What is she talking about? What burning building? Who set it alight? His father, though, seems to understand. It's like he accepts this frightful grilling is his due.

His father tells how a doctor took his measurements. How he had to touch his toes. Drop his trousers.

"That's hernia," his mother says. "He would have made you cough."

She's in her territory here, being the doctor she's always wanted to be.

His dad tells how he had to read some charts. One black and white, then funny-looking numbers in a book.

"That's colour-blindness," his mother says. "Ten percent of men have that. You haven't, though. My father checked you out. What about your blood pressure?"

"They checked all that."

"And?"

"Blood pressure's fine."

"Returning to your pelvis, then..."

"The subject didn't even come up."

"You're sure this was a proper doctor, Ray, not some hack

the fire brigade gets in? Did you see his certificate? Did you see what university?"

"I wasn't there to examine him, Rose. He was there to examine me."

"So was this some Asian? Graduate from Trincomalee?"

"He was a proper doctor, Rose."

"Ray Halliday, the last thing any of us needs right now is for you to be making out you're some kind of hero. It's all most commendable you've wangled your way this far, through some perfunctory medical, but that's step number one. If we're going to do this, Ray, this has to be a serious commitment, and I'd like to know there's more underpinning my future than a nod and a wink from some colonial gentleman. You can't expect to blow one little toot on your plastic trumpet and have the walls of Jericho come tumbling down."

His father looks to him. Please look the other way, he seems to be saying. Don't pin your hopes on me, pal. It's not the kind of message he was hoping to receive from his rescuer.

One thing is clear. They all know now who's actually in charge.

———

It isn't long before the little nothings start appearing, the decorative contraptions his father likes to make from garden wire, bending and snipping with his pliers. He must have brought the makings in his suitcase. A little star, a spider's web, a cross, each dangling from a cotton thread, tied to the landing handrail. In Karnook, Grandpa Doc's verandah used to be infested with these things until there'd be a clean out.

It's so mindless, Ray, his mother used to say. After each

eradication, though, the nothings would start up again. Ray's whirligigs, his grandpa called them. They seemed to underline his general point, that this Ray Halliday was a waste of space. Your flim flam man, he said to Rose one time.

His mother tolerates the nothings now without a word, even accepting the long silences that accompany their making. His father sits out on the landing with his pliers, and she brings him cups of tea.

It's almost like there is a truce between them — but if this truce is real, or only like the French and Germans playing football in the snow on Christmas Day, he isn't sure. He isn't even sure which trench his father sees himself belonging in right now.

So perhaps right now he's really on his own.

———

And so their new life starts, each parent setting off each day in uniform — his mother for her clinic, his father for the fireman training course — while he waits home alone and counts the days till school will start and he can swap his present misery for another kind of woe.

The dead man will not leave him be. The gentleman. He has not told his father, and for all he knows his mother may not have told him either. This present version of his father — the one who has come back all emptied out, who's said he'll live with them — he's not sure he can trust this version to stand up and call out her stupidity like once he might have done. The gentleman, therefore, is his to deal with on his own.

It's not the smell as such that bothers him, unpleasant as its aftermath has been. What bothers him is what preceded that, when the gentleman would have been lying, not yet dead, but knowing it was coming. Lying there and thinking This is it. This is what he could not stand himself — and yet he knows that one day he will lie there knowing too.

This is what he thinks about as he stands in the dingy passageway at half past nine or quarter to eleven, gazing into the porch. At half past one. At quarter to three. He leaves the kitchen radio on, but through the music and the chatter, he can hear the question, loud and clear: what did the gentleman know?

He does have other thoughts that he is working on. He is developing a theory no-one else has ever thought of before. Behind the appearance of all things, it has occurred to him, there must be a deeper, realer thing that he could possibly see if only he could work out how.

He tries new ways of looking in the hallway. He stares at clots and blobs of paint along the skirting board — humble, inoffensive blotches no-one, surely, has ever paid attention to.

What do they mean, these blobs? What is their secret, the thing they will not come right out and say? He stares at them while joists and rafters creak. The shadow of an unseen bird flits over the bathroom skylight. Truly, there is another world behind this world — and he alone, he feels convinced, stands on its threshold.

It is his secret — his alone.

———

HIS MOTHER IS SOON up to her old tricks, making a fool of herself in her new job the way she always does, embarrassing the whole family. She has decided Dr Schlimmicht's clinic looks too bare. It needs a woman's touch.

His father won't engage with her on this, and his lack of interest makes her mad. She's trying to make her way in the world. She needs to impress Dr Schlimmicht. Doesn't he care? It seems, however, he might not. His father is prepared to take this much risk, at least.

To add her woman's touch, his mother buys half a dozen posters at the newsagent's. They're waterfalls. She puts them up about the clinic. When Dr Schlimmicht sees them, he says they make him want to micturate.

"He said what?" his father asks.

"Actually, it means to piss, Ray Halliday."

"It is his practice, Rose. You're just the hired monkey."

"I'm a vital partner in this enterprise. He practically said as much!"

"Take in flowers," his father says. "That's what he really wants."

"I'm not a flowersy person!"

When his mother means to drive a person crazy, there's not much can stop her. She goes back to the newsagent's, and unrolls her purchases on the kitchen table.

Birds.

"You like these, Spookus?" his father asks.

"They're OK."

"Flamingos," his father says. "They're not Australian."

"The brolgas are," she says.

"What's this gooky-looking thing when he's at home?"

"A purple gallinule, that is."

"There's no such thing."

"It's right in front of you."

They've been forewarned this time, but no-one asks. It's

days before his mother finally comes clean. Dr Schlimmicht is not a bird man either.

"A tiger bringing down a wildebeest," she says. "That's what he wants to see. Nature red of tooth and claw."

"He's having a lend, Rose," his father says. "Flowers, that's what he really wants."

Months later, when everything has changed utterly, he will finally get to visit the famous clinic with its cold bare walls. As he waits by the counter for his mother to appear, he will notice a little vase on the reception desk, four inches high, half-filled with pebbles and three plastic tulips.

So is this her famous woman's touch achieved at last, he will wonder then — or another defiant up yours from The Tearful Earful? In a world made up of things, it can be hard to know what any one of them ever truly means.

————

His father's always been a quiet man, hard to get to know — although the useless tools seemed to know him well enough. The one time his father really opens up to him is when he bulldusts. He'll start in on some story that can't possibly be true, then add in detail after detail till he almost can believe it. Then right at the end, when he's sucked him in completely, his father will stick a pin in, exploding the whole thing.

He loves it when his dad does that — when his dad's the centre of attention, everybody listening, wanting to know what happens next — and all the time they're almost sure he's bulldusting them, but they just can't help themselves. At times like this, it's like his dad is spinning one of his nothings out of nothing more than words and air.

He can't help wondering if his father's fireman training stories are like this.

He knows his dad goes off in uniform each morning to where the fireman training happens — this uniform that doesn't have its proper shoulder patches yet — but everything that happens after that sounds quite incredible.

The trainees meet in town, at this place they call East Melbourne. There, if the officer-in-charge is in the mood, they make a bonfire out of cardboard boxes and kero, then they put it out. Another thing they do is carry bags of wheat around. Each bloke gets a bag and has to carry it up a ladder to a concrete place and chuck it on the floor. Sometimes the officer-in-charge makes up a fire in this concrete place, then all the trainees have to climb the ladder and get their bag of wheat and bring it down again. Once they get the bags down, they put them on these stretchers and carry them round the building. When they aren't doing wheat bag stuff or putting fires out, they polish up their nozzles or their helmets, or they read a little book with all the fireman's rules in it. Some days the officer-in-change gives lessons about oxygen and stuff like that. The best part, though, his father reckons, is finding out about the lurks.

"Lurks like what?" he asks.

"Mate, if everybody knew about a lurk, it wouldn't be a lurk, would it?"

"Getting posted out this way," his mother says. "That would be a useful lurk."

Is this really how you get to be a fireman? Will his father eventually stick a pin in this balloon, leaving them fooled all over again? Himself. His mother.

Each day, his father puts his uniform on and walks off to

the station to become a fireman. Is he meant to laugh, or what? It's just so hard to tell.

———

IN THE EMPTY, creaking flat, the holidays drag on. Without a friend like Stevie Bell for company, the gentleman persists in lying on his back, eyes open, waiting for his end.

It must have been the TV room. There are marks of scrubbing on the carpet just inside the door. A whiff of bleach as well, although he has to get right down to pick that up, his nose against the carpet. Lying there with the TV on. The test pattern, most probably. Couldn't even change the channel.

He does his best to drive these thoughts away with 3UZ, turned up in the kitchen really loud.

He lies on his bed, flipping through his World Book Encyclopedia, re-reading favourite articles. How the Titanic hit an iceberg. How the King was crowned at Westminster. All about the fastest locomotive in the world, a steam engine in Scotland. The holy man in India whose fingernails have grown right round his hand.

From time to time he goes into his parents' room and looks out through the window. The tennis racket handle is still there on the verandah. The bits of flower pot. The plastic ball with holes in it. He scans the windows opposite for signs of life, but they are curtained, not for seeing through.

He checks his mother's undies drawer to see if it's still there, the rubber thing. She keeps it dusted with some powder. What is it for? Is it to stop her insides falling out?

Some secret is involved, he's sure. Is this the key to all her crabbiness, this rubber thing?

One morning he steps from his parents' bedroom to find Mrs Green in the back porch, carrying a cardboard box.

"Ah," says Mrs Green. "Up to your tricks, I see."

"Mum isn't here."

"I'm not an utter niddle-noddle. I can see her car's not there. I won't be long."

"Dad isn't here either," he says.

She advances into the hallway.

"You can't just come in," he says.

"Whoever told you that? Was that the tenancy agreement fairy? Has she not told you, this brains trust of a mother of yours?"

"Told what?"

"I hate to say this, child, but I am coming to think less of your mother every day. And this father of yours, he's a turn up for the books, isn't he? Chalk and cheese, those two."

She steps into the second corridor, the one that leads down to his bedroom.

"God Almighty! What on earth is that?"

He follows after her.

"It's a purple gallinule," he says.

"A what?"

"It's a bird," he says.

"I'm not a ning nong, child! I can see it's a bird! What's it doing sticky-taped to my cupboard, that's what I want to know."

"Dr Schlimmicht didn't like it."

"Did Dr Schlimmicht say to go and stickytape this purple whatsit on my paintwork? Go and deface your landlady's property — is that what he said?"

"We could have the brolgas," he says.

"Do I look as if I want the brolgas? I want my cupboard back the way it was. You take it down, and don't you chip my paintwork either. Are there any more of these monstrosities you vandals have been putting up?"

"We've got Niagara Falls."

"And where's Niagara Falls?" says Mrs Green.

"Is it in Queensland?"

"Oh you little monster. Who said that? Was that your father?"

His answers don't seem to be working out so well. He shakes his head.

"That father of yours! He has a way of looking at a woman I don't appreciate. There is a lack of frankness there."

"He isn't colour-blind."

"Is that right?" says Mrs Green. "Mr Green wasn't colour-blind, but he had that look too — as I appreciate much better now. It can take a long time before a man's proclivities truly show themselves, but when they do, young man, you'll soon find out what's what. I won't be making that mistake again."

He squeezes past her and begins to pare the stickytape off the full length door. He knew this cupboard was locked, but thought there must have been some problem with a missing key. He takes the poster down.

"You left an awful mess on my laundry floor the other day," says Mrs Green. "You trying to kill me now, is that it?"

"Not really," he says.

"A woman of my bone structure! I have to be careful where I tread, you understand?"

"You could tip over," he says.

"Tip over? I'm not a spinning top! Go on now, get away.

You turn that radio down! A lady is entitled to her privacy, you know. You go in the kitchen and I'll call you when I'm done."

———

THAT NIGHT, it all comes out at dinner, how Mrs Green was in the porch. How she didn't even knock. The purple gallinule. The tentsy something fairy.

"It's tenancy," his mother says. "Our tenancy agreement."

"And Mr Green," he says. "He isn't colour-blind."

"Isn't, or wasn't?" his father asks.

"She didn't say."

"He's probably in gaol," his father says. "Tried to throttle her, poor bastard."

"Ray, she's not that bad."

"You kidding? Any chance she gets, she corners me down in that yard of hers. Beady little eyes up close. Talk about the third degree. Some women, they just scream throttle me."

"That's disgusting, Ray."

"You ought to hear her. Standing there in my uniform, I am, and on she goes about men in uniform. This Mr Green of hers, you know what he is — or was? Bloody tram inspector! If I find that woman invading when I'm here, I will not be held responsible, I swear."

His mother clears the dishes from the table. This is meant to be his own job, but she's rattled, he can see. She speaks to the window over the sink, her back to them.

"She does have rights, Ray, actually."

"What rights?" his father says. "She doesn't live here. It's our flat for the duration."

She turns, and he just knows immediately there's going to be a scene. He knows it in his bones.

"It's my flat, Ray, actually. I signed the tenancy agreement. And Mrs Green is right. There is a clause we both agreed on. I felt it only fair, seeing we'd got a good deal on the rent."

"There was a dead man," he says. "He stank."

"What dead man?"

"The man is immaterial, but thank you, Ralph. The point is, Mrs Green has private storage space up here, and under our agreement, she's entitled to access from time to time."

"To that bloody cupboard?"

"Yes."

"So she can just come barging in here whenever she feels like it?"

"I'm sure she'll be quite reasonable."

"What's in it, this famous cupboard?"

"I wouldn't know, Ray. Nothing of interest to us, I'm sure."

"Let's have a look then."

"Ray, it's her private space. We have to respect that."

His father has already risen.

"Let's see what Mr Coathanger has to say about that!"

She rushes forward, but she is too late. His father has left the room.

"Ralph, don't you even think about this!"

He almost collides with his father as he hurries past the kitchen doorway, coathanger in hand. He follows, his mother at his heels.

His dad confronts the full length cupboard and gives the knob a shake.

"She's going to find out, Ray!" his mother cries. "You want us on the street?"

His dad presses his weight against the cupboard door, forcing the end of the coathanger into the lock. He writhes and twists until there is a click, then steps back, flinging the door wide open.

"In like Flynn!" he says.

The shadowy cubicle is high enough to walk into. Dusty shelves are stuffed with shoe boxes and rolls of fabric. Looking past his father, he can see an old electric jug. A bakelite contraption with numbered buttons on its face. Two china lamp stands, shaped like cocker spaniels. Standing in the middle of the cupboard is a tall metallic thing, a lady with a great split up her middle. Her torso is lined with coarse grey felt, and her feet are made of rubber, spherical knobs fixed on a ring of steel. From that steel ring, her legs rise up, three metal tubes that reach into her inner workings. The lady has no neck beyond a stub, and no head whatsoever.

"Old Fatguts has a twin," his father says. "Meet Mrs Grey."

"You shouldn't be here, Ray," his mother says.

"I never would have signed that lease."

He tugs his father's trousers, wailing that Mrs Green will know. The next time she comes in, she'll know.

His father drops down to his level.

"How's she going to know, mate? Unless a little birdie gives the game away, huh? A little birdie with a red, red cheek."

"I aren't going to tell," he says.

"That's right," his father says. "So she won't know. But

you be careful, mate. That old biddy is a menace, I'm telling you. A prying, disgusting menace."

His mother walks off, banging the walls with her fists.

His father closes up the cupboard, then he watches, awed and frightened, as his father inserts the coathanger in the keyhole, and begins once more to writhe and twist.

———

Mr Coathanger's depredations notwithstanding, the door of Mrs Green's cupboard seems to be well secured. Sometimes, passing by, he tries the knob, but the mechanism always holds.

Nonetheless, he dreads their landlady's next visit, and tries to steel himself against the funny way she talks. When her grand opinions start thundering down like boulders tumbling down a canyon, will his cheeks give the game away? How can anyone withstand a force like Mrs Green?

By day he thinks of Mrs Green and the expiring gentleman, by night of Mrs Grey. As he is drowsing off, the metal lady hovers in the space behind his eyelids. He knows she is a dummy, but this knowledge makes no difference. Why must she come to him as he is drifting off to sleep? What does she want? Can she really not remain imprisoned in her dark cupboard?

CHAPTER FOUR

One afternoon his mother comes home and announces she has found a friend for him. The friend's name is Theodore.

"You can't just make someone be someone's friend," he says.

"It's the Theodore, isn't it," she says. That's nothing, though. The Americans had a president called Theodore. They called him Teddy. His mother's lovely."

"Everything's always lovely," he says. "What a lovely dress. What a lovely chop."

"I don't say that."

"You should listen to yourself."

"Wait till there's things you actually do like, instead of all this I hate this and I hate that. Wait till you fall in love. That's what I want to see."

"I aren't going to fall in love."

"I pity the poor girl, I really do," his mother says. "She won't get lovely chocolates, will she? Anyway, I like

Theodore's mother very much. It would be great if you two could hit it off."

"Does he have glasses? It's a glasses name."

"You're as bad as your grandfather! The Theo part of his name, that means God, actually, if you must know."

"Great."

She tells him what she knows, how Theo's dad was some kind of missionary, but not a stomping-through-the-jungle type of missionary. He was a kind of helper person, giving out the bibles and the toilet paper. The whole family lived in Tanganyika for two years. Now the father lives in Sydney. They're separated — it's so sad — but he still works in that general line, just not so deep. He's in some warehouse now. He packs up powdered milk and bibles and they ship them off to Africa.

"Don't see what it has to do with me," he says.

"I just thought you might have a bit of sympathy for Theodore. Your dad and I, we almost separated for a bit. That wasn't easy for you, was it? These churchy people, if their marriage goes all wonky, it's a big deal. And Lisa's just a lovely person. You'd really like her. I met her at the butcher's."

"Lovely," he says.

"Well it is lovely. Lisa and I, we have a sort of common interest. She's a nurse."

"Was she practically a doctor too?"

"You cut that out, Ralph. I never said that once!"

"You did!"

"I could have been a doctor if I'd wanted. That's all. And I could have, too. I could have easily. I didn't want, though, that's the point. One doctor in our family's quite enough, I should say. They're either raving egomaniacs or slithery, cold things like Dr Schlimmicht, in my experience."

"I don't need a friend," he says.

———

WASTE OF BREATH, though, that whole argument.

Theodore does wear glasses, it turns out. The lenses are so thick, whenever he looks through to where the ear should be, he sees a door or window behind Theodore, curved and bent. He must be nearly blind without these glasses, and his eyes are like a frog's, too wide apart. His nickname is Thickness, which he really hates.

They sort this out between them in ten minutes.

The kid is obviously a brain. He isn't going to Glendale Tech, he's going to go to Northcote High. He'll get there on a bus. When he gets to Northcote High, he's going to change his nickname.

"My mother wants the kids to call me Reckless."

"That isn't how it works," he says.

"I know."

"And then some kid turns up from primary school, and they all realise you tried to change it."

"They won't," Thickness says. "It's eight miles away."

"They still could."

Thickness wants to know his own nickname. For a brain, he certainly is an idiot.

"I told you mine," Thickness says.

"It doesn't work like that," he says. "People have to just find out. Your mother can't make it up, either."

"Who made up yours then?"

"It just happened."

"Tell me," Thickness says. "What is it really?"

"You have to guess."

"I can't."

"You aren't even trying."

"Spider," says Thickness.

"Why would it be Spider?"

"I don't know."

"There has to be a reason."

"There doesn't," Thickness says. "It can be anything."

"It's Spook."

"How come?"

He tells Thickness then how he used to dress up like a ghost and come into his grandpa's study, terrifying him.

"He wouldn't really get a fright," says Thickness.

"He did. I had a sheet on."

"He would have seen your shoes."

"I didn't wear shoes. I did it in my socks. That's how I got my nickname, anyhow."

"Because your mummy called you Spooky. Mummy's little Spooky."

"It wasn't her! It was Grandpa Doc!"

This all happens on a Saturday. His mother has invited Lisa Howe and Thickness for morning tea while his father is playing billiards.

"I have to give him some leeway," his mother tells Lisa Howe. "He's a country boy at heart, and he's come down here for me. I know he has a bet occasionally with the other fellows, but it's not a lot. He has to have some outlet. You know what they're like."

From the moment he lays eyes on Lisa Howe, he is in love. Her curly hair. Her shining eyes. How such a princess could have got involved with bibles and powdered milk is beyond him.

"At least he has some friends," the princess says. "My Philip — I should stop saying that, I guess — he's always been such a quiet type. Reading, reading, and then if I ever took a peek, it was always Adam and Eve and the covenants and original sin. That side of religion, it's always been like trigonometry to me. I'm much more of a people person."

"If I ever found Ray's head in a book, I wouldn't know what to think."

"Up to no good!" says Lisa Howe.

Ha ha ha. On and on they go like this, shafting their menfolk. Eventually his mother says he and Thickness should go outside and play.

"You can show Theodore your aero engine," she says.

"It won't even start," he says.

"I'm sure one day you'll get it going, Ralph. Maybe Theodore will have some good ideas."

"He doesn't know a thing about it," he says.

"And how would you know that already? You've only just met."

"It's diesel," he tells Thickness. "It's got a high compression ratio."

"Would you know anything about that, Theodore?" asks Lisa Howe. "You're always good at ratios."

"It's not a ratio thing, I don't think," Thickness says.

"You could explain to Ralph about Pythagoras," his mother says. "I've tried and tried. He just sits there and shakes his head."

"It's not about Pythagoras with diesels, I don't think," says Thickness.

"Go on, off you go," his mother says. "There must be lots

of boy things you can get up to. Lisa and I are going to finish off our tea, then we might just have another. Go on, scoot!"

It makes his skin crawl when she talks like this. How Lisa Howe has got sucked into being his mother's friend, he can't imagine.

As soon as they're outside, Thickness asks if he can see his aero engine. They go down to the laundry, and he clears away the Rinso and the other cleaning stuff.

"How come it's nailed on wood?" Thickness says. "You aren't supposed to nail it."

"They didn't give me anything to put it in," he says. "There was a plane in the shop, but they always say You have to save up your pocket money."

Thickness says that maybe he can start it.

"You ever start an aero engine?"

"No."

"It's not a glow plug."

"I know. You said. It's diesel."

"You know what to do?"

"No."

It's obvious this Thickness is a total pain. He doesn't know a thing, but just makes out like everything will be alright. He cannot stand this type of person, but what is he supposed to do?

He fills the fuel tank, sets it on the Velvet.

"You really need the soap?" asks Thickness.

"It's so the fuel can go downhill."

"Have you tried without the soap?"

This is getting pretty maddening.

"You want the soap or don't you?"

"It's too high," says Thickness. "You should turn it so it's flat."

He turns the soap so it is flat.

"That's it," he says. "You spin the prop and it's supposed to start. It's buggered, though. It never goes."

Thickness spins the propeller. He spins it over and over.

"You probably flooded it now."

"I didn't," Thickness says.

"You wouldn't even know. When you flood it, you can't tell."

"So how do you know it's flooded?"

"I just know. It's my engine."

Thickness reckons they should go to this park across the road. He doesn't want to, though. It's just a kids' park. He already knows it.

"So what do you want to do then?" Thickness asks.

They go to the dumb park across the road.

It's tiny, this park. It borders on a lane that runs behind the shops on the opposite side of Blessington Street. There's a roundabout and monkey bars and a seesaw and some swings. There's a little house on one side behind a high wire fence. This house is made of brick, and hasn't any windows. Cables wrapped in tarry stuff come out through a pipe cemented in one wall. They go up to a power line overhead. The whole house hums.

Thickness says there's a big transformer in there.

"It mightn't be that big," he says.

"It is," Thickness says. "It's huge."

"You can't even see it."

"They had to make a house for it," Thickness says.

Thickness argues about everything. It's so annoying.

He reckons they should go back. Thickness says their mothers will just be talking about doctors. He says his mother is a nurse. It's all she ever talks about.

"My mother could have been a doctor. She's a radiographer instead. She works for this Nazi guy. He says micturate."

Thickness tells him how his mother visits people's houses when they're dying. She gives them morphine with a needle.

"Yuk," he says. "They'd get addicted then. I'd never have it. I'd use my willpower."

"Even if you have the morphine, you still can go to heaven," Thickness says.

"Yeah, I suppose."

He can't believe how he's stuck now with this drooby kid, talking about heaven.

They go on the roundabout. They take turns to be the person lying down while the other one pushes. When it slows, the one lying down has to jump off and look between their legs. It's pretty funny.

Eventually they stop and lie back on the roundabout together.

"There isn't really any heaven," he says. "It's just made up."

"There is if you believe," Thickness says.

"I don't believe."

They go on the swings a while and then the see-saw, standing. His mum and Lisa Howe show up. Lisa says they should be heading off, but nothing happens. The mothers go on talking. Finally his mother says they'll all go back to their place and have some lunch.

There is no end of it. He really could scream. This is just exactly how things are when your mother is in charge.

After lunch, he and Thickness go outside and look for stuff to burn. They light a fire in Mrs Green's incinerator.

They poke sticks through the bottom, and once they have a roaring blaze, they throw in snails and slugs and watch as each one oozes goo, then shrivels to a tiny ball.

When the fire begins to die, they take turns hosing water on the embers. Great clouds of ash and steam rise up, swirling in the air. Soon the fire is doused, and all that's left to do is spray the muck that's oozing from the incinerator.

Finally the visitors are gone.

"How was that?" his mother asks.

"It was OK," he says, and goes off to his room.

———

CAPTAIN OATES and he are lying on his bed one afternoon, sheltering from the blizzard, when an animal starts scuffling in the roof above. He can hear the animal breathing.

He growls up through the ceiling, low and menacing, the way Stevie Bell's dad growls at the bull.

"Is boy?" a voice calls down.

It is a man's voice. A man's voice with an accent.

"Wrong place!" he calls. "This is Mrs Green's."

"Si. Mrs Grin."

"Mrs Green, like Zelda. She doesn't live here, though. We do."

"Si, si. Comprendo."

He has placed the voice now. Its owner lives over the side fence. He's heard this man yabbering with some woman. They speak in their own language. Occasionally he makes out an English word. Thomastown. Puckle Street. They must be married.

"You're in the wrong place," he calls. "We're the next door people."

"Si. Antenna boy."

He hears a rattle and a wire appears through the ventilator grille. The wire grows in length until several yards of it are dangling down.

"Is good?" the voice calls. "You want him more? You pull."

"What is it?" he asks.

"For crystal set, si? Mrs Grin, she tell me. Pull him now. I fix him up in roof. Good aerial for you."

He pulls on the wire. Two days before, he found his old aerial wire lying in the back yard. He thought then the string must have broken. Now he's not so sure.

The shuffling in the roof recedes, and soon all is silent overhead. Abandoning poor Captain Oates to his frostbitten fate, he strips the insulation from the wire, and connects it to his crystal set. It works.

———

THE NEXT FEW DAYS, he goes round to the shops quite often. He peers in through the window of the shop next door, past all the fridges and TVs. He never sees a man in there, however. There's just a little woman in a purple cardigan, her yellow hair tied up above her head.

Just once, this woman looks up, seems to meet his eye. There is no look of recognition there, however, of you must be the boy. Just bafflement. He walks away.

CHAPTER FIVE

He's stuck, he understands this now. They're never going back to Karnook. His mother's got away from Grandpa Doc, and if they have to live in a hole, she doesn't care so long as she can keep his dad under her thumb while she gets on with things.

His mother will be the star of their little show now. All the light will be on her, while his dad just puts up with it. Goes off to his training every morning. Comes home every night, washes up their dishes and nods off in front of the TV. There's little fight in his dad at all most days.

He'd like to shake his dad. Stand up to her! he wants to say. Be a man! Can't you get us out of here! He won't do any shaking, though. He's too afraid. He's knows already the response he'll more than likely get.

When he complains of boredom, his mother says he ought to go and play with Theodore.

"We don't play," he says.

"Well pardon me. We used to call it playing when I was little."

Everything she touches, it shrivels. Wherever he turns, she was there before him. He looks up Howe in her Rolodex, all the same.

When Thickness opens his door, he has a French book in hand.

"What you reading that for?" he asks.

"Just to get some idea."

"You can't read school books in the holidays," he says. "It's cheating. If they have a test, you'll know the answers."

"So?"

"Then everyone'll say Der, what a brain."

"They say that anyway."

"Because you cheat!" he says. "I'm only trying to help."

A part-completed jigsaw of a sailing ship is laid out on the living room table. They set to work on it. Thickness gets the bits that fit around the steering wheel, while he goes looking for the pieces that make the edge of the wharf. There's pieces missing, though, or else this crappy jigsaw has been cut all wrong.

He tells Thickness he is going.

Thickness says they can go to the golf ball park. People practise golf there and lose their balls. Once you get a ball, you can smash it up and red stuff comes out, Thickness says.

They go round to this park. It's just a bunch of grass, it turns out, with a few trees, and streets all round. There's a scout hall up one end. There isn't any golf ball person there.

"How many golf balls you ever found?" he asks.

"A few."

"A few. That's three."

"A few doesn't have to be three," Thickness says. "It can be any number."

They walk around the park and come to a shallow concrete basin. It dips down to a drainpipe mouth that's blocked by iron bars.

"Where's that go?" he asks.

Thickness tells him the drain runs underground and joins up with a footpath drain on the far side of the park.

"Go round the other side," he says. "Walk up and down. I'll spook you."

Thickness says it's pointless. He already knows what's happening.

"Pretend!"

"You go over," Thickness says. "I'll be the ghost."

"It was my idea!"

"It's my tunnel," Thickness says. "I found it ages ago."

This is what his mother cannot understand — how this Thickness is such a droob. He is just about to say exactly this when they spot an old lady on the far side of the park walking a Scotty dog on a leash. Thickness tells him to get down. They duck behind the basin rim.

"You get down the drainpipe," Thickness says. "When she's near the other end, I'll say."

"Don't let her see you."

Thickness peeps over the concrete.

"She's really slow. Her doggie's sniffing."

"Give me the rocket countdown."

"She's there!" Thickness says. "Do it!"

He scuttles down to the drainpipe mouth and starts howling through the bars.

"Keep it going," Thickness says.

"Hee hee hee hee, ha ha ha ha, whoo, whoo, whoo!" he calls into the drain.

"Her doggie's stopped," Thickness says.

"Is he scared?"

"I think he's having a poop."

"They do that when they're scared."

"Do it more," Thickness says.

He howls and screeches, giving this haunting all he's got.

"You can stop," Thickness says.

He scurries up the slope and peers over the rim alongside Thickness. The old lady and her dog have walked on.

"Did she shit herself?"

"She sort of bent over."

"She must have seen you."

"She didn't! She didn't see a thing!"

He's so pathetic, Thickness. It's obvious she must have seen him. She must have seen his glasses, but he won't admit a thing.

"We need some little kid," he says. "Some little kid that's really dumb. Then when they come along, we really give it to them — and you keep your head down!"

"I did!"

"Do any little kids come here?"

"It's mostly golf ball people," Thickness says. "Oldie people with their walking sticks."

Stupid Thickness — it's like he doesn't even care. Can't he see how great it would be if they could get some little kid? But Thickness is already walking on, eyes down, looking for a golf ball.

———

Back home, he thinks a lot about this little kid, and how it will be great to make him think there's ghosts. The little kid will tell his mother, and she'll say this bullcrap like Don't be silly, Simon, but the little kid, he'll know.

He could do it on his own, but it's better if there's someone else to see how terrified the little kid will be. But Thickness only wants to go to heaven and do French and find his golf balls. He hardly is a proper kid at all.

One day he goes round to the little park where the humming house is and Thickness is there with a girl. Thickness is lying back on the roundabout with his legs over the side, and the girl is pushing him. She's only short, but already she has tits.

When he says hello, the girl just looks at him, but Thickness sits up really fast. He can tell Thickness is embarrassed.

"I thought you didn't like it here," Thickness says.

"Finished all your books?"

"I don't read all the time," Thickness says.

"He doesn't," the girl says.

"I never said he did. Who are you?"

"Who are you?" the girl says.

"Spook."

"He's Ralph," Thickness says.

The girl and Thickness went to primary school together, it turns out.

"Tina's really smart," Thickness says. "Her mother a real case, though. Her brother got a scholarship to Cranston, but Tina doesn't get the recognition."

"My father's only forty-three and he manages the whole bank," Tina says. "What does that tell you?"

"What?"

"It means he's going places, obviously," Tina says. "That's why we have to live here."

"Where's here?"

"Don't you know anything? We live over the road from you. We saw you on the roof."

"Was that your mother who came round?" he asks.

"D'you get in trouble?"

"Not much. I climb up stacks of places."

"My mother reckons you must be a juvenile delinquent."

Something hot is rising in him. He can feel he is being mocked — mocked by little tits.

"What's juvenile delinquent?" he says.

"It's like yobbo," Thickness says. "They ride a motorbike. They usually have tatts."

"I haven't got tatts," he says.

"I didn't say you have to have," Thickness says. "I just said usually."

"They usually end up in gaol," Tina says.

"They can get saved, though," Thickness says.

Tina jumps onto a swing. He grabs the other one before Thickness has a chance. Soon the two of them are swinging side by side and Thickness has to watch.

He learns a lot this day about the little girl with tits and her many grand opinions. If her views were not so plainly silly, he could almost be in awe of her.

This Tina knows a great deal about robbers. It's because of robbers her family must live above the bank, protecting all the money. Tina's not supposed to breathe a word about the ways they fend these robbers off, but lets on there's a secret buzzer joined directly to the police station, and the minute the cops hear this buzzer, they'll jump in their cars and come around even if there's a red light.

As for why her mother is a case, Tina says her mother hates living above the bank, even if her father is the manager. Her mother calls the people here in Glendale lower class and wishes they were back in Bentleigh where they had a proper house and all the ladies used to set their hair. In Bentleigh she could play this bridge, which if you wanted to play it, you had to be a genius, practically, because you had to count the cards. Above all, her mother dreams of living some place where the people don't say somethink.

"But who says somethink?" he says.

"Everyone in this place."

"I don't say somethink," he says.

"You might say it but not realise it," Thickness says.

Thickness is standing almost underneath him, obviously trying to spoil his turn.

"If I said somethink, I would realise it. It isn't somethink, it's something."

"I just reminded you, though," Tina says.

"I always say something," he says. "Something, some-thing, something."

Thickness starts whining, demanding his turn on the swing.

He's pathetic, Thickness. Anyone can see he's practically in love with Tina, but he doesn't have a hope. Even without his glasses, there's his froggy eyes. She never in a million years would kiss him. Thickness reckons how she is so smart and all this bull, but he's just sucking up. All this crap about her mother counting cards, and all the robbers and their buzzer — as if there's anyone who can't count cards.

Thickness won't let go about this somethink, though. Now he's on the swing, he's telling Tina how the Housing

Commission people can't help saying somethink. Their mothers say it, so then their kids hear that and think it's the proper way to say it.

"But if they go into the bank, the teller says Would you like me to put something in your account, madam?" Tina says. "So then they hear the proper way to say it. But they don't even try. You just go making excuses for them. All they have to do is say ing instead of ink, but they won't."

"I'm just saying they're not stupid," Thickness says. "That's all I'm saying."

"But you aren't even listening to what I'm saying," Tina says. "They can't be bothered. That's all it is! You can tell from the way they speak. They say somethink, anythink."

Thickness is such a dill. He can't even see he's getting on her nerves.

Tina jumps down off her swing and walks towards the lane. Thickness jumps down after her. She turns around.

"You want to come and have some lunch or somethink?" she says. "Juvenile delinquent, he can get up on our roof and fix our TV aerial. Our picture's really crap."

Thickness picks up his bike and follows Tina. Just like a poor pathetic puppy, he thinks. He follows Thickness.

———

WHEN THEY REACH her back door, Tina presses a buzzer, then talks into a speaker on the wall. Something in the door clicks. They go in.

A staircase rises to their left, and there's another door ahead. Thickness says through there is where they keep the money.

"It's really thick," Tina says. "If you had an oxy torch, it would take you the whole night to get through."

They follow Tina up the stairs.

On the upper landing, there's another door, another buzzer. At the sound, Mrs Bexley opens up — the smoking-at-the-window lady who dobbed him in to Mrs Green. Today she's wearing blue, but her hair is very beautiful again, tied up in the French roll.

"Well my goodness!" says Mrs Bexley. "Now all three of you have met, I see."

"Mum, this is Spook. Spook, this is my mother."

"Spook and I have met," says Mrs Bexley. "And Theodore, you're always welcome."

"He isn't really Spook," says Thickness. "He's Ralph."

"Come in anyway," says Mrs Bexley. "I'm sure we're all friends here."

They enter a spacious living room. Two curtained windows look down over Blessington Street. Mrs Bexley picks up a tea-towel and starts flicking low tables, stacking magazines. Her every movement is so elegant, she could be the lady in the Peter Stuyvesant advertisement, the one who half closes her eyes each time she blows out smoke. He wonders if Mrs Bexley knows how beautiful she is. He's never seen a lady quite so like a film star.

Mrs Bexley sits at last, but even sitting down she does a special way. She tilts her legs so as to make him feel... well, he hardly knows exactly what, except he's never seen a thing like this before, not right in front of him.

Mrs Bexley lights a cigarette and breathes it in. Straight away he has the feeling there is going to be a test.

"So," says Mrs Bexley. "Are you boys looking forward to going back to school?"

She blows a donut made of smoke. It drifts across the room.

He looks to Thickness, but Thickness hasn't even noticed.

"I take it that's a no," says Mrs Bexley.

"It's a no," says Tina. "Obviously."

"When we saw you on the roof that day, Spook, we honestly thought you were going to break your neck," says Mrs Bexley. "What on earth were you doing up there? Were you trying to launch a rocket or something? I hope you weren't just showing off."

"He was fixing up an aerial," says Tina.

"Is that so?" says Mrs Bexley. "But couldn't someone else have fixed the aerial, Spook? That would have been far safer, surely."

"It wasn't really dangerous," he says.

"Up on that high roof? I beg to differ there! You won't be going up again, I trust."

"Tina says your aerial needs looking at," he says. "The wires can get this gunky stuff like rust. You have to clean it off. It isn't hard. I did it at my grandpa's place."

"Spook, I have to warn you. Much of what my daughter says, you really must take it with a great big grain of salt."

"Thanks a lot," says Tina.

"And where are you from anyway, Spook?"

"Karnook."

"I don't believe I know a Karnook. Where would that be?"

"It's in New South Wales."

"Ah, New South Wales. When Tina was a little one, we had a holiday in New South Wales. My husband wanted it, so off we went, and guess who got the vomits? Vomit everywhere. Covered in it, she was. Still, she couldn't help it, poor little thing. Bentleigh, anyhow, is where we're from. I'm sure you've heard of Bentleigh. Kevin, Mr Bexley, he's an Oakleigh boy, but Oakleigh's basically Bentleigh East. We're just nomads now, alas. Kevin has to get the branch experience. After that, we'll see. No-one has a crystal ball, but in the bank the rewards come pretty fast for those who earn them. I keep having to tell Tina we won't be putting down roots any time soon, so there's no point getting over-invested, if you see what I mean. Tina's brother, Andrew, that's a different story. Andrew won a scholarship to Cranston, which is on the other side of town, of course, so all of Andrew's friends, they're more or less the Cranston gang, and they mainly come from the better suburbs, obviously. Andrew mixes mainly with the rowing boys these days. Do they have rowing where you'll be going, Spook?"

"I'm going to the tech," he says.

"Oh, I see," says Mrs Bexley, adjusting her position. He is pretty sure he can hear static crackling.

"I'm sure there'll be some excellent teachers there," Mrs Bexley says. "We all need bricklayers and that kind of thing, God knows. There's nothing to be ashamed of there. Our Tina hasn't exactly covered herself in glory, scholarship-wise. We're putting our faith in Our Lady of Sorrows, aren't we Tina? I don't imagine they'll have rowing either."

"Sewing, but not rowing," Thickness says.

"You've such a wicked wit, Theodore," says Mrs Bexley. "You're the one who should be going for the scholarship."

"My mother's not a great believer in private schools," says Thickness.

Mrs Bexley blows another of her smoke rings.

"There's such a lot of prejudice these days," she says.

The smoke ring rolls around itself, growing larger and larger. Mrs Bexley stubs out her cigarette.

"You know I'd be the last person on earth to disagree with your mother, Theodore, but I do think not believing in private schools is a bit like not believing in gravity."

Mrs Bexley smiles, gets up and leaves the room. Tina rolls her eyes.

"Shhh," says Thickness.

Mrs Bexley calls out for Thickness to join her in the kitchen. He follows her out.

"Like her pet rabbit," Tina says.

"Pet frog," he says.

"She'll get him making pancakes, bet you anything."

"Pancakes is OK."

"If you don't look at her legs, she gets offended."

"What about her legs?"

"She reckons they're her best feature."

"Am I supposed to look?"

"Not you," says Tina. "Men."

Tina starts flipping through a magazine. He looks through the pile. They don't have magazines at his place at all. When he has a haircut, he looks though the barber's Pix magazines to see the ladies' tits. Tina's mother just has magazines with Audrey Hepburn and the Queen.

He glances at the Bexleys' television. What if there is a problem with its picture? If Mrs Bexley could open up their window, he could climb up on the roof and loosen off the aerial wires then screw them back again. That would more than likely fix it. Then Mrs Bexley would get him to come back. She'd take him in her kitchen and show him how to make the pancakes. Thickness wouldn't be around. They'd eat the pancakes, him and Tina and Mrs Bexley, and each time Mrs Bexley left the room, Tina could tell him how her mother was a bitch, some thing like that.

Mrs Bexley brings the pancakes out. For a treat, they're allowed to have them where they're sitting. Mrs Bexley puts a tray down on the pouffe. There's sugar in a bowl, and cut-up bits of lemon, and a jug of golden syrup with a special handle that you squeeze to let the syrup out. He draws a swastika on his pancake with the syrup, then squeezes on some lemon juice. Mrs Bexley has half a spoon of sugar and a squeeze of lemon.

Mrs Bexley looks out their window while she eats her pancake, like maybe she is thinking of the statue lady in the ad, the one who holds up the big torch. She has cut her pancake into tiny pieces, and every piece she chews and chews. When she's finished, she dabs her serviette against her lips, then folds it.

"Tell me Tina," says Mrs Bexley. "How are you planning to entertain your friends this afternoon?"

"We're going down The Windings," Thickness says.

"Is that a good idea?"

"It's daytime, Mum," says Tina. "There's three of us."

"Nothing happens down there really," Thickness says. "And it's just a little creek. You'd never drown in it."

"It's just a creek and tracks and stuff like that," says Tina.

"Stuff like that?" says Mrs Bexley. "That's the way you speak now, is it?"

"Everybody speaks like that," says Tina.

she's heard there is a gang down there along the creek. Thickness says the hoons go down and drive their cars around, but that's at night, and mainly up the Broady end.

"The Housing Commission, they're the ones I hold responsible," says Mrs Bexley. "We had the hoons in

Murrumbeena too. Murrumbeena isn't Bentleigh, but it's closer than I'd like. Hanging round the milk bars. Burning up their tyres, making all their silly skid marks. And the girls! Honestly, you just know in two winks they're going to go and get themselves... get themselves in all kinds of difficulties. I blame the parents, I really do."

"Should I have a look at your TV?" he asks.

Mrs Bexley reaches for her cigarettes. She turns towards him.

"I'm sorry, Spook," says Mrs Bexley. "What was that?"

"I could check your TV picture. I could get up on the roof. It's not that hard."

"There's nothing wrong with our TV."

Mrs Bexley rises, gathers up their plates, and takes them to the kitchen.

"What did you make a Nazi pancake for?" Thickness hisses. "She saw you!"

"What Nazi pancake?"

"You made the Nazi sign!"

"It's just a joke."

"They murdered all the Jews!"

Mrs Bexley comes back out, lighted cigarette in hand. She stands there in the middle of the room.

Is this it, then? Is this the end of lunch?

Thickness gets to his feet, like maybe he's going to make some speech, some awful denunciation of the Nazis and their sympathisers. Mrs Bexley goes over to her smoking window. Thickness starts to says how great the pancakes were. He chimes in himself with yeah and thanks a couple of times, but Tina just walks out like they're completely stupid and waits at the top of the stairs.

They follow her, but at the door he hesitates, looks back.

Mrs Bexley has her back to him, her right arm folded, holding up her elbow as she gazes out her favourite window. Her long legs cross each other, sculptured and beautiful. Mrs Bexley is quite unaware, it's obvious, that anyone might be looking at her.

As gently as he can, he closes the apartment door.

———

THICKNESS PICKS his bike up off the grass while Tina gets hers from the shed.

"You'll have to walk," Thickness tells him.

"Walk or dink," Tina says.

"I don't know how."

"I'm not dinking him," Thickness says.

"It's just a pancake," Tina says. "He's sorry."

"He didn't say sorry once."

Tina and Thickness ride off down the lane. When he gets to the end of the lane, he's sees they're just beyond, riding round in circles. Probably they're waiting for him, but they ride away again. He follows. Finally they arrive at a dead end.

"'This is where you have to learn it," Tina says.

For his dinking lesson, he has to sit on Thickness's crossbar while Thickness puts his arm around him. Then Thickness rides. It's revolting. Thickness keeps breathing in his ear, making him pay for the pancake.

At last Tina declares him dinkworthy and they set off properly, riding along the middle of the street. Thickness is really puffing, and little balls of spit go in his ear. When they start going downhill, it's terrifying. Thickness's brakes squeak like anything.

They come out on a major road where lots of cars are whizzing past. Without a word, Tina zooms across, then dismounts on the other side.

Thickness makes him get down off the bike, then wait and wait. By the time they cross, Tina has already gone. They wind on down more side streets and finally catch up with Tina at a row of posts that are blocking off a gravelled patch. Beyond this barrier, knee-high grass and bushes extend in all directions.

"Is this it?" he asks. "Where's the creek?"

Tina gestures ahead, but he can't see any creek. A mile or so away, across the scrub, a slope rises up with houses at its top.

Thickness leads the way, pushing his bike. Before long they start coming across tracks that lead in all directions, crossing and re-crossing through the scrub. In one place where the bushes aren't so thick, they come upon a patch of grass all trampled down.

"It's horses," Thickness says. "The rich girls' horses get out of their paddocks and come in here."

He walks into the middle of the trampled grass. Away to his right, perhaps half a mile off, a massive bridge reaches across the valley, riding on tall steel legs.

"What's that?" he says. "It's huge!"

Thickness tells him it's a bridge for goods trains. He can hear trains sometimes in the night.

"Can you get there?" he asks. "Can you get underneath?"

Tina tells him all the perverts go there, underneath the bridge.

"They come out of the bushes," Tina says. "They show you their thingy."

"How many thingies you ever seen?" he asks.

"I've seen my brother's."

"People go there and get drunk," Thickness says. "They leave their beer bottles."

"Their beer bottles and their frangers," Tina says.

"Their what?"

"Their frangers," Tina says. "Don't you even know what a franger is?"

"It's like a beer bottle top," he says.

"How's that going to stop you having a baby?"

"It's like a balloon," Thickness says. "A balloon, except all crinkly."

He doesn't ask. He's asked enough. Every time he opens his mouth, one of them is down on him like he's an idiot. Still, he likes it down here, with that bridge far off, and the way the bushes hide them. If he could get a secret treasure, he could bury it down here, maybe, and make a map. Then if some emergency happened, he could come and get it.

He is just wondering where he could hide the map when they come upon the creek. The watercourse itself is shallow, but the banks are steep, all sandy stuff with weeds, collapsed in places where there's been a landslide. Bits of muck up in the branches show how high the water must have come.

Thickness tells him how they found a bomb car close to here, Tina and himself. It was all smashed up, but its lights still worked, and when they pressed a button, it made an ahooga sound just like the cars in The Untouchables.

"Did you start the engine?" he asks.

"It wouldn't go," Tina says.

"I could have started it," he says. "You have to use the clutch."

"It didn't have a clutch," Thickness says.

"It has to have one."

"It didn't," Tina says.

He badly wants to see this car. He would like to check it for himself. Tina says the water washes them away, though, or someone comes and pulls them out.

"So how do they even get here?"

"The hoons steal them," Tina says. "They bring them down and drive them round and when they're sick of them, they dump them in the creek."

Thickness says they've found a stack of bomb cars, mostly past the bridge.

They push on towards the bridge, and for the first time in a long while he can't help but feel excited, wandering through this wilderness with a girl with tits who talks about thingies and frangers and perverts. He must be careful, obviously, not to say the dreadful somethink, but all his nerve ends call to him that he has entered a special place where anything could happen.

At last they step clear of the bushes onto hard bare earth, and above them is the enormous bridge. The mighty structure spans the valley. He peers up into its intricate depths, barely paying attention to the others as they drop their bikes and descend to the water's edge.

Above, he can make out all kinds of zigzag steel members bolted together, but behind these shapes all is shadowy, right up to where the railway lines must pass overhead.

Who could have made this bridge? When, and how? And where can it have gone, the giant creature that put this Meccano masterwork together, then left it here to rust, as tiny swallows dart about? The whole structure, he can tell, is tight and zingy. Every now and then, a dinging sound rings out as if the whole creation is wanting to creak under the strain, but can't. He claps his hands, and somewhere up above two shadow hands claps back in answer.

Tina reappears, climbing up the bank.

"Where's all the frangers?" he says.

"They're not here all the time."

"What about the pervert guy?"

Thickness reappears as well, climbing the bank behind Tina. They've probably been talking about him.

"What?" says Thickness.

He doesn't answer.

Thickness and Tina mount their bikes again and set off slowly on a track that follows close along the bank. The creek plain on this side of the bridge is more open, but there's still some scrub around. They're soon out of view.

He doesn't care. He wants to find a bomb car, one to call his own. Soon the track diverges from the creek. He follows close along the bank, stopping every thirty yards or so to walk up to the precipice and check he has missed no hidden treasure below.

On the far side of the creek there are paddocks with proper fences and the occasional horse. Nearer to hand, he begins to notice skid marks in the grass. These must be wheel tracks from the cars the others talked about, the ones the hoons steal and bring down here and drive around like crazy.

He spots a gleaming panel through the willows, and recognises a car shape slanting down the bank. He yells out to the others, but they cannot hear.

He scrambles down the creek bank. The car he's found is not ideal — it's just a Prefect, actually, not even black — but all its windows have been shattered, and its doors are hanging open. He can easily feel around inside. In the crack behind the rear seat he finds several halfpennies and a crumpled cigarette, while there's an old blue tartan slipper on the floor just like his grandpa used to wear. The whole cabin has a people smell, mixed with a smell of mud. The car is pointing down at such an angle he daren't climb properly inside. He scrambles up the bank.

Where are the others? He can't even hear them now. He hurries on, picking up the track they must have taken, and comes upon the two of them crouched over Tina's bike, lying on its side.

"What's happened?" he says.

Thickness is trying to do something with the chain. It seems to have come apart.

"I've found a bomb car. It's great."

"We already saw that one," Tina says.

"It's just got there. I found halfpennies in the back seat."

"It's been there for ages," Tina says.

"There's a slipper in the back seat."

"It was there before Christmas," Thickness says.

"It could have petrol," he says. "We could make it go."

Tina wants to go home. Thickness reckons he could dink her, but she says he can't, it's all uphill. Thickness keeps on trying with the chain. He wraps his hanky round one end and tries to jam the ends together with a stick.

"You should take it to a bike shop," he tells Thickness.

Tina walks off in a snit.

"There's this clip thing," Thickness says. "You have to push it open."

"She doesn't even care," he says.

"I'm just trying to fix it."

He ought to leave them. That's what he should do. Let

them have their little club. Their broken chain club. He doesn't care. He walks away.

The whole thing's getting clearer now. It's been getting clearer for a while. He's meant to be a loner, that's the truth of it. It will be horrible, he realises, but at least he won't have to put up with idiots like these. People always making out they have something he hasn't got, like if they live in Bentleigh or their brother has a scholarship. How they found some real ahooga car.

He looks about him. The bridge is way behind. The nearest house is half a mile away.

It's all so obvious. He is alone. All these other people he must pretend to like, they don't care for him in the least. And — yes, of course! — this is what his father's always known, why he's so strange and hard to reach. It's because he saw this truth a long time back that no-one is allowed to say. All the grownups, maybe, even know. It could be why they are the way they are, so cranky and so brittle.

Even as this revelation is announcing itself, an irritating noise has been competing for his attention. Turning, he sees the top half of a kid bouncing through the grass on what is soon revealed to be a little motor bike, home-made from bits of metal tube.

The kid pulls up in front of Thickness. He goes over to see what's going on. Tina comes back too.

Thickness shows the kid the broken chain. The kid turns to Tina.

"You their sister then, or what?"

"That's my brother fixing up my chain," she says.

The kid says his dad could fix the chain up easy.

"Fix it how?" Thickness says.

"He can fix anything. Who d'you reckon made this? Fuckin' welded, mate. Never break. Fix your chain up easy."

The bike kid is just skin and bone. Sandshoes and no socks. Fraying tee shirt. He leans over his handlebars and drops a giant goobie made of spit.

"Where's your dad?" Thickness asks.

"Not far."

"How far's that?" Tina asks.

"Gees, you want me to get me fuckin' ruler out? Not far, OK? Doesn't bother me if you get it fixed or not."

Thickness looks to Tina.

"I don't care," she says.

"Where you go to school then, anyway?" the kid asks Tina.

"Nowhere you'd be going."

"Got a tongue on her, your sister, mate," the kid says to Thickness. "Where's she go to, anyway?"

"You want us to come to your place or not?" Tina asks.

The kid spits, revs his engine. He rides off a little way and starts doing wheelies. Thickness folds the chain in his hanky and gets to his feet. No-one has expressed the least interest in his bomb car.

They follow the motorbike kid, Thickness and Tina wheeling their bikes, himself bringing up the rear. Every now and then the kid circles back and rides around them like a sheep dog. Once he comes right up to Tina, does a half-arsed wheelstand, then tears off again.

They pass behind a row of houses backing onto creekland, go up a side street, and come out at a little shopping centre. There's a Golden Fleece garage on the corner, a car up on the hoist. The kid points to a guy in overalls working under the car.

"It's your dad," Tina says.

"Not me dad, dipstick. That's fuckin' Brian."

"Is fuckin' Brian going to fix our chain?" Thickness asks.

"Fuckin' Brian spat in me dad's cup of tea. Spat right in it, then he called the cops."

"Did your dad make the tea wrong?" Tina asks.

"Reckoned me dad nicked his fuckin' spanners. But he didn't, 'cos Brian's spanners are Japanese crap for one thing, and if he had of done it, he never would have got caught. The coppers couldn't prove a thing, but fuckin' Brian sacked me old man anyhow."

"Maybe you shouldn't speak so loud," says Thickness.

"You wanna know what happened, four-eyes? You want to know what happened then, or what?"

"What happened?" Tina says.

"Fuckin' Brian, he got very fuckin' sorry. I'll show yez."

The kid zooms off on his motorbike again, then stops a few houses up. He waits for the others to catch up.

"Is this it?" Tina says.

A muddy drive runs down one side of a derelict wooden house. Someone has painted WATCH OUT DOG on corrugated iron gates that block off access halfway down the drive. Beyond the gates, a dog is snarling.

"There should be a comma after OUT," Thickness says.

The kid kills his engine and gets off the bike.

"You the comma copper, are you?"

"I'm not going in if there's a watch out dog," Tina says.

"Old Nipper?" the kid says. "He hardly bites at all. Only takes a nip — unless he doesn't like the taste of yez."

"We're going home," Thickness says.

The kid lets out a bloodcurdling cry. The dog falls silent.

"Only attacks if I tell him," the kid says. "Some dickhead tries breaking in, though, Nipper'll have him for dinner."

"I think we should take it to a proper bike shop," Thickness says. "Somewhere they know about chains."

"Jesus Christ, it's not fuckin' brain surgery," the kid says. "My dad's knockin' back work every day of the week. He can do any fuckin' thing. Engine work, panel work. Fuckin' A grade mechanic, and bloody Brian goes and spits in his tea. And where's all Brian's customers now? You see 'em all lined up at his garage? Bullshit. One lousy car, that's all he's got on his fuckin' hoist, and where do you reckon they all go now? They come here. And they're better off, too. All cash, see. Better price than fuckin' Brian, and a better fuckin' job. You tell your oldies, if they want their car fixed up, bring it here. Save themselves a fuckin' fortune. Anyway, you have a think about it. No skin off my nose. Only trying to help yez."

The kid lets another of his spit balls fall onto the footpath.

Tina looks across to Thickness. The weeds. The sagging weatherboards. The pot-holed driveway and the welded gates. Thickness just shrugs.

"Can you stop saying fuckin'?" Tina says.

"It's just a fuckin' word," the kid says.

"We'll come inside if you stop saying it."

"What's your name?" the kid says. "Can't just tell me dad he's got to fix a chain for Chain Girl."

"Is he even home?" says Thickness.

"Course he's fuckin' home."

"You said you wouldn't say that," Tina says.

"I don't remember saying that," the kid says. "I'm Wocker, anyhow. How long do I have to stop for?"

"Long enough," Tina says.

"You want to see Nipper? Want to see if he bites your finger off?"

"No thank you," Tina says.

"No thank you?" the kid says. "Jesus Christ, it's a joke, Joyce! Leave your bikes. Bring your chain."

Thickness and Tina dump their bikes in the driveway and follow Wocker to his front door.

He leads them down a dingy corridor that stinks of cigarettes and fried food. They pass through a kitchen possibly not cleaned or tidied in living memory, then down a step into a narrow lean-to where nylon curtains flecked with brownish spots admit filtered sunlight. A laminex table is piled high with newspapers. A blood-smeared metal bowl lies near the flywire door, a second china bowl beside it likewise empty but for a dribble of water. Wocker takes the chain.

"Wait here," he says.

Wocker goes out through the flywire door. He peers through the curtains after him.

"Can you see the dog?" Tina asks.

Wocker is walking towards a long, low shed. Inside, there's a Holden with its bonnet up. There is no dog in sight.

"He's chained up," he says.

"My mother'd have a fit in this place," Tina says. "She'd have the health inspectors in."

"You shouldn't even talk to him," says Thickness. "Let us talk to him."

"Don't tell him your name," he says. "He's just cracking onto you."

"He is fixing up my chain," Tina says.

"Maybe," Thickness says. "Wait and see."

Tina returns to the kitchen.

"This is so gross," she says.

The barking starts again, then Wocker comes through the flywire door. His hands are filthy, but he's holding up an unbroken chain.

"Where is she?" Wocker says.

"She had to get a drink of water," he says.

"Who?" says Wocker.

"Tina."

"Ah!"

Thickness gives him a dirty look, just as Tina reappears in the kitchen doorway.

"You like it in our kitchen, Tina Marina?" Wocker says. "You gunna fix us something up?"

She looks to Thickness, then himself. How does Wocker knows her name?

"Bet you got rats," she says.

"That's not very nice. Not when me dad's fixed up your chain, Tina Zina. Not when I stopped saying the magic fuckin' word."

"Thank you," says Tina.

"Yeah, thanks," says Thickness.

"What about seen-a-ghost boy?" says Wocker. "You going to thank me?"

"It's not my chain," he says.

"Four-eyes here, he's not her brother really, is he?"

"I wouldn't know," he says.

"Don't you even know 'em?"

"Not that well," he says.

Wocker grabs a spanner from the table.

"Pack of fuckin' bullshit artists," Wocker says. "Come on."

Wocker leads them back to where they dropped their bikes in the front yard. He loosens the rear wheel of Tina's bike, slips the chain back on, then tightens everything again and stands the bike back on its wheels.

"Give her a spin," Wocker says. "Make sure four-eyes hasn't broken anything else."

Tina grabs her bike, walks it to the footpath, then rides off. Wocker asks them where they go to school. They tell him where they'll each be starting soon.

"Northcote!" Wocker says. "Fuckin' long ride to Northcote."

"There's a bus," Thickness says. "It's worth it, anyhow. They got French and German."

"Fuckin' German? I can speak German. Heil Hitler! See? You want to go to the toilet? Oui oui oui. French too, see? Me and seen-a-ghost-boy, we're the brainy ones. We don't even need to go to school, so we're going to Glendale fuckin' Tech."

"What form you in?" he asks.

"Don't fuckin' care, long as it's not the same as you. Your girlfriend's back."

"She's not his girlfriend," Thickness says.

Tina calls down from the footpath. Her bike is fine.

No-one is around when he finally gets home. He stands in the hallway, and everything is still and quiet. The motor of the fridge starts up and runs a while, then stops. He notices the slanty sun coming through the porch window, how its shadow moves along the floor nearly fast enough for him to see it moving.

This must be what it's like to be a loner. To notice things like this, like how the motor shakes when the fridge stops. He wonders if his dad notices the motor shake.

For just a moment, he has the strongest feeling that everything is very beautiful.

When his mother gets back from Dr Schlimmicht's, she asks what he's been doing.

"Nothing much," he says.

Everything has changed completely, of course. It's like a door has opened onto a whole new world of possibilities — but how could she understand?

After dinner, his mother stays in the kitchen and re-reads her x-ray books. His dad and he watch Rawhide.

CHAPTER SIX

School starts at last, and it is crap.

The playground at the tech is asphalt, covered with overlapping coloured lines, and half are for some game he's never heard of. Even when the lines are for a game he knows, there's so many crossing over it's impossible to tell where one court ends and another starts. There's hardly any balls, either, and half of them are flat.

Inside, his school is crap as well. In every room they have the same type of creamy walls, and on the ceiling there's the same grey stuff with holes drilled in it. Holding up the roof in every room they have these zig-zag metal girder things, and every room has the exact same blackboard and same fan and same desks and benches. The only difference is the scratchings, like where some kid has done a spider or a dick. In every room there's CLUNK LOVES DUNK on some desk or chair. Clunk is Mr McCloskey. He's the principal. Dunk is Mr Duncan. He takes metalwork.

The kids all have to wear this uniform. The uniform is

grey unless you have a jumper. Then you get a stripe around the neck. The stripe is meant to be maroon. It's like dried blood.

This Wocker kid they met down by The Windings, he actually is at Glendale Tech, but in a different form. Wocker's in 1B. He's in Mr Gardiner's form, 1A.

Mr Gardiner is a bit pathetic, but he's nice. This is Mr Gardiner's first school. He tells the kids how he and they are in the same boat. He is new. They are new. There isn't any boat, though.

Mr Gardiner shows the kids his special tie. It's made of wool from a real sheep. Mr Gardiner's mother made it on a loom. It isn't tie-shaped at the bottom. Its bottom is cut straight across, ragged like a scarf. Mr Gardiner's mother dyed his tie in tea and onion skins.

Mr Gardiner is their English teacher. He says stuff like how words are atoms, and these atoms make ideas. It's pretty sad. Anyone can see he's not broken in at all.

The kids at Glendale Tech all know the other kids already. They all went to the same primary school, or else they know some other kid who did. In the playground, everyone has their friends, and whoever their friends are, it's not him. He looks around to see if any other kid could be his friend, but there isn't anyone. This is how he ends up getting stuck with Wocker.

Wocker's name is really William Spink. He reads this on the Gold house noticeboard. No-one ever calls him William, though. Not even Spinky. Even Clunk knows he's Wocker. First day, in assembly, Clunk goes Are you listening to me, Wocker? I hope you are, because you have a reputation. It precedes you. You've been warned.

Wocker must know all the other kids, but Wocker

doesn't bother with the other kids. He's singled out himself. And this Wocker is so pov. He's skinny like a broom handle, and his dacks, they're practically worn out already. He always seems to have a cold, too. He's always sniffling.

Wocker cannot help it if he has a cold. He knows that isn't Wocker's fault. But then Wocker has to come up from behind and kick his ankles. Or Wocker digs his knuckles in his ribs, then starts in with this bullcrap about Tina babe, how Tina is his girlfriend but he has to share. Wocker's always asking him where Tina lives, how big her bra is, all this crap. Wocker says he's going to nick a bra and give it to her. It'll be a black one. He saw one like it in a magazine.

Wocker is disgusting. It's all bullshit, obviously. Wocker must know Tina's not his girlfriend, but he just keeps going on about it, how he's going to fuck her.

He should have stopped this right at the beginning, when it started, but he couldn't somehow, and now he doesn't know what to do. He could tell Mr Gardiner, but that will be terrible. Mr Gardiner won't know what to do either. He can't tell any other teacher, though, because all they care about is making sure the kids aren't mucking up too much. Anyone can see the smoke behind the bike sheds, but the teachers never go there. If he told them how Wocker kicks his ankles, they'd just say Don't bother him, some crap like that. He couldn't possibly tell about the bra.

This Wocker is so pov, he doesn't even have a hanky. If Wocker has to blow his nose, he sniffs it up, or pokes his finger up then blows it out and wipes his finger on his dacks. Wocker reckons this is how they do it in the army. Wocker reckons if there ever is a war and they are soldiers, there won't be any hankies, so they'll have to know some other way. There won't be any toilet paper for the soldiers either,

Wocker says, so they have to be prepared to go without. Wocker reckons if you ever get your dacks at army disposals, you ought to wash them for a week before you even touch them.

Wocker has a million of these bullshit stories.

It isn't fair at all. All he wants is a proper, decent friend, but all he's got is Thickness, and now this Wocker kicking at his heels.

———

His father still can't spell asphyxiation, and even with an easy one like oxygen he gets the x and y mixed up, but in the test he gets enough correct to get his badges. His mother sews them on his father's uniform. Now he only has probation for six months, then he's in for life — a real fair dinkum fireman.

For this first six months, his father has to watch and learn. He gets to hold the hose, but only down the back, not the nozzle yet. He gets to hang the hoses out to dry as well. All the new guys have to do this job. The main part, though, is they'll be watching him. That's what probation really is. They have to know what type of bloke you are. They have to know you fit right in.

Some blokes, it turns out, they're really pyromaniacs. All they want to do is light their matches all day long. These blokes, they get the flick, even if they can tell good jokes and all the other stuff. Another type of bloke, if a cat gets stuck up a tree and someone calls the fire brigade, this bloke, he says Why do I have to do it? This is not the type of bloke they want either. Even if you can't stand cats, you still have to go up the tree.

The best news is, his father's going to be at Glendale. This is great because it's really slack. When they built the Glendale Fire Station, everyone thought there'd be stacks of fires. Then it turned out people started building houses out of brick and got electric stoves. People said they ought to pull this Glendale Fire Station down and move it somewhere else, but the government said no, they built in the right place. They kept hoping there would be more fires.

"The rot you tell this child, Ray Halliday," his mother says.

His father winks. Neither of them dares to tell his mother yet she's sewn the badges upside down.

———

HIS FATHER COMES out of his shell, sometimes, and jokes about, but then he closes up again, and for long periods he hardly says a thing. It's like his father goes away somewhere and leaves behind a replica, a wooden man who has no jokes at all.

Where does his father go?

He's always felt the answer must lie in his father's sad and lonely past. This past is like a sealed enclosure like he's seen in a museum, a dusty diorama behind glass, with plaster dinosaurs and a painted river.

His father's actual past began in Gilberton — a place in Queensland — where his dad was born. After that, his father's mother gave his dad away. She gave him to the Kerricks Home for Boys.

He's heard this story mainly from his mother, not his dad at all. He finds its sadness almost overwhelming. All his dad will say is how there isn't any point or else it doesn't matter now.

Is this, then, where his father goes when he is absent? Back to Gilberton? Back to the Kerricks Home for Boys? If not there, where?

———

ONE DAY, at lunch, his mother says his father's going to take him out. This happens on a Sunday. His father doesn't seem to know a thing about it.

"It'll be good for both of you," she says.

His father leads him down the stairs and asks him where he'd like to go.

"Can we go to billiards?"

"Not on Sunday, mate. I tell you what. You close your eyes and I'll surprise you."

So this is how it starts, their stupid trip with his eyes closed. It's all so weird. His father isn't even meant to drive the Consul. He's been banned. Grandpa Doc made this really clear when he gave the Consul to his mum. So what is going on? If his father's got cancer, why not tell him straight away? Drive around the corner, maybe. Park under a tree. He shouldn't have to close his eyes.

"Did you have an x-ray?" he asks.

They've been driving for about five minutes.

"Why would I do that? Give your mum some practice? She's not that rusty, mate."

"Find out stuff."

"Stuff like what?"

"If you have a mass. Stuff like that."

His father snorts.

"I haven't got a mass, mate. You can open your eyes if that's what's bothering you."

"You said close them."

"Just a bit of fun, mate. No-one's trying to scare you."

Really? Well, he's come this far eyes closed. And actually, he's rather liking it now, this mystery about their destination.

"You worked it out yet?" his father asks. "Where we're going?"

"I know about the egg and seed."

"It's not the egg and seed, mate. Your mum just reckons we ought to spend a bit of time together."

"We're together all the time."

"You tell her, mate. I've tried."

Tried. He can imagine. His father's trieds pass like summer lightning without thunder, in the blink of an eye. He lets it go. They drive in silence.

These situations with his father, the two of them alone together, they're such a strain unless his father has some tease afoot. What if his dad is actually as scared as him? Scared of the empty space where they should know each other, but they don't? He loves his dad, and longs to find a way to heal his pain, but stuck here in the car, pushed into this stupid trip that neither of them really wants — it isn't any good.

He sinks inside himself. From bursts of warmth on his chest and arms, he guesses they are probably travelling west. He hears the ding of a tram, and for a while can feel them juddering over wooden blocks. Following a tramline west, then. But to where?

Suddenly a roar gives everything away. A roar, and a

smell of burning kerosene. Opening his eyes, he sees a tailplane gliding between low buildings.

They turn onto a concrete road. Ker-thunk, ker-thunk, at every crevice. Ahead, a guard stands in a sentry box, beside an open boom gate. His father drives on through.

"Shouldn't we have stopped?" he says.

"Gate's open, mate."

Ker-thunk, ker-thunk. His father has no shame. The drive past open sheds his father says are hangars. Most are empty, but he sees a DC3 in one, a gaping hole along its side.

"Hospital for planes," his father says. "You could work here one day."

His father parks the Consul in a spot marked Commercial vehicles only. They get out and cross together to a cyclone fence that overlooks the airfield.

"Why d'you bring us here?" he says.

"Thought you were plane crazy."

"Who told you that?"

"Your mum."

They look out over baby planes parked at random beyond the fence, their fragile metal skins all bumps and wrinkles. How could you ever trust a flimsy thing like that? The minute your engine stopped, you'd be wishing you'd never taken off. The whole way down, you'd be thinking why did I do this?

"You never talk about your mum," he says.

"Told you all there is, mate."

"Did she ever get a proper husband?"

"Some bloke eventually."

"Is he still alive?"

"Don't know, mate. He isn't anything to me."

"Did she have other kids?"

"Could have. Don't know."

"Will we ever go and see her?"

"It's a long way, mate. You get to Brisbane, you're only half way there."

"We still could go," he says.

"Yeah, maybe. One day."

Half a mile away, the big planes cluster by the terminal as little trains of baggage cars worm their way beneath their wings. Beyond the terminal, a tower rises up, the silhouettes of tiny people visible behind its tinted slanting windows.

"You don't even want to see her," he says.

"Mate, what's done is done."

"Mum wouldn't have to come."

A gust of wind crosses the airfield, stirring the grass into waves. A nearby windsock fills and flaps a moment, then collapses.

"Is it really horrible when you grow up?"

His father spits out a chewed up bit of grass.

"It's different mate, that's all. Enjoy it while you can. It's good to be a kid."

Over at the terminal, they're starting up the engine of a plane. A rising whine becomes a scream, the outer propeller on the wing a lethal whir, and behind those blades a streaming river of hot air, a plane mirage.

"Can we go?" he says.

"You want to see it take off?"

"It's just a plane."

They wait there, clinging to the mesh, as the engines start up one by one. A little tractor pushes the plane onto the runway, then casts off and drives away. The plane taxis across the airfield, rolling along invisible paths. At last, almost a mile off, it slows and turns. Another plane glides into view behind the control tower and touches down with puffs of smoke.

"I want to go," he says.

All the way home, phrases and impressions swirl around inside him, but no coherent sentence makes it to his lips. An unseen hand grips his heart, refusing to let go.

———

MERVYN REYNOLDS STEPS into their life around this time. He is a fireman at the Glendale Fire Station, and their flat is right on Mervyn's way to work. It isn't any inconvenience at all for Mervyn to pick his father up each morning, and even less to drop him back at end of shift.

The car this Mervyn drives is like a slug. It is embarrassing, the way the rear end of his Vanguard slopes down like the back end of a snail without its shell. How Mervyn Reynolds cannot recognise his car is like a slithery thing is just a mystery.

Each morning, his father shines his boots in the porch then washes his hands in the kitchen sink. His mother says Not on the teatowel, Ray, so then his father flicks the sudsy water off and reads the paper with damp hands while his mother fixes up whatever she is getting for their breakfast, whether it is scrambled eggs or Weeties or whatever. Then his father eats this thing and Mervyn Reynolds toots down in the laneway. When he hears the toot, his father drinks the last of his own tea, then fills another cup and stirs three sugars in.

"You run that down to Mervyn, mate," his father says. "I'll bring the toast down in a jiff."

This is how he gets to be down in the lane with Mervyn Reynolds every morning.

Here comes Robur boy. Mervyn says this every morning, then stands there, blowing on his cup, leaning against the fender of his slug car while they wait for his father to come down.

This waiting in the lane with Mervyn Reynolds can get awkward, but usually it isn't, because whatever comes into Mervyn Reynolds' head, he generally starts talking about this straight away. This thing, it could be how he used to do the calling at the Oddfellows' Hall in Ascot Vale, and how the time the lights went out he kept on calling anyway. It could be about how Olive has got cancer in her ear, and Mervyn has to get her heart to eat.

All this calling stuff and Olive stuff, at first it's just confusing, but soon he gets to realise this Mervyn Reynolds, for some reason, thinks he knows all about his life already, so it's not surprising he can't understand. It doesn't really matter, anyway. After enough hanging about in the lane, he eventually figures out that Olive must be a cat, and Mervyn must call out instructions for some kind of dancing when he isn't being a fireman.

Mervyn's conversation notwithstanding, he really would rather not be stuck down in the laneway with this peculiar man each morning. His mother, though, insists he be on hand to retrieve her cup and saucer, and his father says it would be downright rude to leave a bloke just hanging there when a bloke has come to give another bloke a lift.

He's sort of stuck, then — and Mervyn Reynolds' stories always take so long. Just when he thinks one of Mervyn's stories must be getting near the end, it turns out the bit they're getting to isn't really the end at all, it's just the end of the first bit you need to know before you can get to the proper story. And all these stories have so many people in them. If you don't know everything about these people first, you cannot possibly understand why it is so funny what happens in the end, so Mervyn has to tell about them first. All the bits of all these stories are right there in Mervyn Reynolds' head, apparently — he always seems to know exactly which bit should come out next — but then the whole time Mervyn is concentrating on all these bits, he hardly ever has time to drink his tea. Mervyn just holds the cup under his nose and breathes the steam in, and then right when it seems like he is going to take a sip, he remembers some other part he has to explain first, like about how the vet's friend has the shakes, or some microphone that gave a tingle up his arm in Thornbury.

His mother says this Mervyn Reynolds is an old woman. She can't believe his father can put up with him.

"Does he really put out fires?" she asks one time.

"He's a fireman, isn't he?" his father says.

"He isn't just the one they send around to schools to tell the kids not to play with matches?"

"In the big red truck, you mean?"

Personally, he can see his mother's point. Would Mervyn Reynolds really put his teacup down for long enough to chop his way into a burning building and carry out a screaming lady? It seems unlikely, even if a thing like that would make a better story than the unending saga of Olive's ear.

It seems this Mervyn Reynolds really is a fireman, though — and Mervyn certainly wears his love for his fellow firemen on his sleeve.

"Best bunch of blokes you'd ever want to meet," Mervyn

says. "All for one, one for all. Trust my life to a fireman any day."

Eventually his dad comes down the stairs carrying his kit bag and a plate of Mervyn's toast. Once the toast arrives, Mervyn generally gets a wriggle on with his tea. Sometimes he passes the remains across to his dad, who swallows it down in a gulp.

There seems to be some kind of running joke between his dad and Mervyn Reynolds that involves his mother somehow. I'd invite you up, mate, but she's a bit, you know, his dad says, and makes a fluttering gesture with his hand that must be some kind of secret fireman sign.

Eventually the obscene car crawls off up the lane, and he's left holding saucer, cup and plate.

When he gets upstairs, his mother's usually banging crockery in the sink.

"The bloody cheek of him!" she says. "He'll be camping in our backyard next."

"He hasn't got a wife."

"What's he need a bloody wife for? He's got me!"

The way she boils up instantly like this, it bothers him. Grandpa Doc's three hundred miles away. If his father is a mystery bag, his mother is a volcano, sometimes, with a logic all her own.

———

The greatest of his griefs at this time, though, is not his mother or his father. It's Tina Bexley. The bus from Our Lady of Sorrows sets the girls down on Blessington Street around five past four, but even he has the sense to know that hanging around the bus stop is a bit too obvious. He heads for the roundabout park by the humming house instead, because Tina will always have to pass by there to go up her lane.

Tina, though, turns out to be a bitch. That, or else she is completely blind. She never seems to see him, either way. She walks along like she has blinkers on, eyes down, and never once looks over at the swings or at the roundabout. She has to know he's there. She just ignores him.

OK, so she will never like him, probably. Everything about her shouts this out. The little bumps beneath her tunic. The way her mother breathes out smoke. The way she flicks her hair and turns away. All these signs mean something. If Tina ever speaks to him again, he knows already how their talk will go, the snippy way she'll speak, every other sentence like a knife blade, setting him in his place. He doesn't care, though. He just wishes she would notice him.

She doesn't, though. She walks on by.

He goes home, then, to an empty flat and peeps out through his parents' curtains. If only there was something, even once, to see. Tina at a window, taking off her clothes. It never happens though. All he sees are curtains, and occasionally Mrs Bexley, vague behind the terylene.

By half past four, Thickness is usually home. When he gets over there, Thickness is making raisin toast. Thickness's mother gets him raisin bread because she's out when he gets home. That is the kind of mother she is. She makes up for things. When he goes round, they have the raisin toast, then Weeties, then they watch Cisco Kid or Texas Rangers. They make card houses or play pickup sticks.

He doesn't really want to do these things at all. What he really wants to do is say to Thickness Let's go to Tina's.

Instead, he says dumb stuff like I wonder if Tina still rides her bike. Thickness never takes the hint at all.

At last he gets completely sick of it.

"Why don't we go to Tina's?" he says.

"She's not allowed," Thickness says. "She only can have one friend around at a time now. That's their rule."

"But you can still go there. You can go there any time you like."

"I suppose."

"Well do you, then?"

"We're like old friends," Thickness says. "She needs to talk about stuff. She's very mature for her age."

"But talk about what, though?"

"Private stuff. Stuff about her mother."

"If we went round when her mother wasn't there, she'd let us in."

"She has a lot of homework now."

"Bullcrap! In Form One?"

"I don't think she really wants to," Thickness says.

He is such a wuss, Thickness. The raisin bread. The way his mother gives the needles to the dying people. His father practically a missionary. Tina just feels sorry for him. And she's got used to him, because they went to primary school. That's all it is. But now Thickness won't even let him go to her place, and she wouldn't mind at all, probably — not if Thickness was there — and all because he said Why can't we go to Tina's? Thickness probably thinks that he's in love with her. It really makes him mad.

On days he's not completely mad at Thickness, they come back to his place after raisin toast and play cricket in the lane.

Thickness has a proper cricket bat. His father made a

hundred with it when he played for Sydney University. It could have been for theological college. It was a proper hundred, though, with a proper cricket ball.

This cricket bat has linseed oil all over it. The oil is dark, which goes to show the bat is real. The pinky rubber on the handle is peeling off, and underneath it is this string wound round and round the handle. This string was probably made in England. It was probably made at Lords.

To look after his father's string, Thickness has wrapped black insulating tape around the top part of the handle. Whoever holds the bat gets sticky hands in no time, but this doesn't lessen their joint reverence for this relic. Whoever chucks it in the air to determine who will bat first is always careful to make sure it doesn't land on a jutting brick.

Thickness may have this bat, but he is a hopeless cricketer. He just doesn't realise it. On the radio, the commentator is always saying straight bat, but Thickness never listens, he just holds it anyhow. When Thickness goes ballistic with the bat, the ball goes sailing off for miles. He hardly ever hits it properly along the ground. He doesn't even know where silly mid-off is. They put the field positions on the Weeties packet every summer, but Thickness never even reads the packet.

When it's his own turn to bat, he holds the bat completely vertical. It's practically impossible to hit the ball this way, but at least he's playing with a straight bat, and if he hits the ball, he knows he's doing it right. But then Thickness, who can't bowl at all — he doesn't even know what a googly is — he just gets lucky sometimes, so the ball hits a stone or hole and Thickness reckons he span it, and then the ball ends up hitting the rubbish bin by a complete fluke.

There should be a ball hit stone rule, really, but Thickness never will agree to it.

One afternoon, the two of them are playing cricket in the lane when they hear a burst of siren. He looks up to see an ambulance coming along the lane. He lifts the bin out of the way.

The ambulance stops one gate up — behind the place where the migrant people live, where all the TV aerials are up on the roof out front — and two ambulance men get out. They drag the back gate open and slide out their stretcher.

He looks in the neighbour's yard. He's only ever seen a little of it before now, peering through the handhole in the gate. He can see the whole of the long shed now, extending down the far side of the yard, and the garden is more extensive than he realised. Nearly all the plants have pots. There are pots on paving, pots on rusty iron stands, pots on raised up beds with sticks that hold up sheets of netting.

The ambulance men carry their stretcher up the back stairs.

"We should go," Thickness says.

"It's a free country."

"They could be dying," Thickness says. "They could be dead."

The ambulance men enter through the upstairs porch and the flywire screen bangs shut behind them.

"Alright, alright, you lot!"

He spins round to see Mrs Green gesticulating at the shopkeepers who have come out into the lane.

"It's just an ambulance!" says Mrs Green. "You've seen an ambulance before. And you two scallywags, you get on now. It's my responsibility, all this. I'll keep you all informed! Go on, get back to your customers!"

The onlookers hesitate, unwilling to advance, but not yet prepared to concede all priority to Mrs Green.

"Go on now!" shouts Mrs Green. "I'll let you know when there's anything to know. And you two devils — vamoose, I said!"

"We were playing cricket," he says.

"Cricket? Is that what you call it! Blocking up our thoroughfare, hitting your silly balls willy nilly on our roofs! You've probably given this one here a stroke! Do you think we don't hear every word of your silly arguing?"

"We weren't arguing," he says.

"Really? You're arguing with me!"

The flywire door bangs open and the ambulance men carry their stretcher onto the landing. A grey-haired man accompanies them.

They carry their patient down the stairs, a shortish lump covered by a blanket, wisps of yellow hair visible against a pillow. The grey-haired man is mumbling something over and over, crossing himself.

Mrs Green grabs his shoulder, turning him towards her.

"There's an end to all of us, young Sonny Jim. What's your Maker going to say when he meets you? Stickybeak? Is that what you want?"

The ambulance men push through the onlookers crowding around the gate. In the confusion, he catches a glimpse of the patient's face. Her eyes are closed.

"She still could be alive," he says.

"If that one's still alive, I'll eat my hat," says Mrs Green.

Thickness hisses in his ear, insisting they should go because this isn't right.

The ambulance men lift their patient into the vehicle. The grey-haired man goes to climb in after her, and as one of the ambulance men extends a helping arm, his eyes meet the old man's, which he sees now are wet with tears. He looks away, ashamed.

Later, in the kitchen, he waits to hear the news on 3UZ with Thickness. There's no mention of a woman dying from a stroke after listening to boys arguing.

"It isn't always on the news," Thickness says. "People die all the time."

As he is trying to get to sleep that night, the cupboard lady visits him again. She doesn't say or do a thing because she can't, of course. All she can do is hover there before him because she's in a locked up place. He knows he'll have to die himself one day, and if there is a kind of adding up that happens then, he'll have to face it all, the way he's lived, everything he's done. And what if he has lived all wrong? What if he has chickened out of things he should have done, and then it's all too late to change a thing? Will he end up, like Mrs Grey, in a cupboard of forgotten things, the door forever closed on him?

He waits in darkness for a long time, frightened, but at last he passes over to some other place.

———

After the incident with the ambulance, he walks around each day to look in through the window of the shop next door to see what might be happening. There is just a Closed sign hanging in the door, though, and all the TV sets are off. While he is sitting on the back stairs, he sometimes hears a door close over the side fence, but there's no yabber yabber anymore. His mother tells him not to worry. If no-one ever died, she says, there'd be no room for babies.

When Mrs Green comes up one day to do her cupboard business, he asks her what is going on.

"Coronary," says Mrs Green. "And no surprises there, I tell you. You ever seen the guts and gizzards these people eat? All their hung up sausages! Intestines, that's what they're all made of. Your insides! What's the matter with a chop? I said to her one day Chop! Chop! Good for you! They never listen. Minute I saw her on the stretcher, I could tell. Like a little rag doll, lying there."

"Is she alive?"

"Who knows?" says Mrs Green. "All that hocus pocus they go on with, who can tell? Lighting all their candles. Praying to Mother Mary. All their beads and bangles. Saint this one, Saint that one. Concrete and plaster! And the Pope! Don't get me started on the Pope! Infallible my bottom!"

"You think she'll come back?"

"You would have to be the most inquisitive little beggar I ever met! Go on, get out of here, before I take my pinking shears to that long sticky beak of yours."

It isn't fair at all. He and Thickness were the first ones there. He saw a lady who was nearly dead. No-one seems to understand a bit.

He wishes he could talk with Tina. Faced with an event of this magnitude, even snippy snappy Tina would have to... well, he isn't sure exactly, but she would treat him differently, surely. He has seen a lady who was nearly dead.

Maybe he could ring Tina. If her mother answered, he could hang up. If Tina answered, he could say some special thing. He could use his special voice. He could say It's The Skull. Meet me in the roundabout park. Then she'd have to come, to find out who The Skull is, and it would turn out it was him, and he could tell her how he saw the lady on the stretcher and Tina would go all serious, then he could say I love you or something like that, or get her talking about her mother, how she's such a bitch. Stuff like that. It could be great.

The more he thinks about this plan, the better he realises it is. He looks up Tina's last name in the phone book.

Bexley.

Becksleigh.

Bexlee.

Beksli.

Dexley.

Dexleigh.

There's nothing even close in Glendale. They must keep their name a secret so the robbers cannot ring them up.

Nothing ever works! Nothing, ever since they came to this crappy place!

He is sitting on the back stairs feeling sorry for himself when he hears the sound of someone filling up a watering can next door. He goes out to the lane and brings his eye down to the handhole in the gate. The old grey-haired man is just looking up from his watering.

CHAPTER SEVEN

As gloomy as their flat is, sound travels well through the flimsy doors, so Little Mr Big Ears is not bereft of all intelligence. From the pink throne in the bathroom he can pick up conversations in the kitchen pretty well. In this way he learns his mother may have fallen out of love with Dr Schlimmicht.

"A proper thermostat," his mother is saying. "You'd think he could provide a proper thermostat for my developer, wouldn't you? But oh no. You must have set it wrong, that's all he can say. Pre-war rubbish, that's what I have to work with! The voltage meter, I swear that's wrong as well. When was it last calibrated? I said to him."

"What did he say?"

His father's voice.

"If you don't like it, get it checked."

"Maybe you should get it checked."

"Is that my responsibility? We weren't taught that in college."

"It's his clinic, Rose. He's the doctor."

"You wouldn't know a thing about this, Ray. A doctor isn't a god! And this doctor, my God! I get a teeny bit of distortion and he's throwing up his hands. If I can read the films, why can't he? He wants me to call back two patients now! Re-radiate them. What kind of a fool do I look for that?"

"Don't tell anyone."

"This is humiliating, Ray. I'm not some halfwit Pearl Maguire who'll just lie back and take it. He owes me an apology."

"Oh no. Not this again."

"Where's there any again? I've never asked him once for an apology."

"We've been down this road so many times."

"You're sailing very close to my bow, Ray Halliday."

And so it goes. A doctor. His mother. The background music of his life.

———

At school the teachers try to teach, and the kids do their bit, mucking up whenever they can get away with it.

His English teacher, Mr Gardiner, is his favourite, but Mr Gardiner hasn't got a clue. Every day, Mr Gardiner gives the naughty kids detentions, but then he gets all sad when they don't show up. They have to sit and listen while Mr Gardiner asks these kids why they didn't show up for their detention, and they all have their reason, naturally. Then Mr Gardiner gets all frowny, like he's trying to work out if he should believe them when it's obvious they're total liars.

After this, they have to write their letters asking for a job.

Every class, their letter has to start Dear Sir, please find enclosed, which is completely stupid, because if a thing is in the envelope, you'd have to be a moron not to find it. He just feels sorry for Mr Gardiner.

In maths, they have triangles. The right-angled one is easy, but then there are the triangles for smartarses. Obtuse. Acute. Or else it could be equilateral. What is the point? They're all just triangles. That should be enough for anyone.

If it isn't triangles, it's algebra. This algebra, he really cannot get the hang of it. Why do both sides always have to turn out to be equal? What if they just aren't? Plus it's so confusing how the numbers keep turning into letters and vice versa. He says this to Loopy Lennox one time, straight out, but Loopy just says Don't you worry Spookus. You concentrate on woodwork.

The playground is the worst — and it isn't even play-ground now, it's schoolyard, because they're all supposed to be grown up. The kids all know the kids that used to be their friends before, so if he tries to join some game they're playing, they always say there's too many, or if it's a picking type game, they won't pick him till the end. If it's cricket, he never gets to bat or bowl before the bell, just field, and then the next time they play, it's back to picking sides again.

All this time, Wocker Spink keeps hanging round him, saying how he wants to meet his girlfriend, meaning Tina, and how he easily could come round after school and they could go to Tina's place. He has explained to Wocker a million times about the bank and how they have a million locks and no-one can get in, but Wocker just keeps on about it, saying he will get them in somehow.

He is completely sick of this. The kids by now must all

be sure this Wocker is his friend. To put an end to this, he tells Wocker Tina never wants to see him again.

"That's bullshit," Wocker says. "She likes me."

"She doesn't like the way you wipe your nose. How you wipe it on your sleeve, or else you snot in the dirt. She reckons it's disgusting."

"That's how they do it in the army," Wocker says.

"I'm just telling you what she says."

Wocker's disbelief is obvious. Wocker insists they should go and see Tina, clear up all misunderstandings.

"She's only allowed to see one person at a time now."

"That's OK," says Wocker. "It can be just me. I'm telling you, what they say and what they like, these chickee babies, it's two completely different things. You ask me dad."

Wocker is just like a rat scratching at a hole.

One day, after school, Wocker declares he's going to follow him home.

"You can't," he says. "You're not allowed."

"By who?"

"Your dad. He wouldn't let you."

"Me dad's gone bloody roo shooting."

"Bullshit," he says.

"Went last Thursday. Goes every year."

"You can't shoot kangaroos."

"You reckon? Me dad and these guys, they shoot hundreds of the buggers."

"You can't shoot koalas."

"Koalas don't rip down fuckin' fences, mate. The farmers hate the fuckin' roos."

"If you come, you can't spit on our floor."

"What, you live in a fuckin' church or something?"

"It's germy," he says. "And you can't stay long. My mum has to have a nap when she gets home."

"I get it mate. Stealth mission, OK?"

The situation is impossible. Unless he's going to fight Wocker outright in the street, he can see no way out.

He sets off walking as fast as he can, but Wocker keeps up pretty well. At Cox Street, where he usually turns right, Wocker grabs his arm.

"You can't go down there," Wocker says. "We'll get ball bearings in our fuckin' heads. Ninny King and them guys, they live down there. They got shanghais. They can shoot ball bearings through a fuckin' car door. I seen it. Hole this big."

Wocker forms an ominous-looking O with finger and thumb.

"I go this way every day."

"Ninny King and Albert Thomas, mate, they're fuckin' Vultures. Vultures hate the fuckin' Rockets. Who d'you reckon nicked half the cars Turk's doing time for?"

"Who's Turk?"

"Me fuckin' brother, dipstick. He's in Turana for illegal use. Half the fuckin' counts the coppers brung, Ninny King and Albert Thomas, they done 'em. They nicked twice as many cars as Turkie ever done."

"He should tell the cops then."

"He's no fuckin' dobber, mate. He'll fix 'em up when he gets out. The cops, they fuckin' know, anyhow. They just want to put him away."

"How come?"

"His fuckin' turn, mate. That's just how it works. That's justice for you."

"So he's in gaol? Your brother?"

"Fuckin' Turana, mate. Everyone knows Turana. College of knowledge for kids."

"So how old's your brother?"

"Sixteen. Seventeen, the day he gets out."

"When's that?"

"Empire Day. Cracker night. And there'll be fuckin' fireworks this Empire Day, you bet. Ninny King and Albert Thomas, they'll be shitting themselves. There'll be a piss-up and a fuckin' rumble, bet you anything. Rockets versus Vultures, and the Rockets'll kick the Vultures' fuckin' arses."

"So are you a Rocket, then?"

"Jesus, wake up Australia! Turk's me fuckin' brother. What you reckon?"

"So now we can't go down Cox Street?"

"Unless you want a fuckin' BB pellet in your eye. Or else you go on your own."

Really? All he has to do is walk down Cox Street, and Wocker can't follow? But then, who are these Ninny King and Albert Thomas that he's never heard of? What houses do they live in? More to the point, what if they already believe what everyone suspects at school — that he and Wocker Spink are actually friends?

No, he's screwed, he sees it now, and all because of bloody Wocker. They go on back to Blessington Street the long way, bypassing Cox Street altogether.

When they get to his place, Wocker says he'll have CocoPops.

"My mother doesn't believe in stuff like that."

"OK," says Wocker. "Cornflakes then. But only if you've got chocolate milk."

"She doesn't believe in cornflakes either."

"Jesus, mate, they got cornflakes in Turana!"

Wocker has started rifling though their kitchen cupboards.

"What's this shit?" Wocker says. "Weeties? Weeties is for weeds!"

"It's made from proper wheat."

"Proper wheat? She must be a real slag, your old lady. I'll bet she's not a nympho, anyway."

"What's that?"

"My old lady, she's a nympho. Nicked off."

"What is it, though, nympho?"

"Nymphomaniac, mate. Can't get enough of it — the old hokey-pokey. We don't care. Nyah nyah nyah. Clean up your room! Wash the fuckin' dishes! Better off without her, mate. CocoPops for dinner."

"They're just chocolate. Chocolate and sugar."

"Gives you all your energy, mate. What you reckon they got in army rations?"

He makes them toast with peanut butter. The minute he gets out sugar to sprinkle on top, though, Wocker starts licking his fingers and dipping them in the bowl.

How has he ended up like this, as putty in Wocker's hands? If only he had no mother. Then he could be a proper toughie like Wocker. He could eat CocoPops and know what nympho is. How could he have avoided this? What's he supposed to do?

Wocker says they should visit Tina's bank.

"They'll never let you in," he says.

"You go and see her, then," Wocker says. "Get her to come down. Then we can take her somewhere, feel her up."

"We can't. She'll nick on us."

"She wants it, mate."

"She doesn't. She reckons you say somethink. She reckons people that say somethink are povvo."

"I'll bet my dad earns more than her dad any fuckin' day of the week. Twice as much."

"I'll bet he doesn't."

"You wouldn't know. It's cash, see. Nobody knows how much you earn if it's cash. I tell you what. Show us this fuckin' bank and I'll go. How's that?"

Somehow he doubts Wocker will actually honour this promise, but hope is the father of many follies. He leads Wocker into his parents' bedroom and draws back the curtains.

"There's the ES&A, see? That's her dad's bank. They live on top."

"In a shitty old shop flat?"

"It isn't shitty," he says. "It's really nice. They have these big rooms, and carpet on the stairs. Her mother still wishes they lived in Bentleigh, though."

"What's in fuckin' Bentleigh?"

"People who don't say fuckin' all the time."

"Ah. People who say Oooh, would you like some Weeties? and Ooooh, it's germy."

Wocker looks around, bounces on the bed.

"So this is where your mumsie and dadsie make their babies."

"There's only me," he says.

"Oh yeah. Took one look at you and lost interest."

He ought to whack Wocker. Whack him, and throw him through the window.

"Jesus, fuckface," Wocker says. "It's just a joke, Joyce."

Wocker picks up the photo of his dad, the one where he's

on Silverado with his big hat. Silverado rising up. His dad's square chin and dimples.

"That's my dad," he says. "Best horse he ever had. Nineteen forty-eight, won the Queensland Rodeo Championship."

"Oh yeah. Where's his medal then?"

"He had to give it to this kid who had polio."

"Should have given him fuckin' crutches. Anyone can ride a horse. Ride a motorbike, you can ride a horse. No gears on a horse. No clutch, even. What's he do now, your old man?"

"He's a fireman."

"Jesus, that's a slackarse job. Sit round all day and wait for a fire. My old man, he was a racing driver. Drove the stock cars out in Laverton. All the stock cars, vroom vroom. Never had the proper helmet, though. All the other blokes, they kept nicking the best helmets. Got smashed up too many times."

"So then what?"

"Short fuckin' fuse, mate. Every time he shakes his head, he can feel his fuckin' brains rattling. If you want to ask me dad a question, make sure the answer's fuckin' yes, OK? What else they got in here, your mumsie and dadsie?"

Wocker is already reaching for the chest of drawers. He cuts him off.

"Oh come on!" Wocker says. "Don't tell me you haven't had a look."

"It's private."

"Is this where he keeps his titty magazines?"

"There aren't any."

"Ah, Mr Weeties packet knows! Mr Germy. What about their wardrobe?"

"You can't," he says.

He isn't quick enough. Wocker has the door open and has started rummaging through his mother's coats and dresses.

"What about nighties?" Wocker says. "She got any rudey ones?"

"No."

Wocker drops to his knees and pulls a carton from behind his mother's shoes. He lifts a large celluloid negative from the box.

"What's this?"

"It's an x-ray. It's what my mother does."

"Is she a fuckin' doctor?"

"Radiographer. She takes these pictures, then a doctor looks at them."

Wocker holds the film up to the light.

"How come she keeps them here? They porno x-rays?"

"Dr Schlimmicht probably doesn't want them anymore."

"Dr Schlimmicht? That's a kraut name."

"He wasn't a kraut in the war."

"You can't just be a kraut then not a kraut," Wocker says. "You ask Turk. He's read a million fuckin' books about it. Ask Turk anything you like about Heil Hitler."

"Maybe he was a doctor in the war. I don't know."

"I'll tell you why she keeps 'em in her fuckin' wardrobe."

"Why?"

"She fuckin' nicked 'em, mate. Nicked 'em from the kraut."

"She wouldn't."

"What they doing here then, fucknuckle? And what are they even? What's all this smudgy shit?"

He takes the film from Wocker and turns it right way up.

"This is the abdomen, see. This is the bones in the back."

"They're all white. Whitey-bones."

"It's a negative. Anywhere the x-rays can't get through, it comes out white."

"So what's the fuckin' point?"

"Could be looking for a broken bone. Could be looking for a mass. Mass, that means cancer."

"Has this guy got cancer?"

"Don't know. My mum, she could tell you. All this stuff that looks like jellyfish insides, she can tell you what it is. She could have been a doctor, practically. She just didn't want to."

Wocker holds up several more films to the light, then loses interest. He stuffs them back in the box and returns the box to the rear of the wardrobe.

His faint hope that Wocker might finally go home is dashed when Wocker proposes they go out on the landing and pelt some birds.

They go downstairs to pick up stones and have just returned to the landing with some bread when Enrico appears in the open gateway.

"Bugger," he says. "I forgot. I have to help Enrico with his painting. He added a transistor to my crystal set."

"Tell him to come back some other time."

"I'm coming!" he calls out.

"You play your friend," Enrico calls up. "I fix him up, this paint."

"He's a fuckin' dago, mate," Wocker says. "Hey, you know this one? How many gears has an Italian tank got?"

"You'll have to go."

"It's a good one, Spooky. How many gears?"

He stands up, searching his pockets. He pulls out a key.

"I have to go."

"'Thought your mumsie was coming home."

He locks the porch door.

"Oh come on," Wocker says. "How about some cheese?"

"We haven't got any."

"I seen it in your fridge."

"I have to go. Really."

He glances past Wocker towards the gate, but Enrico has disappeared.

"Fuckin' dago lover," Wocker says. "You know how many gears? None forward, six reverse. That's you, pal. Six reverse."

He glares into Wocker's eyes. Should he throw him down the stairs right now? Wocker grimaces back, baring peanut butter-coated gums, then forms a goobie with his spit that slithers down and plops onto the plank between them.

He shoves Wocker aside and runs down the stairs.

"All the blokes kiss each other, pal! Watch out for your bum, Weeties boy!"

He doesn't once look back. If Wocker has any more advice to offer, he doesn't hear it, so loud is the thudding in his ears.

———

"What you thinking, Spook?"

He studies the paint patch on the wall. It is still wet.

When Enrico asked him to pick a colour from the card a few days ago, he followed his first impulse, but now, confronted with the actual colour on the actual wall in what used to be Enrico's shopfront — Enrico has bought four gallons of this stuff, and has already opened two of the tins — he can't help but wonder if his choice may have been a little hasty.

Enrico doesn't seem to share his reservations, though.

"You like him?" Enrico says. "In my country, we have happy colour. Is happy colour, like sunshine, yes?"

He looks from the patch to the open paint tins, then back to the patch. Will the colour hit the eye a little more kindly when it has dried? He could have chosen a pale blue. A palish green. Those are not unhappy colours.

"What you thinking, Spook?"

Four large tins, sitting on sheets of newspaper. Four tins of yellow rich enough to pass as egg yolk.

"It looks great," he says.

"Si! Is good you choose him this one! I tell Maria, Spook, he choose this colour — Spook, my friend next door, you know? Choose him this one for you, Maria. Help you getting better fast. Si!"

"That's great," he says.

"You friend in there, he wanting coming painting also? Help Enrico, eh?"

"He's not my friend."

"Not you friend, that one?"

After that day he chose the colour, he helped Enrico for several afternoons, taping newspapers over the plate glass windows, lugging fridges, TV sets and washing machines to one side, then dragging Enrico's wooden counter and display stands into the middle of the room. Enrico will sell all these eventually, but for now they can stay under covers while they paint.

This afternoon and evening, and much of the next day, he works alongside Enrico, helping transform the former shopfront into a place of recovery for Maria, who won't be able to climb stairs when she gets back from hospital — not straight away, and perhaps not ever.

"Heart kaput now," Enrico tells him. "Little bit, she beating. Stairs no good. Enrico fix-up man, repair man now. No more shop. Comprendi?"

He doesn't fully understand, but the gist is clear. What used to be their shop will be Maria's living quarters now. Instead of mixing sales with repairs, Enrico will just do repairs from now on.

Even knowing this, he is still surprised when Enrico tells him to pull the sheets of newspaper from the windows and start painting over the glass.

"You want me to paint the windows?"

"Si, si. Paint him all over."

"But she won't be able to see out."

"Paint him all glass. Inside, I making beautiful for Maria. Plenty picture. Plenty calendar. Many things."

"There won't be any light, though."

"Like sunshine, Spook! Maria, she like him this colour!"

That may be so, but the plate glass does not like the colour at all. The paint goes to streaks as soon as he applies it, and even after a second coat, the coverage is blotchy and uneven, leaving pinpricks where the outside world peeps through.

"Is OK, Spook," Enrico finally declares at the end of their second day. "No more painting now. Maria like him."

"Did you show her the colour on the card?"

"I know my Maria!" Enrico says. "When she come home, big surprise for her, I think."

———

Mrs Green is also in for a surprise.

"Vomit!" says Mrs Green. "A whole wall of vomit, right next to my gowns — and I hold you responsible, young man!"

It's rare for Mrs Green to visit on a Sunday. His father, having heard the Humber down below, has retreated to the bathroom, but they can't all hide in there. Now Mrs Green has his mother and himself bailed up in the kitchen, her enormous bulk all but blocking the doorway.

"Well?" says Mrs Green.

"It wasn't my idea," he says. "He told me to paint the windows."

"If I told you to jump off a cliff, you little beggar, would you do it?"

"He didn't say about a cliff."

"Don't prevaricate with me, young man! Cliff, window, it's all the same. What on earth do you imagine the Shopkeepers' Association are going to say about all this?"

"I didn't know a thing about it," his mother says. "Perhaps Mr Tangelli could repaint. What do you think, Ralph?"

"I don't want a repaint!" says Mrs Green. "A window is a window! A window is made for seeing through! And you, you little monster — you had the paintbrush in your hand. I have friends who saw you. I'm not unknown here. I was secretary of the Shopkeepers' Association for sixteen years."

"I'm sure you would have been most active," his mother says.

"Don't come that tone with me!" says Mrs Green. "I know a lemon from an egg. And you, you little devil — you can't go hiding behind your mother's skirts forever. You're old enough to know what's what! Puke, that's it looks like, right next to my lovely gowns! I feel defiled!"

"I'm sure none of us wants that," his mother says. "Perhaps you could scrape the paint off, Ralph. It does sound rather lurid."

"It's like the cat's thrown up!" says Mrs Green.

"What do you think, Ralph? Now you can see the effect on other people? You think you could persuade Mr Tangelli?"

"It's his shop," he says.

"It does sound like he values your opinion," his mother says.

"The man's an imbecile," says Mrs Green. "You can't understand a thing he says."

"She has to have it for her room," he says. "When she comes back from hospital. She can't climb stairs."

"What's she doing coming home from hospital?" says Mrs Green. "We're not the Blessington Street Infirmary! I'm sure I'd like to sleep downstairs too. That would be most convenient. But a shop is a shop! That's the law of the land. And a window is for looking through! You can't go covering it up with puke."

"It isn't puke," he says.

"Puke, paint! Paint, puke! If puke is what it looks like, young man, puke is what it is! If Goldilocks can't climb her stairs anymore, that's a pity, I'm sure, but a person's sympathies can only extend so far. Poor little prune of a thing, I feel sorry for her, but she'll just have to go into one of those places. He can bring her all her olive oil and sausage there, and good luck to them. But let's not lose sight of who's the real victim here!"

Mrs Green has a head of steam up, and no-one is getting near the safety valve. In the end, his mother says he must start getting ready for Sunday School because she'll have to drive him soon.

"Sunday School!" says Mrs Green. "Sunday School where?"

"We're trying St Thomas's," his mother says. "We think it might be good for him."

Which of them is more astonished, himself or Mrs Green, it would be hard to say, but within minutes his mother is ushering their landlady through the porch door. As the back stairs timbers begin to groan, the sound of a toilet flushing can be heard within.

"You lied," he tells his mother.

"You want to go to Sunday School?"

"No."

"If Mrs Green asks, then, you'd better have a damn good story, hadn't you? As long as you do, I won't be calling it a lie — and I'd appreciate a similar degree of latitude from you."

———

HE VISITS Enrico often in the following days, helping to prepare for Maria's return. He carries stock and fittings out to the back yard, and helps Enrico cover what won't fit under the verandah with thick tarpaulins. It turns out he's good at working with these heavy sheets, dragging and straightening, tying and untying, even climbing up on a covered pile where necessary to cover a gap with a towel or scrap of plastic.

His real job, though, he understands, is keeping up Enrico's spirits. Enrico seems to be expecting his wife home any day, but every day his hopes are dashed.

"The doctors are the one who ought to know," he tells Enrico. "What do the doctors say?"

"Ah, Maria, she have lovely doctor lady," Enrico says.

"Bellissima! Always smiling for Enrico. We see, doctor lady say. Always same. We see."

"We see, that doesn't mean tomorrow," he says. "It just means she isn't sure."

"Si."

"It means we don't exactly know yet."

"Si," Enrico says. "One day! Two day!"

"Maybe three days. They don't know."

"Si! Three day. Two day, maybe! Maria, she getting better now. Open her eye. She smile. She say my name."

"That's good," he says.

"Si! Two day I think, then Maria, she come home! Just her heart, little problem. I make soup Maria. Soup from my country."

"That's great," he says.

They bring furniture down from upstairs. A single bed — it's difficult, but they manage it. An armchair. A chest of drawers. Enrico hangs some pictures on the wall, brown photos of funny-looking, bent old people in ancient clothes. There are more brightly coloured images of saints. Perhaps they are disciples. There are buildings on a hillside. My village, Enrico says. Not a building in this village, though, is yellow.

Of Mrs Green's remarks, he does attempt to translate the general gist for Enrico.

"Bah, that woman!" Enrico says. "Talking, talking! Shopkeepers' Association, they writing me. What for? This shop, all mine. Enrico's shop! No bank, nothing! Free country, in Australia. Paint my window any colour. You choose him colour, Spook. You telling Mrs Green? Good colour, yes?"

"I told her," he says. "Yes."

"Mrs Green old bag! That what you saying in this country, si? Old bag!"

The yellowish smears covering Enrico's shopfront windows have dried. By day, a dull golden glow fills the room.

One afternoon — Maria is still not back from hospital — Enrico takes him in to show his latest innovation. He has built a partition from masonite and pine and erected this to enclose a narrow area inside the shop's front door. The effect is of a smaller room within the larger room. Within this smaller area, he has set up his old shop counter inside the front door.

"What you think?" Enrico says. "Is good, yes? All the people, when they come, Maria she no see. No bother for Maria."

"It's great," he says.

Enrico points to a button on the counter.

"Is buzzer, see? Also on door, reed switch, see? People come in. Magnet, she make contact — you know contact? Or else people, they press button. Current, she flow in wire. In my workshop, buzz buzz. I hear him, coming shop. What you think? Is good? Good for Maria?"

"It's great," he says.

In truth, he hardly knows how to take these enthusiastic outbursts from Enrico. He suspects Enrico may be heading for a terrible disappointment, but doesn't want to hurt the feelings of this kindly man who has treated him so well.

Now the renovations are complete, Enrico invites him down to his workshop, the long, narrow building set against the back yard boundary that might once have been a garden shed, or even two sheds joined together. Here they sit, side by side, under a batten of fluorescent lights at a pock-marked bench spattered with droplets of solder and roughened from burns and random drillings. Power points peep through holes cut in masonite sheeting. From these outlets, cords run to Enrico's various tools and instruments — two soldering irons, an oscilloscope, a vacuum tube voltmeter, and a thrilling-looking contraption with two large dials Enrico calls his signal generator.

The walls of Enrico's workshop are lined with shelves and racks that hold the myriad components of his trade — capacitors and coils, chokes and resistors, parts of old dials, potentiometers, switches, transformers, rolls of cable, loudspeaker cones, boxes crammed with dusty valves. Steel trays labelled with glued-on bits of paper hold smaller parts — diodes and transistors, tag strips, grommets, nuts and bolts. Chipboard shelves sag under the weight of books and magazines and three-ringed binders stuffed with circuit diagrams and data sheets. Alongside these are piles of dog-eared reference manuals, their covers torn, or smeared with soldering flux.

Heaped in the farthest corner of Enrico's workshop are his repair projects in their various states of disassembly. Radios and televisions, some still in their cabinets, others just naked chassis. Record players. Radiograms. A pop-up toaster. A barrel vacuum cleaner. A tape recorder with two enormous reels. An ancient wooden cabinet with rows of holes in it that might have been a switchboard in an old movie once.

"You really going to fix all these?" he asks Enrico one afternoon.

"All things, Enrico fix 'em up."

Enrico is moving his probe from point to point inside an upturned television chassis. The picture tube is lifeless, but the valves glow underneath, and as Enrico moves his probe, a blue-green line silently tracing across the screen of his oscilloscope jumps and is transformed into a shimmering wave.

"How did you even learn all this?" he asks.

"Many book," Enrico says. "Learn in book, then try him. Many thing to learn, Spook. Ohm's Law. Thermionic valve. Class A amplifier, class B amplifier. All this things. Then oscillator stage. All the waveform. All the voltage. Then transistor. Different from the valve. All new thing. You learn him, then you try. You want learning these things?"

"A bit," he says.

"Which bit you want to learn him?"

"All of it," he says.

"Ha!" Enrico says. "Same me! Same me!"

That afternoon, as he is leaving, Enrico looks out a magazine and hands it to him.

"Good for you, this one," Enrico says. "All things, they making here. All circuit, they explain. You read him. In you brain, you thinking for electron, si? Electron, he go this way, that way. Understand? You no understand him, ask Enrico. This way you learning."

This night, and for many nights afterwards, he pores over the Radio Television & Hobbies magazine Enrico has given him, reading and re-reading every article and advertisement. As he lies in bed and reads, he begins to picture for himself a life in which he has become an expert in megacycles and single-sideband modulation and clamp voltages, even though his understanding of these terms is almost non-existent as yet.

On the back cover of the magazine, a cartoon man sits at a cartoon kitchen table holding several sheets of cartoon paper in his hand. Large worry lines crease the man's fore-head. Bills, bills, bills, the man's speech bubble says. I'll have to earn more. In the next frame, a pretty lady with pointy breasts stands behind the man. John, why don't you take the RCS correspondence course in radio and television, and earn pounds in your spare time? her bubble says. Could a pretty wife with pointy breasts ever care for him like that, he wonders.

He gazes at John's wife a lot over the next few weeks. Apart from her pointy breasts, what he loves best in Radio Television & Hobbies are the circuit diagrams that show components linked by neat, straight lines that either join or cross at right angles. Along these lines, electrons flow, he understands, and these are the electric current. The zigzag shapes are the resistors, where Ohm's Law strangles the electrons. Inside the circles with the plates in them — capacitors — even more peculiar things occur. If the electrons are the alternating kind, they pass straight through, but if they're not, they can't go anywhere.

Would his mother understand this stuff? For all her talk of kilovolts and shielding, he doubts she really understands a thing. His mother just repeats what she has read or what they told her in college, but he is learning from the ground up. And Enrico, who can really fix a television — Enrico will help him, too.

He has finally found a window, he realises, into a secret world even Grandpa Doc would not understand. Each schematic diagram is like a map of a hidden universe where electrons can be tricked into following mysterious laws only he and Enrico and the RCS correspondence school can truly grasp.

One initiate into these mysteries he comes particularly

to admire goes incognito in the magazine. This contributor's segment is called The Serviceman, but for this piece there is no author's name published like there is for all the other articles. The man who writes this article must be a proper serviceman like Enrico, but he lives a double life. He can never can let anyone know who he really is, because if someone took their TV to this secret serviceman to get it fixed, the next month this person could buy Radio, Television & Hobbies and find out how it got fixed. If they knew his name, they could find out all he had to do to get their TV working. He finds the secrecy surrounding the identity of The Serviceman almost as thrilling as the pointy breasts that hover inches from John's shoulders.

Over and over, he reads the case of the television whose picture won't stop rolling. The Serviceman has seen this kind of thing before, of course, so he is not bothered at first. He tries all the usual things, testing and replacing one part after another — but nothing seems to work! Soon he is getting worried. The Serviceman is nearly ready to give up, in fact, but then he has a cup of tea. Suddenly it occurs to him — what about a leaky electrolytic? A leaky electrolytic is the last thing The Serviceman would expect, because he only replaced this electrolytic a month ago when he was working on another problem in this same exact same TV set. But then he tests this new electrolytic, and bingo, it turns out there is a leak! As soon as he replaces this electrolytic, the picture stops rolling.

Night after night, he recommits himself to remembering the lesson of this story — beware the leaky electrolytic, even when it's new — and reaffirms his resolution never to be caught like this himself.

At last he drops the magazine beside his bed, puts on his

headphones, and fixes the alligator clip onto the nine volt battery for what used to be his crystal set. Enrico has rejigged his crystal set entirely, adding a transistor and winding extra turns onto the coil. Alongside the tuning knob, he now has a regeneration control to adjust as well, and with all these changes, the stations are much louder, and he can hear more of them.

In Karnook, he used to listen to Jack Davey and Pick a Box, but now he has discovered 3UZ, where they play pop. The songs on 3UZ are nearly always about love, which he despises somewhat. He prefers more original subjects like The one-eyed, one-horned, flying purple people eater.

Each night on 3UZ they have a voting competition. At half past eight, they play the tune most people voted for the night before, then play two other tunes that are the challengers. To vote, you have to ring up 3UZ. He never could do that himself, but every night he barracks for his favourite, then tries to stay awake until they play the winner.

His all time favourite tune is North To Alaska. If they ever put that in the voting, he will be so happy. North To Alaska is so brave and serious-sounding, and the feeling that it gives him, he would like to have this feeling all the time.

Whenever he hears North to Alaska, he feels he could do some really dangerous thing, like rescue Tina, say, if it turned out some horrible thing was happening at her place and the only person who could rescue her was him. Then he would climb outside Tina's place at night, up on the verandah, and he would have a blanket with him, and a torch, and he would bring some biscuits. Tina would be scared, of course, but he would get her down from the verandah, and while they were doing that, she would probably have to hold his hand, then probably they would go down The Windings and he would make a shelter out of sticks and branches, and he could steal stuff for them to eat until they could get a horse and ride away. North To Alaska gives him all these tingly feelings, especially when the man sings way up north and the other guys sing mush mush mush. It is the best song he has ever heard by miles.

Later, in the middle of the night, he often wakes and finds his headphones have dropped off onto his pillow, so that he can hear the music only faintly, or some guy talking. He unclips his battery then, and thinks about when he'll be dead. He thinks about the pine trees in the driveway back at Karnook, and all the crows up in the topmost branches. The crows will still be there, and he'll be dead.

One night, he wakes and hears an aeroplane circling overhead. It is the middle of the night, and everyone's asleep. Up there, in the dark, the pilot must be flying his plane, looking out his window for some place to land. But how will he find the aerodrome? Who will help him get down? The engines throb, and the big plane flies around and around, waiting for some signal from someone down below...

When he awakes, hours later, grey light fills his room, and on the roof above a bird is walking to and fro, pecking at the tiles.

CHAPTER EIGHT

Mervyn Reynolds has been making progress. From cups of tea and toast down in the laneway, he has worked his way through tea and toast and an occasional orange juice at the bottom of the stairs to tea and toast and juice and scrambled eggs in the upstairs porch. That, however, is absolutely it, his mother has declared.

"Don't bust your boiler, Rose," his father says.

His father would say that, of course. His father's not the one who has to make the extra eggs. He's not the one who has to carry them out to Mervyn Reynolds in the porch, either, plus knife and fork and condiments, now Mervyn's got a taste for the whole caboodle. His father doesn't have to wait out on the porch and chat with Mervyn Reynolds, either.

"He's gone to all this trouble to pick me up, mate," his father says.

Perhaps — but is this really why he has to keep Mervyn

Reynolds talking? Or is it so Mervyn won't overhear what's happening in the kitchen?

Kettle's boiling, Rose.

I can hear it boiling, Ray.

You might want to turn it off, love.

I might, might I?

We could take a chair out Rose. Poor bloke's got to stand.

Over my dead body, Ray.

Mervyn Reynolds never seems to hear any of this, although he does once comment that his mother is a spirited woman.

"Your dad's a lucky bloke to have to her," Mervyn Reynolds says.

This is obviously some kind of fireman's joke.

Now that Mervyn is having breakfast in the porch, he has a lot less room to demonstrate his square dance moves. He can't shout out his calls so loudly, either. When Mervyn grabs his hand now, and leads him through the steps, he has to do it in a much more close-up kind of way, whispering the commands in his ear. That's not so bad, though, because he's really getting the hang of these routines by now — the Come down the middle and the Do sa do and the Four ladies chain — even if the brooms and other cleaning stuff get getting in their way.

Mervyn Reynolds reckons he's one of the fastest learners he's ever seen.

———

He still is so frustrated, though. Tina continues to avoid him, and even Thickness is staying away. Why is Thickness hardly even in the roundabout park these days? Is it because he's up at Tina's place, talking about her so-called problems? Why couldn't they talk about Tina's problems together, all three of them? If he'd never made the Nazi pancake, would things be different? He stands at the window of his parents' room and looks across the street, but the terylene curtains above the ES&A remain frustratingly opaque.

There's the whole Cox Street business now, as well. He can't even go to school the shortest way. Wocker reckons when this Ninny King and other guy fire their shanghais, you never hear a thing. The ball bearing goes even faster than the speed of sound.

It's probably all bullcrap. This Ninny King and other guy, they mightn't even know that he knows Wocker. If he told his mother everything, she'd go to the coppers straight away. You tell this Ninny King my boy is not a Rocket. I'm not leaving till you promise. That's the kind of thing she'd say. Let them know how Grandpa Doc's a doctor. But then next time he goes down Cox Street, all Ninny King and other guy would have to do is hide behind a bush and aim at him, and no-one would hear a thing. He doesn't even know what house this Ninny King is meant to live in.

He stays away from Cox Street.

Since the afternoon at his place, Wocker has backed off a bit, and that's good, at least. Wocker doesn't kick him in the ankles anymore, either, or stand on the back part of his shoe and crush it down. A few times they've played handball in the schoolyard together. It's almost like Wocker finally believes Tina isn't his girlfriend.

One day Wocker tells him they can go and visit Turk.

"What, Turk your brother?"

"How many fuckin' Turks you know?"

"Don't know any."

"Get to see Turana, mate. All the fuckin' crims, they start out there, then they get to Pentridge later. Not Turkie though. He isn't going to fuckin' Pentridge. He's too smart."

"I'll see him when he gets out," he says. "I'll see him at your place."

"He wants to meet you, buddy."

"Bullcrap."

"He wants to meet my friend."

"I'm not your friend."

"Come on, Spooky. Don't get all stuck up on me."

"I can't," he says.

"Why not?"

"I have to do other things."

"What, go and hold some wire for your woggie mate next door? You don't even know what time we're going."

"What time you going?"

"Sunday."

"I have to go to Sunday School on Sunday."

"You don't go to fuckin' Sunday School."

"I do."

"What time?"

"It's in the morning," he says.

"Well goody gumdrops, Spookus, 'cos we're seein' Turk on Sunday afternoon."

"But I don't even know your brother."

"Come on, Spookus. Turk's the guy! The fuckin' Rockets man! I know you reckon I'm a fuckin' weed, but you ought to meet Turk, mate. He's somebody, you get me? And he's my fuckin' brother!"

"I don't know."

"Jesus, Spookus, guys would kill to get inside Turana.

Turana's fuckin' famous — and you've got an invite. Once the kids at school find out you've been inside Turana, they'll all want to know you. You'll be fuckin' famous."

"What about these Cox Street guys? They going to come looking for me then?"

"Fuckin' Ninny King and Albert Thomas? They're fuckin' gutless, mate."

"You said they got shanghais. They can shoot right through a car door."

"They're still fuckin' gutless. They won't touch you mate. They haven't got the balls."

"I don't want to be a Rocket."

"Mate, the Rockets wouldn't touch you with a barge pole."

"I don't want to."

"Mate, your name's on the list. Me dad, he's gone and fixed it. You're fucking Lesley Wedding, OK?"

"Who's Lesley Wedding?"

"Jesus Christ! It's who you are, alright? They don't let anybody in Turana. Family member, that's the easiest. Lesley's fuckin' family, OK?"

"I'm not going to wear a dress."

"It's not a she Lesley, it's a he Lesley. It's me fuckin' cousin."

All he can think of is a car door with a hole through it, and someone laughing behind bushes. He hopes Wocker really is as big a bullshit artist as he suspects.

———

WHEN IT HAPPENS, the fight at school comes out of the blue.

The kid's name is Alex. He's a tall, blond, solid-looking kid with olive skin who often ends up captain of a team when they play their picking-sides type games out in the yard. This Alex likes to grab kids' nuts. He's really vicious with it, diving suddenly and squeezing hard.

He's not the only victim of this Alex by a long shot. Alex goes on rampages, kids doubled over in the yard. The other kids, they seem to cope, but he hates this grabbing of his balls. He feels humiliated and pathetic because he can't bring himself to dob on handsome, blue-eyed Alex. And who could he tell, in any case? Mr Gardiner? And say what? He grabs my balls? It's unthinkable.

This Alex is not a snotter usually, but one day, by the lockers, Alex sticks his finger up his nose and snots him. He cops it on the arm — a blob of greenish-yellow slime.

He loses it completely. Without a care about his chances or what anyone will think, he lashes into Alex, bashing hard, shoving him against the lockers. Alex turns out to be quite soft and warm. He thumps Alex in the guts, and tries to knee him in the balls. Alex pulls his hair, and gets a finger in his lips, which start to burn. All the kids are yelling fight, fight!

Willow and Loopy come out in the corridor and pull the two apart. Willow seems to think it's pretty funny, but Loopy doesn't look amused. Loopy marches them down the corridor, then across to the two hundred block and straight through to the principal's office.

Clunk is in there, reading some letter. He tells them to come in, and makes them sit down opposite his desk. He goes on with his reading, lips moving. After a minute or so, Clunk gets up and walks out, taking the letter with him.

He waits, eyes on the floor. Clunk has gone to get someone, he guesses. He hopes it isn't Dunk. Dunk is famous for his two foot rubber strap, the one with rivets in the end. Everyone knows about that.

How was Metalwork today?

Riveting.

They wait.

Will he get to tell his side of things? It's unlikely. He doesn't care. The fight juice is coursing through him still, the acrid taste in his mouth. He could punch Alex's head in right now, if that's what it will take to stop him. Some animal has been released inside him, and it won't be lured back into its den so easily.

Fucking Alex. At least he's shown him. Whatever punishment is coming, it'll be worth it just for that.

He stares at the lino. The streaky lino eyes stare back. The baying of kids outside is muted by Clunk's venetians. An announcement echoes down the corridor. If Mr Edwards could come to the front office, please. Mr Edwards, front office. Dumbarse Eddo must have left his sandwiches at home again. A ball thumps on the roof, then bounces onto the asphalt. Somewhere up in the valley, a train toots.

They wait.

Riveting or not, he may be suspended. Just for a day, probably, but Clunk will tell his parents. Well, too bad. He'll come up with some story. He'll tell them Alex snots him every day. Makes a habit of it. But then it'll be You should have told us, Ralph. You should have said something to a teacher. Yeah, well. Cross that bridge. Alex knows, that's what matters. Alex knows for sure.

The worst will be if Clunk says Come on now, shake hands. That isn't going to happen. Clunk can suspend him for a week. He can expel him altogether. There's no way he's shaking hands with Alex fucking Villeneuve. Alex Feeler Perv. He should try that one in the yard.

The bell rings. Clunk has not returned. Are they supposed to stay here now, or what?

Mr Edwards appears in the doorway. He's got a woman with him. She's been crying. So not his sandwiches, then.

"What are you boys doing here?" Eddo asks.

"Fight," Alex says.

"Go on, get to class," Eddo says. "Maybe you'll be learning what testosterone is today."

That's it. That's their punishment. No shaking hands or anything.

The rest of the afternoon at school is a blur. He does no work at all, but no-one one crosses his path. No-one annoys him in the least. It's like they know he's not to be toyed with, that he just might knock the block off anyone who gets in his way. A fuzzy warmth suffuses his body. He feels strangely quiet and gentle.

After school, he finds he's in a mood to go to Thickness's. When he gets there, Thickness isn't home. He must have missed the early bus. His mother will be out still, giving people their dying needles.

He goes around to Thickness's back yard. He mucks around with the clothes pegs on the hoist. He clumps them into groups of six on the outer wires, three groups per wire. Thickness has told him about The Beast. He wonders if Thickness's mother will get the joke next time she hangs the washing out.

Eventually he hears Thickness coming up the drive. He goes around and meets him on the front verandah.

"How come you always go and see Tina but I can't?" he says.

Thickness hasn't even taken off his schoolbag.

"What happened?" Thickness says. "What's the matter?"

"It isn't fair!"

"Come inside," Thickness says. "I need to go to the toilet."

Thickness is kind and gentle with him. He makes them bread and treacle, and they have a glass of milk. His glass shakes when he lifts it to his lips.

"What happened?" Thickness asks.

"This Alex kid snotted me, so I whacked him."

"He ripped your shirt."

"We had a fight."

"Your face has all got marks on it. Who won?"

"It was a draw."

"You get suspended?"

"No."

"You get the cuts?"

"No."

"They must have reckoned it was fair," Thickness says. "Fair fight."

"It was."

"Don't worry about it, then."

Thickness has gone all quiet. It's like Thickness knows something awful is going to happen. And it should happen, too. Thickness knows he's in the wrong. Bread and treacle can't make up for everything.

"Have you kissed her?" he asks Thickness.

"She doesn't want to."

"Did you try?"

"I don't think she wants me to," Thickness says.

"Wocker says he's going to fuck her."

"Wocker! He would be the last person! I know she's

mature and all that, but she never would do that unless she really liked a person."

"She still could kiss."

"It would have to be some person she was practically engaged to," Thickness says. "You'd have to be in Form Five at least. Probably Matric. That's the kind of person who could really understand her. That's what she thinks, anyway."

"We still could go around to her place."

"She's not allowed," Thickness says. "I told you."

"But how come you can go?"

"She already knows me. We went to primary school."

"And her mother's practically in love with you," he says. "Because you make the pancakes."

"Listen," says Thickness. "I only help her with the pancakes because she had a sort of nervous breakdown. No-one is supposed to know. You can't tell anybody. You can't tell Tina, especially. It happened when they were in Bentleigh. She took some kind of tablets."

"That's what the actresses do when they aren't beautiful anymore."

"She just has sensitive nerves," Thickness says. "She thinks the people here are yobbos. She thinks I could be a good influence on Tina."

"You?"

"It's because I do my homework."

"Doesn't Tina?"

"She's a total slackarse."

"What about me?" he says. "I'm not a yobbo."

"Her mother thinks you're jittery."

"Did you tell her I aren't?"

"Well you are a bit," says Thickness. "Sort of edgy."

"I'm not edgy! I'm just ordinary. I just want to have a chance."

"Her mother thinks if Tina starts seeing boys around here..."

"What?" he says.

"Well you know what."

"She's going to start having sex?"

"She never said that exactly," Thickness says.

"But she's never going to have sex with you, right?"

"Her mother probably thinks I'm not that kind of person," Thickness says. "She probably thinks I'm more moral. It's not my fault. I just got born like this."

"So you'd only feel her up if she said yes?"

"She probably thinks you're trying to crack onto her," Thickness says. "The first time we went up there, it was OK. But now she just thinks it's creepy, how you keep looking at her all the time, hanging round her bus stop or the round-about park. She reckons you're always looking out your mum and dad's window at them."

"She can't see that!" he says.

"I'm just telling what she says. She's sort of made me promise I won't take you there."

"Because I go down the roundabout park."

"It's the way you go down the roundabout park."

"And I'm jittery. That isn't even a proper word. You can't just make up a word. It has to be in the dictionary."

"It probably is," Thickness says.

"And you haven't even kissed her?"

Thickness shakes his head.

"Holding hands?"

Thickness shakes his head again. This time, he has the awful feeling Thickness could be almost crying.

Thickness makes them toast with peanut butter, then tells him about a kid who's always flicking his bum with the tips of his fingers at school. It really stings.

"Knee him in the balls," he says.

"My mum says a fight never solves anything."

"Yeah, well your mum's wrong."

When he gets back home, his own mother is already there. She gives him all the usual stuff — whatever happened to you?, all this bull — but he just couldn't care. He goes into his room and reads about the leaking electrolytic again. Then he gazes at John's wife for a long time, wondering what it can be she sees in John.

———

ONE AFTERNOON, he looks out their kitchen window and sees Mervyn Reynolds pull up in the laneway driving a cream-coloured ute. His dad is in the passenger seat. They're earlier than usual.

He goes downstairs. His father gestures towards a pile of stuff in the tray of the ute. He says he'll need a hand.

"What is it?" he asks.

"Fire Sale Friday, mate."

"It's Thursday."

"Don't be a dick, Rick. Your mum home?"

He shakes his head. His dad hands him a small suitcase.

"Take it up the landing, leave it there."

"What is it?"

"Offerings of love, mate."

Love's offerings are heavy. He lugs the little suitcase up the stairs and sets it on the landing. His dad and Mervyn

Reynolds are already carrying a large radiogram across the yard. He goes back down the stairs.

"The blue swan, buddy," Mervyn Reynolds says as he goes past. "Bring her up, but careful. She's fragile. Present for your mum."

He looks in the back of the ute for this swan. He can see a ladies' bicycle, and a surfboard with a red stripe along its middle. There's a corrugated stainless steel drainer that goes with a kitchen sink, and an ironing board. He can see an old-style lawnmower, the type you have to push to make it go.

"It's in the bucket, mate," Mervyn calls down from the stairs. "It's got a lampshade on top of it."

The whole unloading only takes about five minutes, then Mervyn Reynolds drives off in the ute.

"What happened to Mervyn's car?" he says. "Did he crash it?"

"Back at the station, mate. Vanguard's no good for Fire Sale Friday."

Upstairs, they rearrange their TV room. His dad pulls the TV along a few feet, then they push the radiogram in beside it. His dad opens the little suitcase and unpacks dozens of LP records. He stacks them in a compartment in the radiogram's side. The record covers are a little grubby, and the radiogram is certainly not new.

"Did you buy it?" he asks.

"Fire Sale Friday, mate. A day early this week, but them's the breaks."

"What is it, though, Fire Sale Friday?"

"It's a fireman thing, OK? Part of the job."

"So you get stuff?"

"Pretty much," his father says. "Stuff nobody needs anymore."

"How come?"

"'It's all been burnt up. It's a fire sale, see?"

His father must notice some look of puzzlement on his face.

"Think about it, buddy. What do firemen do?"

"Play cards?"

"When there's a fire on, stupid?"

"Put it out," he says.

"And when you put the fire out, what happens to the stuff inside the house?"

"Does it get burned?"

"But if we put the fire out?"

"Then it doesn't get burned?"

"You're getting warmer, mate."

"So you can just take the stuff," he says.

"Whoah! Are you kidding? Take the stuff out of a burned building?"

"Yeah, why not. Is that what happens?"

"Mate, if we just took the stuff, that'd be thieving. You can't just go and take stuff. You'd have the cops down in no time. They'd want their share."

"So what, then?"

"Insurance, mate. The beautiful magic of underwriting."

He looks at his father blankly. This isn't making sense at all.

"Listen," his father says. "All the people that are worried their house is going to burn down — house or factory, whatever — every year, they pay this money to their insurance company, right? It's not a lot. They hardly even notice it. And then, each year, hardly any of their houses burn down, you with me?"

"Or their factories. Or whatever."

"That's right. Just one or two. Three or four, maybe. So everyone's happy, see? The insurance company, they get all this money coming in, and the people that are worried their house is going to burn down, they get this bit of paper saying if their house burns down, they'll get a pile of money."

"But then some houses do burn down."

"That's the whole beauty of it," his father says. "We go and put the fire out, and if we get there quick, there's stuff still left. Like the back room, that's charcoal, but up the front, that's not too bad. You get me?"

"So then what?"

"Well, that's where Brendan Cranwell comes in. Brendan Cranwell comes and takes a look. He's the best, but there's others too. These assessors, they look around and figure out what's burnt and what isn't — and I tell you, they're really good at it. A lot of things you and I might think aren't burnt, it turns out they got burned to a crisp."

"How come?" he says.

"Insurance, mate. That's how it works. Crazy, huh?"

"So this radiogram and all these records, did they get burned?"

"The thing you have to remember, buddy, is that pile of money. They got so much money in that pile, these insurance companies, they don't know what to do with it!"

"So how come we get the radiogram and other people don't?"

"We're fire brigade people, right?" his father says. "Your fireman, he might have to risk his life to get inside a burning building. It's only right he ought to get a little extra something, don't you reckon?"

"But how come we get the radiogram and not Mervyn Reynolds?"

"Highest bidder wins, mate. That's how come it's Friday Fire Sale."

"So we had to pay for the radiogram?"

"Bloody oath. They're not handing out freebies. This cost us seven bob. Glad your old man's a fireman now?"

"Does Mum know all this?"

"Your mum knows how the world goes round, matey. No need to spell it out."

Perhaps. When his mum does get home, however, she seems surprised to find his father back from work, and even more surprised to find the radiogram beside the TV, and the blue swan lamp on her bedside dresser. She is so surprised, she takes his father into their bedroom and shuts the door.

He isn't supposed to listen, obviously. But if he isn't meant to hear, why does she have to raise her voice so loud? The boy needs a father, Ray. What am I supposed to do if you're locked up? Whatever his father says to that, he can't make out, but that dimwit bloody Mervyn Reynolds echoes down the hallway clear enough, and even down in Zelda's Gowns, someone can probably hear her shouting Everyone does not do these things, Ray Halliday!

Some sort of truce seems to follow this, or perhaps it's more like hand-to-hand combat. Some kind of muffled, close encounter, anyway.

Then laughter.

His parents come out eventually, and go into the bathroom, then the kitchen.

"Is Dad going to gaol?" he asks.

"He ought to be," his mother says.

"No-one's going to gaol," his father says.

"Do we have to take the radiogram back?"

"It's ours, mate."

"What about the records?"

"I'm just wondering what your father might have chosen for us, actually," his mother says. "He's always had such taste in music."

That night they eat their dinner to the sound of a lady singing about belly high, and other ladies singing about washing their hair. His mother seems to like these songs a lot. She sways her bottom as she washes up the dishes.

Later on, he sees the necklace his father gave to her. The greeny-bluish stones are opals, his mother tells him. She doesn't quite approve, she says, and can't imagine when she'd wear it, but for someone with so little imagination, she doesn't seem too mad about this gift.

For a week after this, they eat their dinner listening to some musical or another, and for a while his mother even stops referring to Mervyn Reynolds as that peculiar person whenever she scrambles up his eggs or squeezes his juice.

———

FOR HIMSELF, their newly-acquired radiogram does not mean South Pacific or Oklahoma. It means Sputnik.

He still remembers the night they saw the little Russian basketball coming up over the peppercorn tree at Karnook as the last glow of sunset was dying on the horizon. A moving star! Grandpa Doc took them inside, then, and found the little Sputnik on his radiogram. Beebledeep, beebledeep, the Sputnik said. Here I am. Now they have a radiogram of their own, he wants to see if Sputnik is still up there and he can rediscover it.

He jams wire into the crevice behind the picture rail in their TV room, then attaches the free end to the aerial screw behind the radiogram. In Karnook, Grandpa Doc only had to touch his finger to that terminal to hear the Sputnik. With a wire aerial attached, the Sputnik should be even louder. He knows the band to listen to already. The Sputnik is on SW, which only radiograms have. SW means shortwave, he knows this from his magazine. The only things he doesn't know are how many megacycles the Sputnik is on, and when it will be overhead so he can have a chance to hear it.

It will take patience, he knows that. But he has lots of patience. Instead of watching Cisco Kid or Silent Service after school, he takes to turning on the radiogram. He switches it to SW, then crouches by the big loudspeaker grille and tunes up and down the dial.

Mostly what he hears is whooshing and crackling, like someone frying bacon. This noise comes and goes, getting louder for a bit, then fading. In one part of the dial, he often hears a sound like a woodpecker chipping away at a tree. In other spots there are proper radio stations, but they are far away. The voices often have American accents. One station is called Radio Luxemburg. Another is called BBC. Sometimes he can hardly hear these stations, then they get louder until they are nearly like 3UZ. In some places, he hears a sound like an aeroplane engine. Other stations just make warbles. One time he hears a man who sounds like Donald Duck. He almost can understand him, but he can't.

Where is the Sputnik though? Has he forgotten what it sounds like — or is he just unlucky, only listening when Sputnik is some other place?

He asks Enrico. Enrico shrugs.

"Only beacon, Spook," Enrico says. "I hear him that time also. Beep beep beep. No message, nothing. Russki battery all kaput now, or she all burn up. Rocket! Rocket! That all Russki care. Biggest rocket! Biggest bomb! Sputnik, nothing!"

It seems Enrico isn't interested in Sputnik. But then Enrico wasn't with them that first time, in Grandpa Doc's front living room.

Hey dumb bum, come and educate yourself a minute.

Yeah dumb bum, come and listen.

You want to hear the Sputnik?

It's great, Mum. Come and listen.

You going to chuck a hissy fit now, missy?

You going to chuck a hissy, missy?

Is Sputnik dead? A flying corpse? Has little Sputnik fallen to the bottom of the ocean? He kneels beside the big loudspeaker and tunes up with eyes half-closed, searching for the tiny craft, lost in a swell of atmospheric static.

CHAPTER NINE

Night shift is the great upheaval in their lives. Even his mother wasn't expecting this one.

"But I told you, Rose," his father says. "It's never been a secret. What were you imagining?"

"Aren't there other blokes can do the night shift?"

"It's a sign they accept me, Rose."

"So now you can be one of the blokes? One of the night blokes."

"You don't have to make it sound like that."

He doesn't have to be Little Mr Big Ears for this one, either. They're arguing it out in the kitchen, right in front of him.

"If you want to be a father, Ray, it's not exactly conducive. If you want to be a husband."

"I'm a fireman, Rose. It's not like selling shoes. A bloke's expected to do the night shift."

"Don't you have any say in this at all?"

"They put you on the roster, Rose. Your name's up there, or else it isn't. That's the say you get."

"You and all the other night shift blokes."

"I can't do it on my own."

"Do you sleep there?"

His father sighs. When at last he answers, his voice is soft.

"If it's a quiet night, yeah."

"So you and all the blokes, you've got your bedrooms?"

"It's bunks, Rose."

They're talking in some kind of code, emitting signals he can't quite grasp the sense of, like the Donald Duck man he heard on the radiogram. Almost intelligible — but not.

This night shift alters everything.

For himself, there's no more learning how the gents swing out each morning in the porch with Mervyn Reynolds, no more Texas Star. If Thickness comes over after school, they have to take their shoes off on the landing and then whisper. Even opening the fridge, they cannot let the door click because his father's beauty sleep can't be interrupted until half past five. Even if they only have a Milo, they have to stir it with their fingers, not a spoon.

As for his mother, it's hard to put a finger on it, but night shift makes her different. It's like she's gone all steely on the inside, getting ready for something he can't see.

Even Mrs Green disapproves of the change.

"Night shift! Did you say night shift?"

"Please!" his mother says. "We have to keep our voices down. He's sleeping."

This is on a Saturday, just after noon. Zelda's Gowns has closed, and Mrs Green has been up for her Saturday inspection. Her cupboard visited, she's parked her great behind in their kitchen doorway once again, rendering himself and his mother prisoners for the duration.

"Sleeping!" says Mrs Green. "All our God-given daylight, and that's what he does with it!"

"If I'd been up all night, I guess I'd need my sleep," his mother says.

"The things these menfolk tell us, honestly!"

His mother has been writing figures in a little book, the one she calls her reckoning account. She sets it down.

"We have to have our fire brigade though, don't we?" his mother says. "And that's a round-the-clock operation. Someone has to do it."

"Oh, the trams, the trams!" says Mrs Green. "Someone has to do it. We've all heard that before."

"It's true though," his mother says. "I wouldn't like it. I'd hate it, probably."

"At least Mervyn Reynolds isn't hanging round so much, I see."

"Do you know Mervyn?"

She is writing in her book again. Writing and writing. She turns a page.

"Everyone knows Mervyn Reynolds! Mervyn Reynolds is notorious!"

"I see."

Her face down, not looking at them, writing.

"Big fish in shallow waters, Mervyn Reynolds."

His mother stops her writing, puts her pen down.

"How do you mean?" she says.

"A man should meet a woman's eye," says Mrs Green. "Meet her eye a certain way, I mean. You'll not get that with Mervyn Reynolds."

"I'm sure he hardly drops by on my account," his mother says. "It's purely a convenience. He gives Ray a lift."

"Anyway, they're separated now," says Mrs Green.

"I don't quite catch your drift."

"Well, your husband's on the night shift now."

"And so is Mervyn. They're rostered on together."

"Ah," says Mrs Green.

His mother closes her book and turns towards him.

"Ralph, why don't you go outside and have a play."

"Melbourne's so lovely in the autumn," says Mrs Green.

He eyes the fat lady. What is this certain way a man should look at her? With a death ray, perhaps?

"I want corned beef," he says.

"You can have that when we have our lunch. Go on now."

"I want some now."

"Mrs Green and I are talking, Ralph. You can have the it later."

Mrs Green is tapping her foot on the lino.

"I want some water."

His mother shrugs. He fills a glass at the sink, then sips it slowly, glaring at her.

"I really must be getting lunch," his mother says to Mrs Green.

"I don't believe I ever told you about Mr Green."

His mother gets to her feet.

"Quite like your husband in a lot of ways," says Mrs Green. "Men in uniform."

"Yes, my husband told me. Tram inspector, I believe. I'm sorry things didn't work out between you. These things happen, don't they."

"Men in uniform and their night shifts," says Mrs Green. "I can tell you a thing or two about that."

"Mrs Green, I have no idea what you might be suggesting, but my husband is a fireman, not a tram inspector. Whatever happened between you and Mr Green, I'm sure there must have been fault on both sides. I don't know how they do things in the tramways, but I assure you the Metropolitan Fire Brigade is a different organisation entirely, with altogether different entrance standards. My husband had to undergo a rigorous examination before he was accepted, and I'm sure that's true of all the men, even Mervyn Reynolds. Your concerns are perfectly well-meant, I'm sure, but they're entirely baseless, I assure you, and I would thank you to give us the space and privacy now to get on with our day."

"I thought we might deal with this one woman to another," says Mrs Green. "I see I'm to be relegated, however. Well, I've tried, my dear. I've tried."

His mother gets Mrs Green out their door at last. She starts preparing lunch.

"When Mervyn Reynolds showed you all those dance steps," she says, "did he do them in the air, or were you more like partners?"

"You have to get a good grip, Mervyn says, or else you could go flying anywhere."

"So did Mervyn dance the man's part, or the lady's?"

"If you're going to call a dance, you have to know both parts."

"Was there anything else?" his mother asks. "Anything I should know about? He is a little odd, I realise that."

"He has this way of sucking up his tea where the tea leaves get stuck on his teeth. He says it's his vampire trick."

"I see," his mother says.

"Maybe Mrs Green doesn't think we should have our radiogram."

"The sooner Mrs Green is out of all our lives, the better. There's just a few things we must sort out first."

"Like what?"

"You just be a kid, Ralphie. Enjoy it while you can. It doesn't last forever, believe you me."

———

When Thickness hears about Turana — how he's going to go there, how he'll have to make out he's Lesley Wedding — Thickness makes out Turana's no big deal at all.

"It's just a kind of school," Thickness says. "A school with beds for all the kids, and walls to keep them in."

"But they have guards," he says. "They must have."

"The guards are probably just like teachers," Thickness says.

"But it's practically a gaol. Wocker reckons half the kids in there, they end up in Pentridge."

"That isn't the idea at all," Thickness says. "They get a chance to change and not do bad things anymore."

They're walking round the drain park, looking for a golf ball to smash up. They haven't found a golf ball here for weeks.

"What did Wocker's brother even do?" Thickness says.

"He nicked cars."

"He'll just be a dickhead like Wocker. I don't get why you want to go and see him."

"He's practically the leader of the Rockets."

Thickness picks up a long stick and begins poking through leaf litter under a shrub.

"Not everyone has to be a goody goody all the time," he says.

Thickness straightens up.

"So now you're going to be some great tough guy, are you? Because you hit some kid at school, and now you're going in Turana."

"You're just jealous," he says.

"Yeah, I really want to go and visit some dickhead in Turana."

"You want to find out what it's like?"

Thickness just walks off, whipping the grass with his stick.

———

The afternoon of his visit to Turana, he tells his mother Thickness and he are going down The Windings. She gets all gooey, saying how it's wonderful he has this friend to do his boy stuff with.

"We go there all the time," he says.

"I didn't realise. You never talk to me."

"It's just a place we go."

"Your father and I, we hardly know what you get up to, half the time."

"I don't get up to anything."

"I could pack a snack. I could give you some cordial in a flask."

He's supposed to meet Wocker at the bus stop on the Wallace Street corner at half past one. When he gets there, there's no car. He sits down in the bus shelter.

This whole idea of meeting Wocker's dad, he's not too thrilled about it. Wocker's dad will probably have tatts and smoke and say fuckin' all the time. His dad will take one look at him and know he's just a mummy's boy. Then what? Give him an Indian burn? Wocker reckons, though, if Lesley Wedding doesn't show, the guards will get all narky and take it out on Turk. It's probably just crap. This whole Turana place, it's probably just like a kind of school, like Thickness says.

He feels the spaceship before he sees it. A low throb rattles the shelter walls, then a two-toned chromium-plated monster slides into view. White-walled tyres. Gleaming metallic strips along red and cream flanks. Vertical fins, just like an aeroplane's. Behind the open driver's window, Elvis Presley has suddenly grown older. Slicked-back hair above a creased and leathery face. Ageing Elvis turns towards him.

"You getting in or what?"

The words come out without a single movement of the lips.

"Back door, Spookus!" a more familiar voice calls from inside.

Within the spaceship, a radio is playing It's now or never. He pulls the rear handle and the enormous door swings open. Inside is a wide red seat, long enough to sleep on. Venetians with little draw cords cover the rear window.

He climbs in. Whooom! With a tremendous growl, the spaceship takes off, throwing him sideways as they turn into Wallace Street.

He can hear Wocker cacking himself in the front. Wocker reaches over and whacks him on the thigh.

"What'd I tell you, mate? Vee eight, dickhead. Dual

carbies, cigarette lighter, every fuckin' thing. She can go alright. Automatic, three speed."

Avoid the mirror. That is all he has to do. The minute he looks in the mirror, Wocker's dad will be looking back at him, right into his pathetic son-of-Rose-Halliday soul. Anywhere but the mirror. In twenty minutes he'll be Lesley Wedding.

It's obvious Wocker's dad loves his spaceship car. Every time they come to a corner, Wocker's dad slows her down, then swings his arm around the enormous steering wheel and whump! whump! whump! they're off again, headed for the moon.

Wocker's dad is wearing a short-sleeved shirt. His thick strong arms don't show any tatts at all.

Just act natural. Avoid the mirror.

"You going to introduce me to your friend, Weed?"

"Dad, this is Spook. Spook, this is Dad."

One of the mighty arms reaches over from the front. The arm's hand hovers before his chest. What is he supposed to do with it? The angles are all wrong. He cups the mighty hand in his own two little hands, then finds himself held in a fierce grip.

"Don't fuck with him, Dad. I told you, he's a pussy."

Pussy?

The fierce grip tightens, then releases, and the great arm withdraws.

Pussy. Jesus. He should have said he couldn't come to Wocker straight off. Told him how his Aunty Pearl has cancer. How they've only just found out. After Sunday school each week they have to go to Brighton. He has to walk Mitzy on the beach. It's to cheer his aunty up.

Yeah, right. Then Wocker would want to come too. He'd want to bring Nipper.

Avoid the mirror. Just act natural.

He looks out the side window, hoping to see some sign of envy or astonishment on a pedestrian's face. There must be lots of people who'd like to be riding where he is right now. He'd gladly swap places. The footpaths are deserted, though.

He succumbs at last and looks — and there, in the rear view mirror, are two brown eyes waiting for him. One brown eye winks.

"You got your name right, buddy?" Wocker says.

"Lesley Wedding."

"D'you bring your dress?"

"You said he was a guy!"

"Don't get your knickers in a knot," says Wocker. "These Turana pricks, they probably won't even notice."

———

TURK TURNS out to be a proper jumping jack. His right leg is either swinging in and out like crazy, or jigging up and down like he's got ants in his pants. Turk bites his fingernail at the edge, chewing on it, and his head is tilted over like he can't bear to the see the world the same as everybody else. He has oily brown skin like his dad, and muscles, too. Big muscles, thick. He doesn't look like Wocker at all.

"What about Brucie Ellis?" Turk says. "Brucie been around? Or George? What's Georgie up to? Still got the ciggie thing going? Has his uncle found out anything?"

"His uncle's been around," Wocker's dad says.

"So?"

"What d'you fuckin' think?" his dad says. "He's not impressed. You think the whole world revolves around you?

It doesn't, dickhead. You're here to smarten up. No-one tell you that?"

"Fuckin' dobber Ninny King, that's why I'm here."

"There's always dobbers, dickhead. And for every dobber, there's some dickhead gives 'em something to dob on. You need to watch your step. You're not some little kid, you know."

"Stick it up your arse."

Turk and Wocker and their dad are sitting at a table, one of many in a large high room with timber flooring. He is standing a few feet off, still not properly introduced, and trying to look like he isn't listening. Wocker's dad beckons him over.

"You didn't know Weed had a friend, did you?" Wocker's dad says. "This is bloody Lesley, if anybody asks."

"Lesley who?"

Turk looks away, avoiding eye contact.

"Lesley your fuckin' cousin, dickhead. Lesley from Bunyip."

Turk turns towards him now and looks him up and down, head tilted sideways, leg still jigging.

"Gidday," Turk says.

"Gidday."

Turk works his jaw like he is chewing gum. He doesn't think there's any actual gum there, though.

"So what did Brucie Ellis say then, anyway?" says Turk. "Anything about fuckin' Ninny King or Albert Thomas?"

"You ought to leave those pricks alone," his father says.

"Mate, they're the reason I'm in here."

"Am I some fuckin' record goin' round and round?" his father says. ""You're in here because you're a fuckin' dickhead. If you want to nick a car and take her for a spin and take her down the creek, leave her in one fuckin' piece. You're just asking for it."

"And you never did," says Turk.

"I never got myself locked up in fuckin' Turana."

"Yeah yeah. Difference between you and me — I got initiative."

"You? All fuckin' spark plug, no fuckin' ignition."

Turk spits on the floor, then glances to the doorway, where a man in a grey uniform is sitting at a table, laying down cards in front of him from a deck. He turns to Wocker.

"What you been up to, Weed?"

"Got a piece for you," Wocker says. "Chickee babe. She wants to meet you. She's fuckin' dying for it."

"Jesus, Weed," his dad says. "You got your end in now?"

"Tell him, Spookus."

"Tell him what?" he says.

"Jesus, you're the one who's always going on how mature she is. She lives over the road from Spookus here. Her old man's in the bank. She isn't interested in Spookus, obviously. She's looking for a more maturer kind of guy. Guy who's been around a bit. Guy who just happens to be getting out on Empire Day, and it's his bloody birthday too. "

"She never said that!" he says.

"Spookus, mate, you don't know half what goes on in that chickee's brain. I know. I got the knack."

"Porkie little pigs might fly," his father says.

"You wouldn't know. You're out of touch. I practise every day. Practise in the mirror. And Ninny King and Albert Thomas — little birdie tells me they're just waiting for you, mate, they're that ready to rumble."

"I'll give 'em fuckin' rumble," Turk says. "First night I get out of this shithole. Down The Windings."

"She really wants to meet you, Turkie. Seriously, mate."

"I don't think she does," he says.

"Jesus, who brought him?" says Turk.

Wocker catches his eye and jerks his head sideways. So what's that supposed to mean? Is he supposed to be a mind-reader now?

"How old's this chick?"

"She's old enough, mate," says Wocker.

"Is she a slack moll, or what?" says Turk.

"She won't come out," he says. "Her mother won't even let her come down the swings."

"See?" says Wocker. "Got a hot one for you, Turkie."

Turk turns to him, swinging his whole body around in his seat this time, and looks him up and down.

"Remind me," Turk says. "What you even doing here?"

"They brought me."

"Why don't you go and play with the light switches or something?"

OK, he gets it now. He gets it. He moves away, out of earshot.

He looks around. This cavernous space they use for visiting hours is probably a basketball court at other times. Broken-looking women — mothers, grandmothers — are talking with wary-looking kids who'd fit right in at Glendale Tech. Chairs scattered everywhere. Lots of unoccupied tables. Over by the double doors, the guy in uniform is rearranging the layout of his cards.

So this must be real life. This is what you're left with when you take away manners and all the other crap his mother's always going on about. A wooden floor marked out with half-obliterated lines. Four walls of concrete blocks. Four tiny windows, way up high. Four sets of fluorescent lights behind wire grilles. Two broken window winders. Chuck in the feral kids and whatever family they've got left, and this is Wocker World.

It's awful, obviously, this place, but it does have one redeeming feature. At least it's unquestionably real.

———

AFTER SCHOOL NEXT DAY, he goes around to Thickness's, where Thickness turns out to be pretty interested in Turana after all.

"Did the guards bash up any kids?" Thickness asks.

"There was only one guy in the visiting room. He was playing patience."

"Did he have a gun?"

"He was playing patience, I said. Wocker reckons Tina wants to fuck his brother."

Thickness nearly drops his raisin toast.

"Wocker reckons he's got her all lined up to be Turk's birthday present when he gets out."

"That'll never happen."

"That's what I said."

Thickness stuffs the rest of the slice in his mouth.

"When does he get out?"

"Cracker night," he says.

"Empire Day?"

"Yeah."

"She won't. She wouldn't."

"That's what I said. Turk just told me to shut up, basically."

"So what did you do then?" Thickness says. "Did you call the guards?"

"What for?"

Thickness flushes down the toast with the remains of his glass of milk.

"Why did they even want you there?" Thickness says.

"I don't know. Wocker had a piss behind a car when we were leaving. His dad says to me how he really appreciated me coming. He calls Wocker Weed."

Thickness runs a finger round the insides of his gums.

"I ought to warn Tina," Thickness says.

"I'm the one who found out!"

"Yeah, but I'm the one her mother believes in."

"Tell her to believe in me, then!"

Thickness stands, collects their plates and glasses.

"She thinks I'm like a Bentleigh person," Thickness says.

"Tell her you're not! Tell her you're not a Bentleigh person at all!"

"I should warn Tina, anyhow, not her mother."

"You weren't even there! You don't even know what Wocker said."

"But you just told me."

"I didn't tell you all of it," he says. "We both should see her. Then she'll understand it's serious."

"I suppose," says Thickness. "If she had to have a baby, I'd feel awful."

"Her mother would just hate it."

"She would."

"So can you ring her up? Make her come down and talk to us?"

"I'll tell her it's really serious," Thickness says. "I won't tell her you'll be there."

———

THE PHONE CALL WORKS. When they meet Tina at the roundabout park, she doesn't even seem annoyed that he is there with Thickness.

The two of them explain the situation. Tina seems to think it's just hilarious.

"Wocker's brother!" she says. "Why would I want to meet Wocker's brother? Wocker's such a drivel face!"

"But his brother's nothing like Wocker," he says.

"Does his brother do goobies all the time?"

"He's completely different," he says. "He's much more muscly. He jiggles."

He shows her what he means, jerking his knee up and down.

"He must be highly strung," Tina says. "Emotional type people, they're like that. They can't help it. They're just born that way. They feel things all the time."

"He steals cars," Thickness says. "He's always worried he'll get caught. That's why he's highly strung. He's a criminal. He has a gang, too."

"How do you mean he has a gang?" Tina asks. "Like, is he in a gang, or is he the boss of the gang?"

"They don't have a boss," Thickness says. "They just all decide what they're going to do whenever they're going to do it."

"They're the Rockets," he says. "There's this other gang, the Vultures. They're like the enemies of the Rockets."

"I get all that," Tina says. "But is he just one of the Rockets, or is he like the leader guy?"

"They take a vote on everything, I think," says Thickness.

"I think he's the boss," he says. "He kept on saying What about this Brucie guy? and What about this Georgie guy? I reckon he's the boss."

"So this was in Turana, right?" says Tina.

"It's no big deal," says Thickness. "It's just a school, really."

"Everybody knows about Turana," Tina says.

"Yeah, but they get the wrong idea," Thickness says.

Tina jumps off the roundabout. She starts to push it around, turning the boys.

"Turk's getting ready for a fight with the Vultures when he gets out," he says. "This fight, they call it a rumble. They'll be down The Windings. Ninny King and Albert Thomas and all these Vulture guys, they'll have their shanghais and ball bearings and their BB guns. They can shoot ball bearings right through a car door."

"All these Vultures guys?" says Tina.

"Yeah. Those guys."

"Like who?" says Tina.

"I don't know," he says.

"You say all these Vultures guys, but you don't even know who they are."

"He definitely wants to have sex with you," Thickness says.

"He doesn't even know me!"

Tina gives the roundabout a final shove, then walks toward the swings. The boys dismount and follow her. Tina is already airborne.

"What's he really like, Wocker's brother?" Tina says. "Apart from highly strung and muscles. Is he good looking?"

"He isn't that good looking," Thickness says.

"I thought you didn't even go there," Tina says. "I thought it was just Spook."

"I'm going on what he said."

"He's average looking," he says.

"Has he got tatts?" Tina asks.

"No."

"What about a girlfriend?"

"He isn't that type of guy," Thickness says. "He's the type of guy that gets any girl that comes along, then he tries to make her be his girlfriend."

Tina scuffs her shoes along the ground, bringing her swing to a halt alongside Thickness.

"You haven't even met him," she says.

Something is going on between Tina and Thickness, something without words. He doesn't quite understand what it can be. Thickness seems embarrassed.

"I don't have to," Thickness says. "It's obvious."

"Is that the type of bloke he is, Spookus?" Tina asks.

"I don't know. Probably."

"Jesus, Spook!" Thickness says. "You're the one who wanted Tina to come down. You're the one who said we had to warn her!"

"Was that your idea, Spook?" Tina says.

"It was both of us's idea," he says.

Tina starts to wind the swing she's sitting on. She winds and winds until the chains will twist no more.

"It's very sweet of you," says Tina. "Both of you. I really appreciate your thoughtfulness."

She lets the swing go and spins, legs forward, head thrown back, her long hair flying.

Well, she has been warned.

———

BACK AT THICKNESS'S AGAIN, Thickness is beside himself. Why couldn't he do all the talking? It would have been so much better. But people hate it when you are a brain. They never will admit you have the best ideas.

"But you weren't even there," he says. "You didn't even see Turk."

Thickness says there isn't any point in arguing. The main thing now is saving Tina.

"Maybe we should call the cops," he says.

"What's the point?" Thickness says. "He's in gaol already. Not gaol. Still, Turana."

"Maybe we should tell her mother."

"Then what if her mother takes sleeping tablets?" says Thickness. "She already saw a psychiatrist one time, Tina reckons. I don't reckon we should tell her mother. We should just rescue her."

"But rescue how?"

Thickness says he'll think about it.

"I'll think about it too," he says.

So this becomes their plan for now. They're going to think about it, both of them. And so they go away, and think.

CHAPTER TEN

One afternoon as he is making a snack he notices an envelope tucked behind the bread bin. The envelope is empty, but the sender's name in printed on the front. It's from the Medical Registration Board.

When his dad gets up at last, he sees this envelope.

"Where did you find this?"

"What is it?"

"Nothing, I hope."

When his mum gets home, his dad shows her the envelope straight off.

"So?" his father asks.

She says it's nothing.

"Medical Registration Board? It can't be nothing, Rose."

She tells his dad she gets letters all the time.

But didn't she once report a certain medico to this Medical Registration Board, his father wants to know. He demands to see the letter. She says she burned it.

"So is this your father all over again?" his father says.

"This has nothing to do with my father."

"Great. So what's the this this time?"

She flings her things onto the table. Potatoes roll onto the floor.

"You come home, Ray, and crash when I get up. Then when I get back from work, you go to work. And now you're suddenly interested in my private correspondence?"

"Changing the subject a bit there, Rose."

"Fine. Fine. I reported certain anomalies to the Board. Certain clear anomalies, in my opinion, regarding Dr Schlimmicht."

"Jesus Christ, Rose."

"I have a duty, Ray."

She picks up the potatoes.

"I get it, Rose. Dr Goebbels is giving you a hard time. It's because you're a bit rusty, Rose, that's all. Just smarten up your act. You'll be fine."

"I am not a bit rusty, Ray Halliday. I do not need to smarten up my act. I know a mass when I see one."

"Rose, Rose, you're on thin ice. That's his job, not yours."

She throws the potatoes at his dad.

"The man is a belittling, supercilious know-all!" she shouts.

Most of the potatoes miss, but one hits his dad in the belly. He scuttles between them, scooping up the battered spuds before anything worse can happen to them.

"You've changed your tune pretty fast," his father says.

"He's always been an arrogant so-and-so. I needed to get out of Karnook, Ray. I had to have a job."

"So how far up this creek have you paddled?"

"I sent a confidential enquiry, Ray. CONFIDENTIAL

in capital letters, underlined. You'd think that would mean something, wouldn't you?"

"And?"

Real tears are running down his mother's cheeks.

"This is so unfair, Ray. I let you back into our lives, and now the minute I get back from Dr bloody Schlimmicht's, here you are, ripping into me like you would know the first thing about anything! These are people's lives at stake here, and for your information, I am not some hot-head who goes rushing off to the Medical Registration Board for no reason. I am not going to be treated like some kind of blind, dumb idiot who doesn't know what's going on, and I most certainly am not going to be patronised by you!"

She rushes from the kitchen.

His dad doesn't follow her. For himself, he hardly knows where to look. He's seen some meltdowns in his time, but this one is up there with the best of them.

They can hear her in the bedroom, opening drawers.

"You should get her, Dad."

His mother storms down the hall. The back door opens, then slams. They can hear her feet on the stairs.

"She'll calm down," his father says.

A car door closes. An engine starts.

"Jesus Christ," his father says.

They look out over the sink. The Consul is backing through the gate.

His father sighs.

Together, they unpack the onions and greens from his mother's shopping bags and put them away in storage, where it's unlikely they'll be touched for some time yet.

———

THREE DAYS LATER, his mother still has not come home. His father reckons she's at Aunty Pearl's.

"Have you rung her?" he asks.

"Mate, the more you prod and poke, it's like stirring up a fire. All these sparks, going up the chimney."

His father is cooking them something at the stove.

"I could ring," he says. "Aunty Pearl always talks to me."

"Your Aunty Pearl'd talk to a gate post, mate. Who do you reckon helped write the letter when your mum took your grandpa to the Board?"

"I don't remember it."

"Your mum and all her tricks, mate — this goes way back."

His mother's absence is not without its compensations. Chief of these is man food. This cuisine originated in Queensland with drovers and rodeo riders. There are no vegetables in man food. The main requirements are a frying pan and lots of dripping. The possibilities are almost endless. Fried bread. Fried eggs. Fried bread and fried eggs. Fried eggs and fried baked beans and fried bread. Something like this is what his father must be cooking now.

"I still don't get it with the CONFIDENTIAL," he says. "Why is that so bad?"

"Your mum has this idea how Dr Schlimmicht is missing stuff. Missing tumours. Not reporting them to patients, other doctors. I said Rose, forget it, he's the specialist, but Aunty Pearl and her, they probably reckoned if she put this CONFIDENTIAL in her letter to the Board, the Board wouldn't straight off ring up Dr Whatsit and tell him everything."

"Is that what happened?"

"I wouldn't mind betting."

His father brings the sizzling pan across and scoops his share onto a plate. Fried bread and eggs. Two blackened sausages. Fizzing shards that might once have been bacon.

"Go for it," his father says.

"Where's your plate?"

"I'm sick of all this washing up, mate. Easier to have it from the pan."

———

HIS MOTHER RINGS around quarter past eight. It's the first time he's heard from her since she left.

"Did your dad get off to work OK?"

"When you coming home?" he says.

"You going to watch Sea Hunt tonight? I know it's Sea Hunt night."

"It's better if you're here," he says.

"It's not that scary. You're a big boy now. If Lloyd Bridges didn't make it, there wouldn't be a show next week, would there?"

"I know," he says.

"There's cameramen there with him. He isn't on his own at all."

"I aren't stupid," he says. "Are you coming home?"

"Are you missing me?"

"No."

"What has your father had to say about all this? Do I even have to ask?"

"He says you're bloody stupid."

"Your father's not a medical person, though, is he Ralph?"

"You're not a doctor. You just wish you were a doctor."

"I don't know where you ever got that from, Ralph."

"I aren't Ralph. I'm Spook."

"You're getting all cross now, aren't you? I can hear it in your voice. You know I love you very much."

"You coming home, or what?" he says.

"Everybody needs to feel that people like them, Ralph."

He doesn't say a thing.

"Aunty Pearl and I, we're going to have a little... We're going to have a little celebration of our long friendship, Ralph. A little cheer-me-up — because a person does need cheering up from time to time. After that, I'll be home."

"Tonight?"

"You make it sound like someone died, Ralph. No-one died, you know."

She hangs up.

He goes into the kitchen. He makes himself a chocolate drink. He has it, then he makes himself a second one.

He doesn't like these nights here on his own.

He thinks about John Ford from Night Beat. Every time the coppers hear there is a smash at night, they ring John Ford and tell him where to go. Then John Ford gets there with his tape recorder. When they've put the smashed up people in the ambulance, John Ford asks the driver Where to, driver? St Vincent's, I suppose? — and then the driver says That's right, John. St Vincent's from here. Every ambulance driver in Melbourne must know John Ford.

John Ford could watch Sea Hunt on his own. John Ford wouldn't care if Lloyd Bridges was fighting a giant squid and the bad guy came along and cut his oxygen. He wouldn't care if Lloyd Bridges got the bends, and this time, in the decompression chamber, he really won't make it. This is how he wants to be one day, like John Ford, knowing all the answers in advance. Maybe caring just a bit, but definitely not too much.

The cardboard box is where it's always been, in the bottom of his parents' wardrobe. The lady with the baby skeleton inside her, folded up and bent. The person with the wire in his arm. They're all still in the box. He checks. Images of jellyfish and mush. Because of one of these, his mother's gone and dobbed in Dr Schlimmicht, but now she's coming home.

He goes into the TV room. Sea Hunt should be over now. The thrashing giant squid and flashing knife and bubbles in the water — all his deepest fears, packed into half an hour. By now, Lloyd Bridges should be back at the helm of his boat, rocking gently on the water, talking to the camera before the ads.

He turns the TV on.

The Untouchables will be next. He's never allowed to watch The Untouchables when his mother is around. He only ever saw it once, with Grandpa Doc one night in Karnook when his mother was out.

The picture tube hisses to life, revealing Eliott Ness climbing stairs. Eliott Ness has his hat on. Wallpaper is peeling off the walls. The music is very serious. Something bad is going to happen. Elliott Ness knocks on a door. A lady inside the room rests her forehead against the door. She does not answer. She looks really worried. Eliott Ness says Laura! The lady opens the door. Elliott Ness goes in. He takes off his hat. The lady says Will you have a drink? Elliott Ness says You know I can't do that. The lady says Johnny Sacramento sent you, didn't he? Eliott Ness takes off his jacket. He is wearing a great waistcoat. He hangs his jacket on a chair. Leather straps cross his back. These must hold his holsters up. A truck pulls up outside. A man inside the truck sticks out a tommygun. The tommygun goes katakatakak. The window of the lady's room is all shot up. The light gets shot up too. Elliott Ness throws the lady in the corner. She is going to scream. Elliott Ness puts his hand over the lady's mouth. Their eyes are open really wide. Suddenly it's day time, and Elliott Ness is walking down the front steps of a large old building. He has his hat on. Zillions of photographers run up to him. Their flashbulbs go pop, pop, pop. Eliott Ness half closes his eyes. There are more flashbulbs. A telephone is ringing.

Ringing.

He is awake now. On the TV, Kevin Dennis spreads his arms in front of all his cars, excited about his low deposits. The phone is still ringing.

He goes out to the hall and picks it up.

"Hello?"

"You're up late, shweetiepie," his mother says. "Aunty Pearl, she shed He'll be there waiting up for you. And there you are, you're waiting up for me."

"You're drunk."

"Happy, shweetie. Everything is good now. Everything's alright."

"You coming home?"

"Ha! That's what I shay! Your Uncle Paulie, though, he wants a word, lovie. Shober as a judge, he is. Shober as a magistrate. Wants a word. Probably wants a whole enshy-clopedia."

He hears a clunk — the handset being dropped, perhaps — then Uncle Paul comes on the line.

"Hey Scoop, Uncle Paul here. How's it going? Everything OK your end? How's school and all? Haven't seen you for a while. Busy busy, you know how it is."

"I'm OK."

"Mitzy's been missing you, mate. Remember all our walks? Remember the old Plimsoll line?"

"I remember."

"Thing is, mate, we don't want you getting all worried. Your mum, she's fine. She's had a few, that's all. I said to your Aunty Pearl, You're temptin' fate, love, she's not used to it, but your Aunty Pearl, she likes a sherry, and one thing leads to another, you know? Hate to have seen them in the old days, I really would. Oops! Hang on mate, I might just have to put the phone down for a sec. Not the towel, love, get the bucket. Bucket and hot water. Gor. Sorry mate, there's been a bit of a... The mop, Pearl, not the towel. Get the mop from out the back. Jesus. Mate, your mum, she'll be fine, she will. I just don't think she's drivin' anywhere tonight, OK? So go to bed mate, rest up, and your mum, she's in good hands, alright? Hang on, I think your Aunty Pearl wants a word."

He hears a crashing down the line that could be furniture tumbling over. Someone is saying Rosie, Rosie. Aunty Pearl comes on the phone.

"Poppet, is that you? Listen, your mum's fine. She's got a big heart, Ralphie — too big for her own good sometimes. There's more towels in the laundry, lovie. Get a clean one."

"Did she sick up?"

"Little bit spewsie-woozie, Ralphie. She'll have a whopper in the morning. She loves her family. That's the main thing, ay? Now you just put the phone down, lovie, and go back to sleep, and all this will work out in the morning, OK?"

"Is she there?"

"I think she's dropped off for a little nap, sweetie. We'll leave her, shall we? It's probably for the best."

He hangs up. He goes into every room and turns on all the lights, then retreats to his bedroom, takes off his shoes, and climbs into bed.

Before too long, Elliott Ness is climbing stairs in a dim, dark place. Elliott Ness knocks on a door. Within, a woman kneels over a bucket. Laura? calls Elliott Ness. Mum?

———

Someone is standing in his bedroom doorway.

"You awake, Ralph?"

The voice is a low whisper. He opens his eyes and takes in the first light of day. There is no-one in his doorway. He throws back his blankets and finds he is fully dressed. He hears the toilet flush down the hall.

He gets up. His mother is in the kitchen, getting stuff down from the medicine cupboard. He flicks the light switch and the fluorescents stutter.

"Don't," she says.

He turns the switch off and studies her from behind as she tears a strip of metal foil, then drops two tablets in a glass of water. Bubbles starts to fizz. She doesn't turn.

"So he reckons I'm a bloody idiot, does he?"

"You always have to tell people off. Even if we just go in a shop, you have to tell the person off."

A haggard, older version of his mother turns to face him. She is going to say something, he thinks, but then she hesitates.

"What?" she says.

He doesn't dare to tell her. How she looks. Who she has become.

"I embarrass you," she says. "Your mother is a frightful, dreadful person, as far as you're concerned. Unfortunately, other people's lives just happen to be at stake though, Ralph. Did that come up in all your man-to-man conversations these last few days?"

"He doesn't talk like you do all the time."

"You can say that again."

She swallows down the cloudy, fizzing liquid.

"Have you got the sack? Can we go back to Karnook?"

"Wouldn't that be lovely? Back and back and back."

"Can we?"

"That isn't how it works, Ralph. There's no going back."

"Is Dr Schlimmicht mad at you?"

"Dr Schlimmicht and I had a difficult conversation. You could say we laid our cards on the table."

"What cards did you have?"

"There are no cards, Ralph. It's a manner of speaking. So what have you been eating, anyway, these last few days? Fried bread? Fried bananas? Fried ice-cream?"

"We didn't have fried ice-cream."

"I'm going to run a bath," she says. "When I get back, I want to see this place cleaned up."

She leaves the kitchen.

He looks inside the fridge. She hasn't even bothered bringing up the milk. He can hear her bath running.

He descends the back stairs. Soon his father will be home, and what will happen then? Another argument. She'll be crying. They'll send him to his room. And all for what? What really? Because his dad is dumb and she isn't? Because he's just a fireman? Lots of people are firemen. He's got a job, at least. Isn't that what she went on about for years? Why did she even marry him if all she wanted was to tell him off? She could have let him stay in Queensland. He could have gone on being a cowboy. Why does she have to make everything different from how it's meant to be?

He gets their milk and paper from the laneway. The bath is still running when he comes inside.

He puts the milk in the fridge and turns the radio on. He runs hot water in the sink. If only Dr Schlimmicht would sack her. Finally she might understand how other people can't stand her.

The Vanguard pulls up in the laneway a few minutes later. His father climbs the stairs.

"Rose?" his father calls out as he comes in through the porch.

"She's in the bath."

His father goes on up the hallway. As for himself, he doesn't have the heart to linger. He shuts the kitchen door and finishes the washing up, then starts in with the tea towel.

Eventually, someone pulls the plug out of the bath. He hears a rush of water down the pipes, then after that the water glugs and gurgles, then trickles and drips, until finally there is no more water left in the drain at all.

CHAPTER ELEVEN

Next door, Maria has come home from hospital.

She sits propped up on pillows and cushions in what used to be her own shopfront surrounded by a golden glow, a wizened, scowling little creature devouring cartoons and kids' shows on Enrico's twenty-one inch Astor. In her left hand, Maria grips a length of wood to which Enrico has attached a push button. If she presses this button, Enrico will come up from his workshop, but for some reason — spite, or stubbornness, or sheer forgetfulness — the little woman never does press the button, preferring to croak out Santa Maria! at seemingly random intervals.

His own duties from four to half past five on Mondays, Wednesdays and Fridays comprise manning the shop counter, keeping up Maria's supply of raisins, and preparing two glasses of Pimm's Number One Cup for her, one at four fifteen, and the second an hour later.

For his performance of these duties he gets scarce acknowledgement from Maria, who eyes him with dark suspicion or ignores him completely. As for his role at the front counter, he soon finds there is more to winning a customer's confidence than writing their details on a pad, along with the make, model and serial number of their appliance and a description of the problem. Nearly every time, the customer wants to talk to Enrico about it all, so the whole point of his being there is lost, it seems to him. Nonetheless, each time he sees that telltale look of doubt in a customer's eye, he steps back through the partition curtain, crosses the no-go zone between the senora and her favourite show, and goes to fetch Enrico.

Enrico doesn't seem to mind, though. As Enrico tells him often enough You want to be repairman Spook, all starting like this.

His favourite time at Enrico's is the half hour after they have closed the shop. By then, if he is generous with the second Pimm's, Maria will have begun to snore, and he can go back to Enrico's workshop and continue his education.

Sometimes Enrico is totally absorbed on these occasions, not even aware of his presence, it would seem. Enrico will prod and probe inside a chassis, then solder or unsolder components, glance at his oscilloscope, hiss his disappointment or surprise, murmur numbers under his breath. These must be the difficult cases, he guesses, just like the ones The Serviceman takes on each month in Radio Television & Hobbies.

On other afternoons, Enrico is chattier, happy to comment aloud as he goes about his work. Enrico can tell that a resistor is all burn up just by looking, that a capacitor is leaking like bambino bottom, see? At other times, there seems to be more guesswork involved. Change him this valve, I think — got bad feeling this one, he might say, or something loose in here, I think, followed by a tapping spree with his insulated screwdriver.

This is when Enrico likes to set him challenges. He might point to a resistor hidden under a tangle of soldered joints and quiz him on its value.

"Four seventy ohms," he'll say. "Plus or minus ten percent."

"Ohms! Four seventy ohms? You think? What colour, number three band?"

"Orange? Is it orange?"

"You think is brown, this one?"

"Orange."

"So?"

"Four seventy K."

Sometimes the quizzing is even more demanding.

"Across this one, Spook, I measure him twenty-four volt my VTVM. What current flowing this one? You work him out. What formula?"

"E equals I R."

"So then?"

He'll take a pad and pen, and try to solve the puzzle.

If Enrico's in the mood, these sessions can go on for ages. Other times, Enrico set him physical tasks, vacuuming dust from a chassis, or loosening off the pot knobs and nuts that hold a chassis in its cabinet. One time, Enrico challenges him to draw the components and connections around a TV valve socket that he's been working on as for a circuit diagram.

"Hard thing, this," Enrico says, after he has struggled for a while.

Enrico looks over his attempt.

"You got PL81. Is pentode. Good. So then, what else?

Filament for this one, she got no power yet! How she going to get hot, eh? And now you got high tension in the grid. All blow him up, Spook, kaboom! Anode for this one on top, see? Little hat. You touch him this one with you finger, you go dead!"

"I get it now," he says.

"You doing good, Spook. First thing, Ohm's Law. You knowing Ohm's Law now. Is good. Take long time, all this. You learning, Spook."

Sometimes he gives up altogether, and simply watches in a kind of trance as Enrico stoops over a chassis, tinkering, muttering, measuring. He loves to see the valves lined up, their filaments aglow. The flickering image on a picture tube — just rows of dots, Enrico has explained to him, little phosphors lit up by electrons. Whoever could have guessed that's all that makes up Superman?

"Too close now, Spook!" Enrico whispers. "Back! Too many volts for you."

When Enrico touches his probe on a soldered joint and the trace on the oscilloscope jumps to life, it's like they are in an operating theatre, probing a living heart.

"Si, si," Enrico will say at such a moment, under his breath — while he knows better than to utter a single word.

———

HE FIRST MEETS Mrs Dahlenberg the day she comes into the shop to get her record player. Mrs Dahlenberg is old, but not the usual way. Her hair is pinkish blonde. A warm cream glistens on her cheeks. Little gold shapes dangle from Mrs Dahlenberg's ears.

"It's just a smallish one," says Mrs Dahlenberg. "It's a

Philips, I believe. A portable. It's red. Enrico will know. He rang to remind me. I'm going to take it with me to New Guinea."

Mrs Dahlenberg seems to have all the time in the world. When she smiles, her smile is gentle. Mrs Dahlenberg has nothing to prove, no point to make.

Dazzled, he backs out through the partition opening and runs the gauntlet between Maria and Felix the Cat to find Enrico in his workshop.

"Si, si!" Enrico says. "Mrs Dahlenberg! I get for you."

Enrico pulls the small red portable record player down from a shelf and places it in his outstretched arms.

"No charge for Mrs Dahlenberg!" Enrico says. "Me check him all. All good. Mrs Dahlenberg, nice lady. You say for me, Very sorry Mrs Dahlenberg, this job. Enrico promise him two weeks ago. You tell him this for Mrs Dahlenberg. Is good! No charge!"

He carries the record player back into the shop and sets it down on the counter, then translates Enrico's message as best he can.

"You tell Enrico I am very grateful," says Mrs Dahlenberg. "Do pass on my best wishes to Maria too. You must be Enrico's new helper."

"Sort of."

"Well, you know who I am."

"Mrs Dahlenberg."

"And what's your name? Can I ask that?"

"Spook."

"Spook. That's a good name for a boy."

"It is," he says.

Mrs Dahlenberg's smile seems a little sad, like maybe she

is thinking of some other boy. If so, this other boy is very lucky.

She steps forward to pick up her record player.

"I can take it," he says, and comes around the counter.

"It's hardly anything. You can open the door, though. That would be wonderful."

He opens the door. Mrs Dahlenberg steps out onto the footpath, carrying her record player.

"Thank you, Spook."

He waits there in the doorway, watching, as Mrs Dahlenberg crosses the street. She approaches a black Mercedes. She puts the record player in the Mercedes' boot, walks to the driver's door and gets in. It's hard to see through the window reflections. Mrs Dahlenberg seems to be looking down, putting on some glasses. The Mercedes' indicator light begins to flash. The car pulls out onto Blessington Street and drives away.

———

Thickness comes into the shop one afternoon while he is on the counter. The Texas Rangers are shooting up baddies behind the partition but Maria is snoring. Thickness's eyes are red about the lids.

"What's up?" he asks. "Did you see Tina?"

"It isn't that," Thickness says.

"What then?"

"It doesn't even matter."

"Did some kid bash you up?"

"They found out. There must have been some kid that went to Glendale Primary."

"They found out who you really are?"

"It isn't who I really am! Thickness —why do I have to be Thickness?"

"You want some raisins?"

"No."

He goes back through the curtain to the inner sanctum. Maria's eyes are partly open, yet the old lady is snoring, head thrown back. He lowers the volume on the TV, then clears lozenges and tissues from a little table. He brings the table back and offers it to Thickness as a seat. Thickness waves it away.

"Once you get a name, that's it," he says. "It's just a name, though. It doesn't matter."

"Thickness. I'm not thick. I'm not stupid. I'm not fat."

"You have got glasses, though" he says. "Are they going to bash you up?"

"They could."

"You just have to whack them. Whack them in the balls, like I whacked Alex."

"I can't. I'm not allowed."

"That's when they bash you, though, when they think you're not allowed."

Thickness starts kicking the legs of the little table, nudging it across the floor.

"Did you see Tina?" he says. "Did you tell her what happened?"

"Sort of."

"So what happened?"

"She says we just have to be friends," Thickness says. "Plus her mum, she's really mad at Tina. She reckons Tina went out with this Simon Goodluck. He's in Matric."

"Jesus!"

"Tina's mum didn't even find out from Tina. She found out some other way."

"What did Tina say?"

"She reckons this Simon's a total dick brain. She reckons he's immature."

"Did you tell her how you're going to get bashed up?"

"She wouldn't even care," says Thickness. "I don't even think she likes me anymore."

"She probably never did that much."

The little table is copping quite a kicking. He whisks the table away from Thickness and sets it on the counter.

"She gets infatuated," Thickness says. "That isn't proper love, though. It's just infatuated. That's what my mother says."

"Everyone doesn't have to love everyone, though."

"She really hates her mother. She'd do anything to annoy her."

"Like go with Turk?"

"You kept on making him sound really great. Like he's this great gang leader."

"I didn't."

"You did!" says Thickness. "You don't even realise it. He's just a criminal."

"Well tell her mother then."

"What's that going to do? Anything her mother says, she'll just do the opposite."

"I don't see why you even care about her," he says.

"I know," Thickness says. "If you really care about a person, though, you just do. And you have to do what's right."

"Like what?"

"When the Vultures and the Rockets have their rumble

down The Windings, we should be there. We should save her."

"How?"

"Throw spears," Thickness says.

"But then they'd shoot us with their shanghais."

"We could make a fort. We could grab her in the dark and take her to there."

"She'd yell out, though."

"We have to do something," Thickness says. "Tomorrow, after school, come down The Windings."

"Santa Maria!" a voice croaks out beyond the curtain. "Cisco Kid!"

He grabs the little table off the counter. He has to go, he explains to Thickness. It's time for Maria's special medicine again.

———

Next afternoon, he and Thickness go down to The Windings and look for car ramps near the bridge.

Thickness reckons when the Rockets and the Vultures rumble, they'll bring their stolen cars down here and drive them up these ramps that they have hidden somewhere. They'll go flying through the air. They'll all be drunk, and if there's any girls, they'll make the girls go in their cars. If there's a smash, Tina could die.

They can't find any ramps, though.

"They could be anywhere," he says to Thickness. "They could be right up the Broady end."

"There isn't any wood up there," says Thickness. "When they have a rumble, they always have a fire. It's like the Indians and their war dance. You come down here some days and it's all charcoal where their fire has been. You can see their beer bottles and all their wheelie marks. Their frangers, too."

"Right here?"

"Right here. They fight each other. They have bike chains. Whoever gets the girl, they go off in the bushes with her."

"Tina wouldn't like that, though. She'd go home."

"She couldn't," says Thickness. "It'd be too late."

Thickness walks up and down.

"You know what we should do?" Thickness says. "We should make a bomb. Then if the Rockets get Tina, we yell out Give her up, or we let off our bomb."

"What if they don't even think we have a bomb?"

"OK," says Thickness. "We have two bombs. If they don't believe us, we drop the first bomb off the bridge."

Could this work? He looks up to the top of the bridge where the railway lines must pass overhead. That must be four stories high.

"So we're up there, and they're down here?"

"This is where they have their fires," Thickness says.

"But what if a train comes along?"

"There's hardly any. It's only freight trains. I'll do it on my own if you don't want to."

"I dunno."

Thickness marches off towards the rocky slope that rises up to the far end of the bridge. He stops and turns.

"You have to save the other person, Jesus says! Even if you don't want to!"

Jesus? How did Jesus get involved with this? He chases after Thickness, if only to talk some sense into him.

The slope up to the bridge proves hard climbing. There's

thistles among the weeds, and the edges of the rocks are sharp. By the time he's halfway up, Thickness is already out of sight.

When he finally gets to where the railway lines and sleepers are, Thickness is well onto the bridge. Bloody hell! If a train comes now, he'll have no choice but to jump onto the other rails. And if two trains come at once?

"This is stupid!" he shouts. "What are you doing?"

Thickness doesn't answer, just keeps on walking.

He looks around. The nearest houses are several hundred yards away. If someone in those houses is looking out their back window, they'll see him and Thickness on the tracks for sure. What they're doing is just completely dumb.

He's scared enough up here already, that's the truth, and he isn't even on the bridge yet properly. Erecting an aerial was a piece of cake compared to this. If a train comes, it won't be able to stop. He knows this much from Casey Jones. Even when Casey makes his wheels go backwards, his engine still keeps going nearly to where the bad guys have pulled up the tracks — and that's on a steam engine where the wheels can go backwards.

Look down at the sleepers, that's what he'll have to do. The sleepers and nowhere else. The bridge is wide enough if there aren't any trains. It's just a long way down, that's all, so if he falls, he'll die for sure. A footpath made of sleepers, that's what he has to think of. Walk along that footpath, and not trip on any stones.

He's already feeling cold and sick. He sets out, shivering, and almost straight away — he cannot help it — he catches sight of the ground below and sees how far away it is. Without any warning, his knees begin to shake, and soon he has no choice but to stop and hang onto them and hope they will behave. He must look ridiculous, he knows, stooped over, quite unable to straighten, while Thickness goes on ahead.

"You should come back!" he calls. "I can hear a train!"

But Thickness shows no sign of hearing him at all.

"It isn't funny, fuckface!"

Thickness finally pauses and turns to look up the valley. He must be nearly over the creek, that's how far he's gone.

Can't Thickness just come back? He tries a little step, and finds that he can move a bit, but the shaking in his legs is terrible. If a train comes now, could he even make it onto the other track?

"You're a fucking idiot!" he yells.

The yelling seems to help a little. He slides his hands up onto his thighs and keeps on going. Great currents of electricity are whirling in his head.

When he finally reaches Thickness, he sees that Thickness, like himself, is shivering all over, and that his cheeks are wet with tears.

"Come back," he says.

Later, searching Thickness's garage in the dusk, they find two tins of house paint. They tip their contents down the gully trap and set them up to dry. Their plan is underway.

CHAPTER TWELVE

A few days after this, Enrico tells him they are going to shut up shop earlier than usual and pay a visit to Mrs Dahlenberg. She has a problem with her TV picture.

"What about Maria?" he says. "What if she needs someone to change her channel?"

"Just one hour, Spook," Enrico says. "Maria, we leave banana. She be OK. Mrs Dahlenberg, she wanting see you, Spook. Enrico, bring you helper, she say to me."

"How come?"

Enrico shrugs.

"Liking you, maybe."

The drive to Northcote takes a while. They go in the old Commer van.

"Mrs Dahlenberg, she sad I think," Enrico says. "Doctor Dahlenberg, I never meeting him. Mrs Dahlenberg, she come my shop. Some person telling her Go see Enrico, Enrico good. Dr Dahlenberg, he die."

"When?"

"Last year. Fall over desk. Kaput. All finish."

"But how come? Did he have a coronary?"

"Spook, I fix him up TV. Not person doctor."

"I'd think about it all the time if I was old, how I could die."

"For you, Spook, many years. Later, you worry for that. Not now."

They have pulled up at traffic lights. He looks across to where Enrico's veined hand rests on the long vibrating gear stick. Enrico must know he is getting near to his end, and Maria to hers, and yet Enrico has come away and left her with just Parer the Magician and a banana for company.

Will he ever have the kind of deep-down steadiness he can see in Enrico? What is the secret of that?

———

MRS DAHLENBERG's house is on a corner behind tall trees and bushes. All he can see of it as they pull up is a high slate roof and two chimneys capped with chimney pots just like the ones at Grandpa Doc's.

"I'll stay here," he says.

"Mrs Dahlenberg, she want to see you," Enrico says.

"I don't feel like it."

"Come all this way."

"You fix her TV. I'll stay here."

Enrico gets his tool case from the back, then returns past his window.

"Wanting change you mind, Spook? Come inside?"

He shakes his head.

Enrico walks through the picket gate on the corner and disappears from view.

Is Enrico disappointed with him? Probably. Well, it's just too bad. He needs some space from all the upset people in his life. Now it turns out even Mrs Dahlenberg is grieving. The day he met her in the shop, she seemed so nice. Floaty, like she was on a cloud. But she probably comes home and cries all day. She wouldn't want to see him, anyway. People just say that when you're a kid. She wants to see Enrico, really. It's Enrico who can fix her TV set.

He starts flipping through one of Enrico's spare parts books. There are pages and pages of graphs for valves with labelled lines — Vg_1, Vg_2, Vg_3, Ia(mA). That last one probably is current, milliamps. But where do all the milliamps go? There's so much of this he'll never understand.

He glances up to see Mrs Dahlenberg approaching. She is wearing a pink cardigan and matching jumper. The same ashy-pink hair that he remembers. She comes right to his window. He winds it down.

"You're looking very snug and comfortable in there."

"I am."

"Good thing. I'm all in favour."

"I'd just be in the way inside."

"You're probably right," says Mrs Dahlenberg. "We mustn't spoil his concentration."

"Don't you have to show him what's gone wrong?"

"It's pretty obvious. My television's got the stripes disease, whatever that is called. I wouldn't really know."

What is Mrs Dahlenberg expecting from him, standing out here like he is maybe going to talk to her or something?

"Can I bribe you with some chocolate?"

"I don't like chocolate."

"That's a pity. I've got caramello. I've got ginger chocolate. I've got white chocolate, too."

"You've got a lot of chocolate."

"I'm a kind of chocolate witch," says Mrs Dahlenberg. "Still, if you don't like chocolate, I won't be able to cast a spell on you, will I? Not a chocolate spell, anyway."

"You won't."

"I'll have to have the chocolate all myself. I've got mint chocolate, too. Did I mention I've got mint chocolate?"

"Why do you have so much chocolate?"

"Oh, that shouldn't be any concern of yours," says Mrs Dahlenberg. "You don't like chocolate anyway."

"I don't."

"I have some goldfish too," says Mrs Dahlenberg.

"What kind of goldfish?"

"They're quite large, some of them."

Mrs Dahlenberg holds out her hands, eight or nine inches apart.

"I'm a goldfish witch as well," she says.

"Are they in a tank?"

"They're in a pond. They hide under the lily leaves. If you wait, though, eventually they come out and swim around at the bottom. They're very beautiful. We call them goldfish, but actually they have reddish sides. They swim around down there, and no-one has the least idea what they're thinking. It's just their own private place down there, under the lily leaves."

"Do you feed them?" he asks.

"I do."

"Have you got any biscuits?"

"I might have."

"Have you got any creme-betweens?"

Mrs Dahlenberg thinks she has.

"It won't take a minute to check," she says. "Would you like to come and have a look?"

He follows Mrs Dahlenberg through her front gate. It has a little roof and vines growing down each side. Beyond the gate, Mrs Dahlenberg's bushes have grown over her path, leaving it a shady tunnel. Four wide steps lead up to her porch and a tall flywire door. On either side of her door are long, narrow windows made of swirly red glass.

"Is this where all the patients come?" he asks. "Where they came?"

"Ah, Enrico's been filling you in, I see. No, Dr Dahlenberg had a dull little place on Station Street I was always hoping he might pretty up a bit. This was never his surgery, though. It was always just the two of us here."

"My grandpa, he's a doctor," he says. "We came from New South Wales. My mother, she takes x-rays."

"You'd know all about it," says Mrs Dahlenberg.

"I do."

She says that seeing he's her guest, he should open the flywire door.

"Seeing you're the chocolate witch," he says.

"Exactly."

They enter a dim hallway that smells of wood polish. Mrs Dahlenberg invites him through to see her fish.

He follows her through the kitchen into a room with a cork-tiled floor. A large fish hangs on a wood-lined wall. She opens two narrow glass doors and steps down onto a paved area outside.

He joins Mrs Dahlenberg underneath a high old tree with spreading branches. Before them is a lawn of soft dark grass. In the far corner, a lily pond, its surface ruffled by a sprinkle from a fountain.

"What makes it go like that?" he says. "Has it got a battery?"

"Well that's a question," says Mrs Dahlenberg. "It's got a pump and motor, I believe. You'll have to talk to Clive if you want all the details. Clive's our pump man in Darebin. He has all the bits and pieces for these things."

"Does anyone catch your fish?"

"I should hope not!" says Mrs Dahlenberg. "I'd murder them first. Some of our birds are pretty interested, though. And there's an old ginger tom next door who comes and has a look every now and then."

"I used to have tadpoles," he says. "When we were in Karnook."

"What happened to your tadpoles?"

"I don't know."

"I had tadpoles when I was a little girl," says Mrs Dahlenberg.

He steps onto the lawn.

"Can I see the fish?"

"Of course."

He walks towards the pond and peers over the edge. Red-sided fish are gliding under lily pads, while others just hold their positions in the water. They dart away as Mrs Dahlenberg joins him.

"Did Dr Dahlenberg like your fish?"

"You know, I never asked him that. Maybe if we had a little boy who got to be a big boy like you, he could have asked Dr Dahlenberg that question. My husband's greatest love — apart from me, of course — was almost certainly a kind of fish, but not this type. He loved brown trout. The days he spent casting flies to catch an old brown trout. And then he'd let it go!"

"Is that what's on the wall?"

"Oh, that old fellow!" says Mrs Dahlenberg. "Old Stinky, I call that one, though he doesn't stink so badly now. He's a rainbow. My husband's father caught Old Stinky — and my husband's father wasn't a let-them-go type fisherman. Eat 'em or mount 'em, that's what he used to say. I do believe I promised you a biscuit, though, didn't I?"

"Because you're the biscuit witch," he says.

"I am. And we should see how my TV is getting on."

They pass back through Old Stinky's home and Mrs Dahlenberg's kitchen into the large front room where Enrico is working on her TV set. He has removed the back cover, and is poking through his toolcase when they come in. Mrs Dahlenberg asks Enrico if he would like a cup of tea.

"Si, si," Enrico says.

Mrs Dahlenberg goes out.

There is a Liberace-type piano at the far end of this room, its lid raised up, and bookshelves crammed from carpet to ceiling occupy each corner. The walls are covered with a stripy wallpaper, and nearly all the wall space is filled with paintings in golden frames. One painting shows an old town with a river running through it. Another has a lady in an olden days dress that goes down to her feet. She's holding an umbrella, even though it isn't raining. In the rudest one, a lady with no clothes is lying on a couch. She's turned away, but he can see she has the biggest bum.

"Have you fixed it yet?" he asks.

Enrico clicks a switch, then comes around to the front of the TV and waits for it to warm up. The tube hisses and bars flicker across the screen, but won't settle into a proper picture. He can hear Gerry Gee talking to Ron. A fragment of the Tarax jingle. Enrico turns it off.

"Can you fix it?"

"We take him back workshop, Spook. You talking Mrs Dahlenberg?"

"I guess," he says.

"She like you, Spook."

Enrico starts screwing the masonite cover back on the TV.

"She's sad for Dr Dahlenberg," he whispers to Enrico.

Enrico puts his finger to his lips.

"Kitchen just in there, Spook. Shhh."

———

HE ONLY HAS two squares of caramello left when they pull up at the level crossing gates. He breaks one off and passes it to Enrico.

"Why does she have to go away at all?" he says.

"Do something for the people, Spook. Not be good for nothing, useless. That what she telling me."

"But she's really nice."

"Big house. Plenty money. You see her car? Mercedes Benz. But Mrs Dahlenberg, she say I want to help the people. Helping the people in New Guinea."

"Why in New Guinea?"

"New Guinea, no clothes even, those people. The lady, wear the skirt made from grass, you know? Bone through their nose. All their house, grass. Big storm, blow him all away. All they eating, sweet potato. Vegetable."

"How can Mrs Dahlenberg help, though?"

"She nurse. Nurse like in hospital, long time ago. She go help the people, be their nurse."

"She didn't tell me anything about it."

"You waiting in van, Spook. You no want come in."

A train rumbles through the crossing and passes out of view. The dinging bells fall silent. A man in a uniform comes out of his little house and drags the big gates open.

———

WHEN THEY PULL into the lane, the creamy-coloured ute is up ahead, blocking their way. It's the Fire Sale Friday ute — but it's only Monday.

"It's my dad and Mervyn Reynolds," he says. "I'll get them to move."

Mrs Green's blue Humber is still in the back yard when he walks through the gate. His mother's Consul isn't, but then she's been working later and later recently. When he looks up, he's surprised to see Mrs Grey standing on the landing, half way up the stairs — his nightly visitant, looking oddly vulnerable out here in the open air. Mervyn Reynolds comes barging through their porch door juggling a stack of shoe boxes.

"You've timed your entrance!" Mervyn calls. "Bit of a situation we've got here."

"Where's Dad?"

Mervyn starts on down the stairs, holding the boxes out in front of him.

"Old girl's gone a bit ballistic, matey. Your dad's inside."

"Who's ballistic? Mum?"

"The old cheese, matey. Buggerlugs."

They meet on the landing half way up. Mervyn Reynolds holds out the boxes to him.

"Take these down the laundry, mate. Put 'em somewhere dry."

"What's going on?"

"Need a place to store a bit of stuff, that's all. Just temporary. Somewhere no-one would think to look especially."

"You mean her cupboard? Mrs Green's?"

"Me arm's dropping off, matey."

"Enrico's in the lane," he says. "He has to get past. Can you move the ute?"

"Jesus, if it's not one thing, it's something else! OK, I'll be back."

Mervyn Reynolds puts the boxes down and hurries past him down the stairs. He keeps on climbing.

"Dad?"

There is no answer.

"There you are, you little devil!"

He turns to see Mrs Green at the foot of the stairs, brandishing an envelope.

"Where's your mother when I need her, that's what I want to know! We have an agreement!"

"Dr Schlimmicht makes her stay for extra stuff."

"Extra stuff! I'd be doing extra stuff, if I was married to that one. What am I supposed to do now, call the police?"

"Don't call the police!" he says.

"Ah! You seem quite sure of that! So what have our two nancy boys been up to?"

"They're not up to anything," he says.

"Spook!"

The flywire door crashes open. His father emerges with rolls of fabric in his arms.

"Just shut it, mate!" his father says. "Not another word. This bloody situation's gone on long enough."

His father brushes past and starts on down the stairs.

"There is no agreement!" his father yells down at Mrs Green. "You can stick your special clauses up your arse. You want to catch this lot?"

"Don't you dare!" cries Mrs Green.

"Go on, call the cops, you biddy! They'll sort you out in no time. They know a bloody nosy parker when they see one."

"I'll nosy parker you!" says Mrs Green.

"You want this lot, or in your washtub?"

They're toe to toe, the two of them, at the bottom of the stairs.

"I want this back in my cupboard! My legal cupboard — my cupboard that's in writing. What's in writing, that's the law — and your wife, she agreed!"

"Your legal cupboard is required for other purposes," his father says, and dumps the rolls at her feet. Pink stuff unfurls across the gravel.

"You ever hear of privacy?" his father says.

"You think I don't know what you get up to in your privacy? You and your night shifts! The Melbourne Metropolitan Tramways Board, that's where I learned about you lot!"

"Olive! Olive, love!"

Mervyn Reynolds rushes forward from the laneway.

"Olive, this is unbecoming!" Mervyn says. "We have to sort this out! Have you got a Bex or something?"

"I don't need a Bex, you craven ninny. A man who can defend my rights, that's what I need!"

"Olive, love..."

"You get your hands off me, you snake!"

His father is climbing back up the steps.

"We can discuss this," Mervyn says.

"Spook!" his father calls up. "Come on down. Give us a hand with Mrs Grey."

"You leave my mannequin alone!" cries Mrs Green. "Some things are sacrosanct! The Fire Commissioner is going to hear of this. The Fire Commissioner, you hear me?"

He hurries down to the halfway landing, where his father has already tilted Mrs Grey off balance.

"Big heave, mate," his father says. "One good heave, and we end this now."

"Dad, we should wait...!"

"Right at her, OK?"

"Mum!!"

Too late. Mrs Grey, upended, is already crashing down the steps, and slides to rest just feet from Mrs Green as his mother, in the gateway, looks about her, taking all this in.

"Can I ask what's going on?" she says.

CHAPTER THIRTEEN

The period that follows is a bleak and empty time, with lots of fried bread and arguments about the washing up — it's not a cupboard, it's a sink, his father complains, as if he is the chief offender — and many late nights in the TV room all on his own.

There's not a show that anyone can stop him watching now. No program is too violent or too adult. Alfred Hitchcock, Perry Mason, Heart of the City, The Corrupters, The Untouchables — all the worst life has to offer, he confronts it every night. No matter how bitter this cup that has become his life — a cup over which the shadow of divorce now hangs with grim inevitability — he will down it to the dregs. In his own mind, he is like John Ford from Newsbeat now, roaming through the darkness, paying attention to all disasters and shirking no horror. This, he has finally come to understand, is the true business of being a man.

As for Dr Schlimmicht and his mother — that unlikely pairing! — well, apart from the sheer ridiculousness of the situation, he hardly knows what to think. Nymphomaniac is Wocker's verdict, but Wocker seems to think every other woman suffers this condition. In the world of late night television, this might be true, but as he cases the Blessington Street shops by day, the women he sees don't look too desperate to him. Bored. Busy. Irritable, perhaps. As for his mother, he's never heard her say a single thing about sex in her life, unless You'll be getting sticky stuff soon counts in this connection.

There it is, though, all the same. His own mother and Dr Schlimmicht — the cold fish Nazi who couldn't see a mass when it was under his nose.

They should go back to Karnook now, his dad and him. Grandpa Doc would take them in for sure. The Tearful Earful was always the real problem. With her out of the picture, Grandpa Doc wouldn't hound his dad half so much. He could get back along the creek with Stevie Bell. Him and Stevie could go to school together on the bus each day. To Berinjup High, most likely. That would be OK. Wherever Stevie is going to school, that would be fine with him. At night, he could listen to shortwave on Grandpa Doc's old radiogram. When no-one was around, he could pull Diseases of Women off the shelf behind Grandpa Doc's brown leather couch and look up all the pictures of the naked ladies hanging upside down.

His father tells him it could never work. They're city people now. His mother will come to her senses, more than likely. Dr Schlimmicht certainly will.

"Have you even met him, though?" he asks his father.

"No."

"He might be real good looking."

"So?"

"Don't you even care?"

"She's the one who left, mate."

"Have you talked to her?"

"I told you. She's at Aunty Pearl's."

"But have you? Have you rung her up?"

"She's in a snit, mate. She'll come round."

"What if she's just infatuated?"

"Infatuated? You kidding me? She's pissed off."

"Because of a stupid cupboard?"

"Cupboard and some other stuff, mate."

"Is she a nympho? Is that it?"

"Mate, your mum's no nympho. She's pissed off, that's all."

"But why?"

"We just have to wait it out, mate."

Thickness reckons they are equals now. Thickness only has his mum. Now he just has his dad.

"Doesn't make me anything like you," he says.

At school, Mr Gardiner has been trying to start this thing he calls his Washing Machine Club. This club, it's just for Form One kids. Mr Gardiner reckons if he can get an old washing machine that someone could donate, all the kids in Washing Machine Club can pull it apart after school. Mr Gardiner asks him if he wants to put his name down for the club.

"What night is it?" he asks. "I have to work Mondays, Wednesdays, Fridays after school."

"That's a lot," says Mr Gardiner. "What are you doing?"

"I fix televisions. It's like a serviceman."

"Could be dangerous, with all those volts in there. I hope you take good care."

"You just have to know where to put the solder."

"Washing Machine Club might be a bit bubsy for you, I guess" says Mr Gardiner. "We haven't got a washing machine yet, but we have got a lawnmower engine. Would you like to help pull that apart?"

"What night is it?"

"I was thinking Tuesdays," Mr Gardiner says.

"Is Wocker Spink doing it?"

"Wocker's dad gave us the engine."

"I'll think about it," he says.

He doesn't. Dumbarse Mr Gardiner and his Washing Machine Club — he couldn't care less about bubsy stuff like that. The bomb he and Thickness are going to make, that's more important than any Washing Machine Club.

Thickness wants their bomb to be a dynamite type bomb. Thickness has been looking up Encyclopedia Britannica at his school.

There aren't any good instructions in the encyclopedia for dynamite. It just says mix nitroglycerine with kieselguhr. When Thickness looks up kieselguhr, though, it says siliceous earth. When he looks that up, it says like diatomite. It just goes on and on like that.

Thickness says he wants a bomb where they can light a fuse. If they have a fuse, they can yell out Give her back, or we'll light the fuse. Then if they light the fuse, the gang people will be really scared. They'll see they mean business. Then he can stamp the fuse out, and they won't even have to let the bomb off.

"Or I could stamp it out," he says.

"It's my idea," says Thickness. "You're just helping."

Thickness says they should put motor mower fuel in their bomb. This fuel explodes inside the motor mower,

Thickness says. That's what makes the engine go. He's read this in Encyclopedia Britannica.

"It doesn't explode," he says. "It just ignites."

Thickness doesn't agree. He says all the professors read Encyclopedia Britannica because it's always right. Thickness says they use it on Pick-a-Box to decide the correct answer.

Thickness wants to test the motor mower fuel so they'll know how much to use. He gets the can of two-stroke fuel from his mother's garage and pours some into a bowl. He sets the bowl in the middle of the lawn, then goes inside to get some matches and some string. This string will be their fuse.

He looks around the yard while Thickness is gone. He's sure this motor mower fuel won't explode at all, but just in case, they ought to shelter somewhere. Round the corner of the garage should be OK. He'll close his eyes and block his ears, just in case.

Thickness comes back with matches and a length of string. He soaks the string in motor mower fuel, then trails it over the edge of the bowl and along the grass.

"You want to light it?" Thickness says.

"We probably should go behind the garage."

"Yeah, but someone has to light it," Thickness says. "You said you want to."

Thickness hands him the matches.

He explains to Thickness how in Casey Jones they always have a handle thing to push down when they're going to blow a train up. They should have a thing like this, he says. Thickness says with two-stroke, it has to be a match. He's going to go inside the garage.

"You sure there isn't too much in the bowl?" he says.

"It's just the right amount," Thickness says. "Just make sure you light the fuse at the end, not halfway up."

Thickness retreats to the garage and closes the side door.

"You ready?" he says.

Thickness yells out from the garage that he cannot hear, he has his ears blocked.

Something doesn't feel good about this. He lights a match, then steps back and tosses it. The match falls through the air as he is running backwards, then lands harmless in the grass, its flame extinguished.

"What happened?" Thickness calls out.

"You want to have a go?"

"It's your turn," Thickness shouts. "If you want to, you can run in here. Just close the door real fast."

He thinks of Tina. He thinks of all the gratitude she'll feel when they have saved her. Of his right hand, resting on her breast. He lights another match and chucks it and stumbles back, hitting the ground just as the match lands in the bowl. The petrol mixture flares up with a whoosh as he scrambles to his feet and rushes back until he's thoroughly entangled with a daisy bush. Black clouds swirl up, billowing in the air.

"You going to light it yet or what?" Thickness yells.

He staggers from the daisy bush.

"Encyclopedia Britannica is wrong!"

———

In fact, the actual situation is much worse than either of them has realised. It's Thickness who gets wind of this first. Thickness visits him in the shop to break the news.

"She went and saw The Parent Trap with Wocker!" Thickness says. "Her mother even knows!"

"She went with Wocker? When?"

"They went to Moonee Ponds. Her brother went as well. Her mother told me now. I've just been there."

"Did her mother let her go?"

"She's seeing this new doctor now. He's like a specialist in the human heart. This doctor says she has to loosen up the reins."

"Is Wocker like the horse?"

"I think Tina is the horse."

"But Wocker's in the saddle!"

"We need a bomb," Thickness says. "We need a proper bomb that really can go off."

"We should use crackers."

"How much pocket money you get?" asks Thickness.

"Two and six. Except my mum, she usually pays me, and she's gone."

"We need threepenny bungers," Thickness says. "Tie them all together, that'll make a bomb. We can't just go in the shop and only buy the bungers, though. The newsagent guy, he'll be going Ooo, you'll blow your eyes out boys. We'll have to get some girlie stuff as well. Catherine wheels. Sparklers."

"How much pocket money you get?" he asks.

"We have to give our money to the poor people," Thickness says. "I get one and six."

"Gee. Can you tell your mum we need more for cracker night?"

"She wouldn't like it if she knew we were making a bomb."

"What you got saved up, then?" he says. "I got about ten bob."

"About six shillings. We ought to use your plane fuel as well."

"I need that for my engine."

"You want to save Tina or not?"

Next afternoon, they buy up crackers at the newsagent's. Each goes in alone, then they meet together on the footpath outside.

"Did he say Ooo, you'll blow your head off?"

"He said I hope you'll be responsible with these, young man."

Thickness already has the paint tins with him. He gets his aero fuel from home, then Thickness dinks him and they go down to The Windings.

Under the bridge, they lay their crackers out.

"I could be going to another school soon," Thickness says. "Somewhere miles away. My mum has to see about it."

"Further than Northcote?"

"I don't care how far I go," Thickness says. "I just want to go somewhere decent."

"They'll still find out."

"They won't. Not if I go far enough."

"Someone always finds out."

Thickness doesn't want to talk about it. He just wants to make their bombs.

Thickness has brought rubber bands. His big idea is how they ought to wrap the bungers all together then put them in each tin. After that, they'll pour in all the gunpowder from the jumping jacks and penny bungers, and on the top of that they'll sprinkle in some aero fuel. For a fuse, they can tie together all the fuses from the jumping jacks and make one longer, proper fuse.

"Make a hole in the bottom," he says. "Then make the fuse come through the hole. Then it doesn't have to be so long."

"But then you have to light it underneath," Thickness says. "If the fuse is short, it could go off too soon."

"So how long should it take to go off?"

"I don't know," Thickness says. "Twenty seconds."

Thickness starts bundling threepenny bungers together with rubber bands. While Thickness is doing this, he pulls some jumping jacks apart and tips the grey stuff from their middle onto a paint tin lid.

Eventually, they get a kind of bomb prepared. A couple of dozen threepenny bungers are clustered in the bottom of a paint tin, bound together with rubber bands. One of Thickness's brown shoelace holds their fuses together, while with the other he has tied on several additional fuses from smaller crackers. Over the top, they've sprinkled gunpowder and a capful of aero fuel.

"Where do you want to let it off?" he says. "You want to take it on the bridge?"

"It's just a test," Thickness says. "We can let it off down here. Light the fuse and run. You can light it for the test."

"Is this a twenty second fuse?"

"About," says Thickness. "We can find out."

"Give us the matches then."

"I thought you were bringing the matches."

"You didn't say bring matches."

"But it's obvious," Thickness says. "I've brought our bomb tins. We've got crackers."

"It isn't obvious. You didn't think of it."

"I didn't think of it because I thought you were bringing them."

"But you don't have to blame me."

"I'm not blaming you," Thickness says. "It's just annoying. It's very annoying."

"But you are blaming. When you say annoying, that's blaming."

"It isn't blaming," Thickness says. "I know what's blaming."

"Get annoyed at you! Don't get annoyed at me!"

"If you'd brought the matches, we could let it off. I even said you could light it."

"Yeah, 'cos you're chicken. You don't even know if it's a twenty second fuse."

"I'm not a chicken. It was my idea to have a bomb. I'm the one who thought of it."

"You are a chicken. You're a nancy boy. That's how come you got your nickname. 'Cos you've got glasses and you're a nancy boy!"

"I aren't a nancy boy! You're a nancy boy!"

"You're a nancy boy!"

"Spooky is a nancy boy!" Thickness says. "Spooky boy! Nancy boy!"

This is too much. He crashes off through the bushes, shoving branches out of his way. Fuck bloody Thickness!

"This isn't fair!" Thickness yells. "You should have brought the matches, that's all I said!"

No, bugger Thickness! Thickness and his stupid ideas. Doublecrossing him with Tina. Seeing her the whole time, then making out so nicey-nicey. Why should he go back? Thickness should go fuck himself! Thickness should go well and truly fuck himself!

———

HIS MOTHER still has not come home, and already it's term holidays.

Mrs Grey, bent and mangled, stands propped in the corner of the laundry near his abandoned aero engine. Upstairs, Mrs Grey's former prison cell is bare, the door latch broken, and the door itself hanging permanently ajar. The perpetrator of this outrage is still on night shift.

His mother phones from work one day, pretending all is normal, like she only wants to know how he is getting on. Is he seeing friends from school? Is he seeing Theodore?

"I don't have any friends," he says.

"That isn't true," she says. "Lisa and I, we still talk on the phone. Lisa tells me you and Theodore have been getting on so well. And I know you see that other boy from school — the one who's so poor and unfortunate."

"I don't," he says.

"Well pardon me."

"Are you getting a divorce?"

"Goodness!" his mother says. "A divorce. You make that sound like it's the most terrible thing. It's just a word, really. If there was some other word that could mean I made a mistake, Ralph — a sad, unfortunate mistake — if there was some word like that, Ralph, would that make it easier?"

"We should go back to Karnook," he says.

"We're not doing that."

"I don't mean you. Dad and me. Go back like we were before."

"But it wouldn't be like we were before, would it, if I wasn't there?"

"It'd be better," he says.

She can't say anything to that. That's because he's right. She never can admit it when he's right.

"You still there?" he asks.

"Manfred would like to meet you."

"Who's Manfred?"

"You know who Manfred is. My boss. I've already told him so many things about you. How you love your aero engine. How you've got yourself a job with that funny old fellow next door."

"He isn't funny. It's not a job."

"Well excuse me. You spend enough time in there. And you're forever reading those magazines of his. Have you ever considered how I might know about these things you find so interesting too? I studied physics at college, you know."

"It's not the same," he says.

"Of course not. Not if I'm involved."

"Is that it?"

"He really would like to meet you, Ralph. I think you'll find he's very... He's got a fine mind, Ralph. He's not at all like your father."

"He's like a fish. That's what you said."

"I never said that."

"You did. You said he's like a cold fish."

"There's never any shades of grey with you, Ralph. Manfred is often quite restrained, but quite restrained is different from being a closed book. Some men never let you even open the covers — whereas Manfred, it's more like he holds himself on a leash, but when that leash comes off, my God! Talk about the tiger and his wildebeest. Kingly. Proud. It gives a person a new perspective, Ralph."

"Are you the wildebeest?"

"I shouldn't even be talking about these things."

"He's still a Nazi."

"He's not a Nazi, Ralph. This is just ridiculous. The day will come — and I just hope it comes before I'm an old, old woman — when you finally begin to understand what it might be like to stand in my shoes, for once, instead of this constant carping of yours, this cruel, critical way you have of always..."

He slams the phone down.

Wildebeest. Books and covers. Shades of grey. Always putting him down, telling him how he knows nothing — this is her whole way with him.

She will ring back. She always rings back. She always has to have the last word.

She'll ring back with her if. There's always that if, like he just imagined she said something horrible, when really she didn't at all. I'm sorry if. Well, he isn't going to cop it, not this time. This time, when she rings, he's finally going to put her in her place. Nail her. Nail her to the wall.

Any minute now, the phone will ring. He'll pick it up, and this time he will really give it to her.

But the phone doesn't ring.

It goes on not ringing for a long, long time.

———

IT SEEMS like pretty much everyone can see he's in a shit these days. People are just a bit on edge when he's around. Mrs Green. His dad. Even Enrico, sometimes. It's like everyone has the sense he's ready to explode. Not that anyone comes right out and says so, but he can tell. And this should be a good thing, because people can obviously see he's not a patsy anymore. It should be great, this change. He's finally got what he wanted — but now he's not sure he even wants it anymore.

His father says he can spend a few days at Aunty Pearl's if that is what he'd like.

"Doesn't bother me if you want to see your mum, mate," his father says. "No skin off my nose."

"You want to get rid of me."

"Don't come all your sad-sack bull with me. Go and see her or don't. I don't care."

"Aren't you even going to try and get her back?"

"There isn't any point, mate. We're just not compatible."

"What's that even mean, though, not compatible?"

They're having this discussion in the hallway, which his father has decided for some reason needs a mopping. He's never seen his father use a mop in his life.

"Just means we're different types of people, mate. Sheep and goats. Like we're spraying water on an electrical fire."

"But who's the fire?"

"There isn't any fire, mate. Fire's out."

His father runs the mop through the wringer, squeezing the dirty water out.

"Are you a nancy boy?" he asks.

"A what?"

"A nancy boy? Like Mrs Green says. Nancy boy."

His father lifts the mop and nudges the bucket along the hallway with his foot, then goes on mopping.

"There's nothing like that, mate."

"Nothing like what, though?"

His father stops and turns to face him.

"There's nothing like anything, mate. This Mrs Green's, she's just a ... Jesus, mate, you've seen her. Terrifying specimen of humanity, that's all I can say. Mrs Green and her bloody cupboard — when are we ever going to hear the end of it?"

"Mum reckons when I'm older, I'll understand."

"There's nothing to understand, mate. Sheep and goats. That's it."

His father kicks the bucket into the bathroom, then goes on mopping in there.

Sheep and goats. Fire and water. If the whole problem can be boiled down to such simple elements, why the hell doesn't it make more sense?

CHAPTER FOURTEEN

The change of seasons is well advanced. The shadows cast by walls and trees are lengthening, and even by eleven in the morning, a golden haze still hangs in the air.

On all sides, preparations for cracker night are under way. The thud of someone letting off a bunger or the crackle of tom thumbs can sound up the lane at any hour, bouncing off the high brick walls.

In the roundabout park, third and fourth grade kids are gathering sticks and branches, heaping them in piles to go on the bonfire, shouting and shrieking in ways he seems to have lost the knack of. He leans against the wire fence by the humming house, his face turned up to catch the sun, and tries to picture the current flowing back and forth inside the copper coils of the transformer. These screaming kids could not begin to understand such a hidden, pulsing force. Is this kind of secret knowledge the compensation life has to offer for his sorrows?

Mrs Green corners him as he is returning through her back yard.

"Come on now, don't be silly," she says. "I'm not going to eat you."

He pulls up as she approaches, determined to look her fiercely in the eye, given the emphasis she has placed on such matters of etiquette.

"He probably hasn't told you, has he?" says Mrs Green.

"Told me what?" he asks.

"I've given him my notice. Your father. Notice in writing. Thirty days, and that's being generous, all things considered. So no saying you didn't know, OK?"

"Is it in your window? The notice?"

"Not in my window, nincompoop. Right in his hand — and Mervyn Reynolds is my witness, too. You have to leave, that's what it means. But I don't direct this personally at you. You probably think the sun shines out of his backside."

"I don't."

"Well that's good, because it doesn't."

"Is that it?"

Mrs Green glances down, kicks away a stone.

"You probably think I'm horrible. Horrible Mrs Green."

She sniffs, looks up again, meets his eye.

"Come on, I'm not a complete babe in the woods. Cat got your tongue?"

"Not horrible," he says.

"Ha! That's fine. You lie away. Everyone must tell their lies. Some do it better than others. That's the human comedy, you know that?"

"No."

"You will," says Mrs Green. "So what you doing on cracker night?"

"Don't know."

"Don't know? A boy on cracker night?"

"I don't," he says.

"I'll tell you where we go," says Mrs Green. "Morley Park. You know that park where the big drain goes under, and all the kids play their silly ghostie games? You probably don't even know it. You go down Gowan Street. Everyone will be there. It's a real community event. The Boy Scouts, they'll be there. They'll have their tents up, I dare say, and their flag pole. You should see that. It's made from a real tree with bark on it. They'll have milk bottles for everyone who wants to bring their rockets. A community event like this, it really brings us all together. You should think about the Scouts. That could be good for you, you know. Get some proper role models, for a change."

"I'll think about it," he says.

"I'll think about it," says Mrs Green. "That's excellent. Not everyone can fib to Mrs Green like that. I have high hopes for you, I really do."

Later, he sits out on the stairs with bread and peanut butter and watches the sun creep up the wooden steps as he chews. It's the whole world that's slowly turning, really. He does understand that.

Where will they go now, his dad and him? To Mervyn Reynolds'? They could do, for a while at least. He's never laid eyes on Mervyn Reynolds' house, but he's heard enough about it. For days, Mervyn Reynolds talked of nothing but his wall-papering and his new curtains in chartreuse velour. They could go and live with Mervyn Reynolds and his chartreuse velour for a bit, then head back to Karnook.

Everyone must tell their lies.

When he gets to the roundabout park, the kids have gone. Tina's laneway is empty.

The gate behind the bank is stuck, but when he shoves hard enough it gives way, scraping against the concrete. He steps into the yard and looks around for any sign of visitors — a certain bicycle, perhaps — but there is none.

Some do it better than others.

He presses the back door button. Mrs Bexley comes on the intercom.

"Is Tina there? It's Spook."

"I'm sorry, Spook. Tina's not here. Would you like to leave a message?"

"You sure she's not there?"

"If I say she's not here, Spook, she isn't here."

"I'll wait," he says.

He sits down on the step.

They're not getting rid of him this easily. Not anymore. It's time people started listening to him for a change. He glares at the clothesline. Forty-seven pegs, he counts — and which is the peg for the famous bra? Has Wocker gone and given her that already?

Some do it better than others.

Wocker is a rotten liar, actually. How could anyone believe a word he says? They have no hankies in the army. Soldiers just eat chocolate. They don't have toilet paper. It's such bullshit. Why do people believe this crap? Is it just because they feel sorry for Wocker with all his sniffles? Or are they really lying too, only pretending to believe him when they don't at all? This special bra that Tina's going to get supposedly — the black one Wocker's talked about so often — does it even exist, in fact?

He hears a creak inside and stands. The door opens, and there is Mrs Bexley before him in blue jeans and a hairy coarse brown jumper. Mrs Bexley's skin is like a crumpled piece of paper today.

"What's all this, Spook?"

"I have to see her."

"She's not here, Spook. I told you."

"Is she with Wocker?"

"You can't just come asking this sort of thing, Spook. That isn't how things are done at all. I don't believe she is with Wocker, as far as I'm aware, but that is not the point. What's up?"

"Nothing."

"Then what are you doing here on our doorstep?"

"Did she go to the pictures with Wocker? Did they really go and see The Parent Trap?"

Mrs Bexley presses her fingers to her temples and massages her skull. Then just as suddenly as she has started this odd movement, she ceases it.

"Spook, I know this isn't easy. Since you're here, I'll spell it out. My daughter is a scatterbrained little minx who will probably break a lot of hearts before she's finished. A lot of hearts, Spook. Which is cruel. All this anguish, and for what? I don't know, Spook, but I'll tell you something I do know, and it's taken me a long time to find it out. You can't control another person, Spook. You simply can't."

"Is she really not here?"

"She really is not here, Spook. I don't know where she is."

He walks home in a daze. Mrs Bexley, wearing jeans! And that awful jumper made of prickle hair!

At home, he throws himself down on his bed and weeps.

Eventually, a kind of calm returns. He pulls his World

Book Encyclopedia down from his bedhead and opens the covers of the old red volume. The book's insides are parting from the binding, he notices now, revealing an ugly gap of bandaging stuff smeared with glue.

He turns the pages, anyway, and starts to read once more about the coronation of the King.

———

He wakes to the familiar sound of footsteps on the back stairs. This morning, though, there is no hoo roo from Mervyn Reynolds and no whining from the Vanguard's gearbox in the lane. Moments after he hears the footsteps, he senses his father's presence in his bedroom doorway.

"You awake?"

"No," he says. "Where's Mervyn Reynolds?"

"Other fish to fry, mate. Special day today."

"Empire Day," he says.

"Commonwealth Day now. Big night for us. We'll all be down Morley Park. Serve the old dears cups of tea. Run the ladder up."

"I'm still asleep," he says.

"How about a day for us? Father and son?"

"You got us a place yet?"

"All this whole schemozzle, mate, we need to have a talk, you and I. You snooze on a bit. I'm going to catch forty winks. Then we're going out, you and me. Special treat, OK?"

"OK," he says.

His father seems to linger in the doorway — his father who never lingers anywhere.

He closes his eyes, pretending sleep. He could not be more wide awake.

———

A couple of hours later, his father says to follow, so he follows. Out to the lane they go, but where they're going after that, he has no idea.

"Do we have to walk to this place?" he says.

"Where's your sense of adventure?"

"I haven't got one."

They emerge onto the street. The cream ute is parked under a prunus opposite.

"We getting nicked stuff?"

"Don't start all that again," his father says. "Nothing's nicked, I've told you. Our turn for a treat today."

"Treat like what?"

"If I told you that, where's the surprise?"

"I don't want to go to the airport."

"Bugger. And I was going to take you for a plane ride."

His father opens the ute door. He walks around the other side. He can see a few empty briquette bags lying in the tray. Under the cabin window there's another hessian bag with something in it.

He climbs in.

"We getting Mervyn Reynolds?"

"Why would we be getting bloody Merv?"

"Don't know."

"Merv-free zone today, mate. You'll have to do the dancing on your own."

They set off. The ute's a real rattler, it turns out. His

father has to use the clutch a special way each time he changes gears. He swears each time the lever won't engage.

They're driving mostly south, he guesses, into parts of town he's never been. His father offers little by way of conversation.

"We going near Bentleigh?" he asks at last.

"Don't reckon. There's nothing in Bentleigh, mate."

There's so much he'd like to ask his father, but his father's like a wall. He's like that high stone wall he saw around the prison they drove past that day he went to Mrs Dahlenberg's with Enrico. Pentridge. Lookouts at every corner. A big brown door with iron slats. Not a sign of anyone coming or going. This is what his father is like — a locked up man.

"Is this the fire brigade's?" he asks.

"This old shitheap? In a manner of speaking."

In a manner of speaking. Meaning what, exactly? Everything's always riddles with his father. Riddles or joshing.

"Don't make 'em like this anymore," his father says. "Thank Christ, I say."

How long has he understood all this about his father? Since forever, probably. It's not his father who has changed, who has grown impatient, frustrated. Something horrible and awful has grown up inside himself, and this something is getting bigger and stronger every day. He wishes it would go away, but it won't.

And yet this day, this autumn day, is proving beautiful in a way that almost makes him want to cry. The sky is palish blue behind thin curtains of mist. Leaves flutter down from roadside trees, flickering in the air. Other leaves are mouldering already in gutters, wettish cakes of brown and yellow. An orange sun whispers secrets to the glowing bitumen.

Again, like on the day they visited the aerodrome, they find themselves on tramlines, the ute's front wheels juddering on wooden paving blocks. The whole vehicle bucks each time his father misjudges his line, but then he brings them back on course.

They quit these tramlines eventually, and veer onto a side street that becomes a boulevard. Soon they are driving alongside playing fields encircled by white fences, each oval separated from the next by a stand of poplars. These are all but naked now, clothed only in a scattering of yellow leaves.

Where are they? What are they doing in this place? Is this where his father is going to make him into a man?

On and on the ovals go, the road winding through them, and barely a soul in sight. In the distance, beyond the playing fields, he can see a cluster of darker trees still in their full foliage. He knows these from the day they put his grandma in her grave.

What kind of tree is this one, Spook?

Don't even start that, Dad.

Cement tree!

His mother's fingernails, piercing his palm. They're cypresses, Ralph. They remind us of eternity.

Cypresses, then — and under these reminders of eternity, he can see two long, low buildings that look like sheds, or toilet blocks, or changing rooms. Past them, a glistening band of water. A river.

They pull onto the soft mush under the cypresses and his father turns off the engine.

"Is this it?" he asks. "Are you going to tell me this thing?"

"What thing?"

"The thing you're going to tell me."

His father climbs out.

"Grab the tank, mate. It's in the back."

His infuriating father and his riddles! Stringing him along! He promised!

This tank, it must be in the hessian bag under the cabin window. He gets out and pulls the bag towards him. The contents are heavy, clunking over the tray ridges. He lifts the bag out and sets it on the ground. Inside is a red steel tank with plastic tubes attached. A smell of fuel.

"We cutting grass?"

"Come and see our mower."

His father walks past the block of changing rooms, waits for him at the far end of the building.

"There's our mower."

Between the buildings, someone has left a dinghy on a boat trailer.

"It's a boat," he says.

"No flies on you, mate. And it's our turn."

"Turn for what?"

"What do you bloody reckon?"

"Whose is it? Who does it belong to?"

"It belongs to people, mate."

"What people?"

"People that have a boat."

"Is it nicked?" he says.

His father pulls a key out of his pocket and holds it up.

"This set your mind at ease?"

"No."

"No-one's missing Bindy, mate. Bindy's like an orphan. Lost her parents. It's a bit of a long story, but there it is. A few of the blokes at the station, we look after Bindy. Find her somewhere safe to stay."

"Like here?"

"Not here, mate. Not any longer. I've found another place. First, though, Bindy needs to get out and about. She needs some fresh air."

"I'm not going," he says. "You take her."

"Jesus wept. Give a bloke a break."

"I don't like boats."

"Get the chain undone, anyhow. You can help us with that, at least."

His father hands him a little key. Inside the boat, an Evinrude outboard motor is chained and padlocked to the crossbench. Two oars lie in the bottom.

"Are there floatie things?"

"We're not going to Tasmania, mate."

"I can't swim."

"I've bloody seen you."

"Not in a river."

"Mate, we've got a boat. Boat, float — you get it?"

"I don't want to."

His father lifts the fuel tank into the boat, then takes back the key and unlocks the chain.

"I'm going to need a hand, mate."

"What am I supposed to do while you're gone?"

"Don't know, mate," his father says. "That's your problem, isn't it."

He helps his father drag the dinghy off the trailer. They carry her to the bank, then slide her down the grassy slope to the river's edge. His father takes off his shoes and socks and tosses them into the boat, then backs into the water, dragging the boat after him.

"You'll have to push," his father says.

He adds his weight, pushing until the dinghy is three quarters in the water, only her nose still on the mud.

"Hold her front," his father says.

His father climbs in, lifts the outboard and slots it over the stern plate. He tightens the holding clamp, then brings the fuel tank nearer and attaches the two plastic tubes.

"You want to start her up?" his father asks.

"I'm not coming."

"'Two bob you can't get her started."

"You start her," he says.

His father pumps a button and a yellow serum advances through the plastic tubing. He pulls a knob, then, behind the engine and yanks hard on the starter handle. Nothing happens on the first attempt, but then the engine coughs to life, emitting clouds of smoke. His father twists the throttle, and the engine snarls.

"Going to be gone a while!" his father shouts. "Want to change your mind?"

He shakes his head.

"Give us a push then!"

He gives the boat a shove. It slips away so rapidly he nearly topples over as he follows through, stumbling into the shallows. With one further, not-quite-intended step he suddenly finds he is much deeper than he meant to be, frighteningly deep. He grabs at the boat's side, trying to save himself, and as he yanks down hard he ends up tumbling over, landing in the bottom, sopping wet.

The outboard roars. The boat tilts, and suddenly the pallid sun is in his eyes.

"Bloody classic, mate!" his father yells. "Lloyd Bridges'd piss himself with that one!"

He struggles to sit up, trying to find something to grab hold of as the boat bounces along.

"Get on the bench!" his father calls. "Rest your bum."

Fuck his father. He lies back, taking his chances where he is, but the oars are painful under his back. Their knobby parts jut into him, and he has the outboard chain under his head as well. He pulls the chain away and flings it towards his father.

"Don't be a dickhead!" his father yells. "Sit up!"

He closes his eyes. Soon the engine drops back to a softer putter, and the slapping against the hull subsides to a gentler rushing sound. He eases himself up.

"Want to drive?" his father asks.

He shakes his head. He does get up onto the crossbench, though, facing back towards his father. Rockin' Ray, rodeo rider. Fencing hand and fireman. Bullshit artist. Liar. Rockin' Ray twists the throttle and off they go again.

The smallest ripples on the river's surface are enough to set the little boat to bouncing. He grips the seat beneath him and eyes the banks on either side. Which will be the closest if he has to swim for it?

Boat, float. He hopes his father's got that right, at least.

The cypresses and changing rooms are slipping out of view around the bend, and now sheds and fibro stables take their place. Opposite, a rock wall rises up, covered by creepers. Occasional house roofs peep through the shrubs and trees above. A concrete staircase, edged with rusty railings, zig-zags down to the water's edge, but there's no jetty at the bottom. A staircase to nowhere.

"Where are we going?"

His father's eyes are fixed on the horizon, and he does not answer. Has he even heard him?

He turns and slips back down again until he is sitting on the bottom of the boat once more, his back to his father, shoulder blades against the crossbench. He is cold. His shoes and socks and pants are wet, and though there is no actual breeze, their movement creates one. He shivers.

More playing fields are passing by. The creeper-covered wall has given way to a promenade of houses that face the river across an ordinary street. His father must have upped their speed again because the little boat is whacking the water now quite hard, lurching noticeably. The eerie mist is breaking up even as they enter it. Ahead, just feet above the water, patches of fog are dispersing into wisps that twist and twirl and disappear as he watches. The sun's rays feel warmer on his face and arms.

They round another bend. On their right, ahead, he sees a grassy wilderness that slopes up all tussocky and uneven behind a double cyclone fence. Partly buried concrete bunkers are dotted along the hillside.

"Explosives! That's where they store them, for the army!"

He doesn't turn or acknowledge his father in any way. The army and all its ways, real or imagined, are nothing to him. Explosives. Chocolate. Toilet paper. Who gives a damn? The outboard throbs, and they go on.

Float, boat.

He looks up into the guts of a bridge as they pass under. Pipes and cables. Rusty bolts and rivets. Always the same question comes to him when he sees these old structures — who made this? Were they like the workmen who made the Flying Scotsman in his encyclopedia? Men from the olden days with bowler hats, smoking their pipes? How can this bridge be here, so present, when those who made it have vanished?

They round another bend.

Ahead, a tall brick chimney towers over a low factory. Wagons in the factory yard are stacked with large glazed pipes, the kind men lay in muddy drains. Opposite, across the river, white railings extend in sweeping arcs across a wide green field, overlooked by a long, tiered grandstand.

They pass beneath more bridges, two of them quite low. The outboard echoes loudly in the gloom. Past these bridges are metal buildings, grey unpainted storehouses of some kind. There are dozens of these, surrounded by large parking bays. Forklifts bounce along, bearing drums and pallets. Some yards hold railway wagons, through from down on the river he can see no tracks. In one yard, a giant yellow insect crawls along on six enormous wheels, its yellow insides hollowed out as it hunts for prey.

The river is widening and changing colour, getting dirtier. The first seagulls fly across their path. A smell of oil and kerosene is coming off the water now. They round another bend and pass a farm of giant oil tanks, rusty white and red, with tiny ladders spiralling up their sides. Each tank must be twice as high as their flat over Zelda's Gowns.

This river must be getting seriously deep. Beyond the oil tanks, a green cargo ship is pulled up at a wharf. No river bank is visible at all now, just rows of blackened timber pylons, and wooden barricades, grey and tarred.

He turns towards his father.

"We have to go back!" he calls out. "I can't swim!"

"Don't rock the boat! Shut your eyes."

"Can we go back?"

"Sit still. Think of England!"

England. He makes himself look down into the bottom of the boat. Greenwich, with its line no-one can see. Thomas Edison. Mary Queen of Scots, before they chopped her head off.

He could drown. And then, what if there's a shark or

giant squid? He doesn't even have an oxygen tank. The oars are wood. He could throw them over — but are they floating wood, or sinking wood? If he had to grab an oar in the water, he'd probably panic. Would it hold him up? One gulp of water and he'd be gone.

Stonehenge. All those people dragging stones and hardly any clothes on. Just the druids in their robes and sandals. Artist's impression of a solstice festival.

He is thinking of those sandals, who could possibly have made them, when the green wall looms out of nowhere, startling him with its huge rivets close enough to touch as they drift past.

He gapes up at the flanks of the iron monster. Columns of white numbers, each a foot high. Symbols with red lines through them. Meaning what? To whom? Water — or is it something else? — dribbling from gashes in the monster's side, trickling down the iron platework.

As they glide in under the ship's bow, he cranes his neck to see the claws of the giant anchor, held in its recess by a chain whose links are thick as his own legs. At a railing high above, a man stands peeing into the river.

"This better?" his father calls. "You like it slower?"

"We going home?"

His father revs the outboard and their little craft sits up as they head back into the middle of the river.

On either side of them, more ocean-going vessels are tied up at wharves. Some are black, or red and black. One, blotched with rust, is meant to be a creamy colour. Another is a filthy blue. All are painted the same pinkish red just above their waterline in memory of Mitzy and the Gas and Fuel.

Ahead, a low, squat vessel with a tall funnel is bearing

down on them, creating quite a bow wave. He glances round. Has his father seen it?

"Hang on!" his father calls.

"Go round him! Slow down!"

His father shakes his head.

"We have to ride it!"

The fat green tug is only fifty yards off now. His father hasn't changed his course or slowed.

"Hang on!" his father shouts.

He can see the driver of the tug boat clearly through the glass. His dark blue jumper. His crumpled cap. This driver isn't even looking at them. Straight ahead, ignoring them, and his tug is getting wide and high, its engines really throbbing until his chest is pounding with the beat and they hit the wave and fly and fall back with a crash, rocking and dipping like crazy while the tug boat, all indifferent, glides past.

This tug boat — it could have sunk them easily. It didn't, but his stomach is in his throat as he turns to his dad, whose cheeks are flat like dinner plates, his eyes like empty windows in this moment until he notices his son is looking at him.

"Shit yourself?" his father calls.

"You did!"

"No way!"

His father swats away a fly that isn't there, glances up at the sky. For himself, he settles back, shoulders to the cross-bench, as they continue on up the river, leaving the ocean-going ships behind. The chills in his body begin to drain, leaving an empty, hollow feeling.

They pass more wharves where barges are tied up in pairs, then slip under a bridge so low he could almost touch its underside. The noise of their engine in here is like a thunderstorm.

When they emerge, they are in a new place altogether. Beyond a further bridge, he can see tall buildings rising up — the famous city, where John Ford roves at night grilling his ambulance drivers, where his mother has always threatened to bring him for a proper outfit.

Will he ever get to tell his mother of this journey? On the phone, it will sound so lame. He never could explain.

They pass beneath another bridge and now, on his left, two red electric trains are racing each other, neck and neck, until a third train, coming out of nowhere, zips between them going in the opposite direction.

His father throttles back the outboard, and the city sounds begin to make themselves heard. A vehicle with squeaking brakes. A clanging tram. A background noise that's somewhat more than murmur, less than roar.

" Street station," his father says. "See it?"

Following his father's outstretched hand, he can make out a compact settlement of low roofs, and under these what must be railway platforms. A couple of red trains. People standing on platforms. People walking. He hears a toot, and one of the trains begins to move.

"This is it, mate. Melbourne."

"So what you going to tell me?"

"Mate, it's a beautiful day. We're out in it. I reckon that's enough, don't you?"

"You said you'd tell me something."

"I don't know about that, mate."

"You said we had things to talk about. You said Merv-free zone."

"There's nothing about Merv in any of this, mate."

"In any of this what?"

"In anything," his father says. "In anything, OK?"

"You ought to stop the night shift! You ought to be just ordinary!"

"Mate, we've been over this. The day shift, it's a joke. It's like your mum says. Checking fire extinguishers. Going round to primary schools. Telling the kiddies not to play with matches."

"You could do that."

"Mate, I know you love your mum and all that, and you want her back. But your mum, she's got her own ideas about things, and they're not the same as mine."

"Like what?"

"There's just a lot of stuff, mate."

"Stuff like what? You said you'd tell me!"

His father glances toward the river bank. They're close in underneath the railway station, moving from a patch of shadow into sunlight. Eddies of froth and straw are drifting up towards a high stone bridge where a tram goes rumbling over.

"Mate, you've had your say," his father says. "And fair enough. And I've had mine, OK? That's how it is, alright?"

"This is bullshit," he says.

"I can drop you off. You can go home on the train."

"I don't want to go on the train!"

"It's Flinders Street Station, mate. Famous."

"I don't want to go in Flinders Street Station!"

"Thought you didn't want to drown."

"Fuck you!"

"Jesus!" his father says. "No need to scare the shit out of everyone. Just sit up on the seat. Or sit back here with me."

"I'm fine!" he says.

His father turns the boat around, and they start heading back. Back under the bridges. Past the ships. Past the warehouses. They're approaching the racecourse and the pipe factory when the outboard sputters and gives up.

He turns about, and immediately he can see the reason. The plastic tubes from tank to outboard motor are completely clear.

———

ENRICO DRAWS a map and writes down street names for him. Enrico adds the numbers of the buses he will need to catch — there's two — and marks where he'll need to get off for each.

"Is holiday this afternoon, though, Spook," Enrico says. "Not so many buses, maybe. I ring first, make sure she home."

He tells Enrico no, he's going anyway.

"Least cleaning up you pants," Enrico says. "Dirt and mud, no good."

He says he doesn't care. He's in a hurry. He must go.

The map is helpful, it turns out, and the buses are running. In ninety minutes he is there.

The sun is low and close to setting as he comes around the corner and sees the high slate roof and chimneys with their chimney pots, nestled behind shrubs and trees. There is something new, though, outside the house. A large sign against the fence. This magnificent residence. For Sale.

So she is really going.

What will he tell her of all that has happened? That he didn't drown, after all? That he smashed his oar to pieces, and threw the pieces at his father and he doesn't care at all?

He doesn't know. The words will come out somehow.

She is the only person he can think of he can blub all this out to. Blub out everything.

He passes through the picket gate and up the foliage tunnel. Up the red brick steps onto her porch. Shafts of sun are penetrating the bushes, lighting up the red panes of glass beside her high front door. He pushes the button and hears what sound like chimes inside. He pushes again to be sure.

Behind the flywire screen, a door is opening. With dappled sunlight on the mesh, it's hard to see through.

"Spook!"

The screen door opens wide and there she is, in gardening gloves and apron.

"I was just out in the garden, cutting flowers," says Mrs Dahlenberg.

"I came to see your fish."

"My fish! Goodness, you've come a long way for that. Come on in — although I can't stay very long. I'm expected at the church. I'm helping Mrs Dowsie with the flowers. Come on, come in. We'll see if we can find you any creme-betweens. And you're in luck with my fish. I haven't fed them yet."

He follows Mrs Dahlenberg through her kitchen, down into the room where the big fish still hangs with his goggle eye. The narrow doors that lead out to her garden are already open. He follows her onto her lawn, where a bucket stands half-filled with flowers beside an open pair of seca-teurs. Mrs Dahlenberg fetches a box of pellets.

"There you go," she says. "A pinch is all they need. Spread it wide so the greedy ones don't get it all. I'm nearly done here."

He stands at the pond edge, still and quiet. He can hear the snip snip of the secateurs, then a dull rattle as flower stalks fall into Mrs Dahlenberg's bucket. He wants the fish to come out of their hiding places down among the weeds. He wants the fish to trust him, to come out and let him see their reddish flanks. But the fish are wary this evening, and show themselves only in flashes.

He tosses them their dinner, anyway, scattering the pellets as best he can. For half a minute the water boils as the fish rise to the surface, tumbling and darting — but soon every pellet is eaten or sunk, and the disdainful creatures retreat to their world of weeds and shadows.

He turns to find Mrs Dahlenberg waiting for him, bucket in hand.

They go inside. Mrs Dahlenberg takes off her gloves and locks the long thin doors.

"How did you get here Spook? It's a long way."

"I got two buses. Enrico showed me which ones to get."

They go into her kitchen. Mrs Dahlenberg puts her bucket in the sink and fills it with water. She puts away her gloves and secateurs, then opens a cupboard.

"I've nearly cleaned out all my biscuits now. We'll have to see if you're in luck."

"How come?" he asks.

"We're on the market now. I don't know if you saw the sign. I've got a fine young man from Buxton's, Andrew Young his name is. Andrew's handling the sale for me, and we're getting close, he says. There's two couples especially interested, but they're both still talking with their banks. It possibly won't be sold even when I fly out, but I have every confidence in Andrew. All the cleaning out and everything, Andrew can handle all of that. You're looking rather shocked. Didn't you know?"

"Is this because you're going to New Guinea?" he says.

"Yes."

"When are you going?"

"Oh, we're very close," says Mrs Dahlenberg. "Next week I fly to Sydney for two days, then from Mascot to Port Moresby, and then to Popondetta in a tiny little plane. We're going right up in the mountains. That's where I'm going to meet all my head-hunters, and pray to God they don't want to eat me. If they do, they'll be in for a very disappointing meal, I should think, and I won't get to help them, either, with their sores and burns and babies. Still Enrico, I think, must have explained some of this."

"Did he ring up?" he asks.

"He did suggest you might be coming. You've had quite a day, I gather. You go in the front room, now, and turn on the TV. I'll get changed and bring us both a snack."

He goes into her front room, where everything is just as he remembers it. The piano and the books. The paintings on the wall. The naked lady with her big pink bottom. The other lady with the umbrella. What will happen to all this? Will Andrew get to keep these paintings?

Mrs Dahlenberg comes in carrying a tray. She has changed into caramel slacks, and has brushed her pink-gold hair. Her lips have that cream on them again, glistening and moist.

"Can you believe I haven't got a creme-between in the house?" says Mrs Dahlenberg. "That's what we've sunk to, I'm afraid. I do have crackers, though, and cheese and drinking chocolate, so we're not completely bereft, are we?"

"How come you have to take the flowers to church?"

"They're giving me a farewell this Sunday. A special sending off. Have you ever been in church?"

"When my grandma died we went. That was in Karnook."

"That must have been very sad," says Mrs Dahlenberg. "When was that?"

"I was seven."

"And did you like your grandma?"

"She was always sick. My mum was supposed to be looking after her. She had this thing that was the matter with her, and they were always trying to fix her up. Sometimes she was OK."

"Sounds like me," says Mrs Dahlenberg.

She sets her tray down on the pouffe.

"You're OK," he says.

"Ah, looks can be deceptive, Spook. We're not here forever, any of us. Would you like a cracker?"

She holds out a plate of dry biscuits. They have slices of cheese on them.

"How come you call them crackers?"

"Oh, it's just a name. What would you call them?"

"Biscuits."

"Would you like one? I'll leave them here."

She puts the plate down on the tray. He picks a biscuit up.

"Would they really eat you?"

"I'm told they're lovely people, Spook. I hope they don't — but if that is their idea of how I can be of use, who am I to say?"

"You shouldn't go!" he says.

"Oh Spook! The age you are — it's such a strange time, isn't it? It's like you're standing in a doorway. Behind you, this enchanted place we call your childhood — and ahead, this great immensity that you know hardly anything about.

So what are you supposed to do? Step forward? Step back? It's the most precious, scary time. Meeting my cannibals, Spook — that will be nothing in comparison."

He chews his biscuit and sips chocolate milk.

Mrs Dahlenberg takes a biscuit up and separates the parts, the cheese in one hand, biscuit in the other. She nibbles on the biscuit.

"You must be on school holidays," she says.

"We are."

She takes a sip of chocolate milk, then dabs a hanky to her lips.

"Enrico did ring, Spook. He says you're not so happy with your mum and dad right now."

"That isn't it!"

"No? Well, maybe that isn't it, either."

"It isn't!"

Mrs Dahlenberg folds her hanky and slips it in her sleeve.

"You should finish these up yourself," she says. "I had the most enormous afternoon tea. I was very naughty."

"You'll get fat."

"All the better for the cannibals!" says Mrs Dahlenberg.

He picks up the remaining biscuits and swallows down the last of his milk. Mrs Dahlenberg takes the tray.

"Would you like come with me to the church? You can come and meet Mrs Dowsie. I'll tell Mrs Dowsie you're my young friend, and she'll be greatly shocked. There are few things under heaven that don't shock Mrs Dowsie."

"Is she an old biddy?"

"You'll have to meet Mrs Dowsie and form your own conclusion," says Mrs Dahlenberg. "She's very good with flowers."

"Why do you take flowers?"

"Oh, it's a thing we do. A tradition, I suppose. We beautify the house of the Lord."

"I should get going," he says.

"Well, if you must, of course. If you'd like to come with me, though, you're more than welcome."

In the end, it turns out Mrs Dahlenberg needs his help, and so they go in her Mercedes. He has the bucket of flowers on the floor in front of him. The bucket has water in it, and he has to stop it tipping over.

Mrs Dahlenberg's Mercedes is an automatic. She doesn't have to change the gears at all. She doesn't even have to use the clutch. Her Mercedes has leather seats, and her radio has buttons that you push to get a station. Mrs Dahlenberg doesn't want to listen to the radio, though. She wants to listen to him.

"But what about?" he says.

"Anything at all."

"I can't think of anything."

"There must be something," says Mrs Dahlenberg.

He can't, though, think of anything. Not now. Not like this. When another person says a thing, he can always think of something to say back. But just like this, to start off cold...

"What's a nancy boy?" he says. "Is that a robber?"

"There's an interesting subject for a conversation!"

"Is it a robber? Is it a kind of crook?"

"Did someone call someone a nancy boy?" asks Mrs Dahlenberg.

"Mrs Green. She has this dress shop. We live on top of it. She said this Mervyn Reynolds is a nancy boy."

"And this Mervyn Reynolds, is he a friend of yours?"

"He takes my dad to work. He's a fireman."

"Ah, I see."

"So is it a robber, then? If he's a nancy boy, would he have to go to gaol?"

"I wouldn't say that exactly, Spook. Nancy boy, it's more a silly thing people say sometimes."

"It's like a girl's name."

"I suppose it is," says Mrs Dahlenberg. "There's a town in France called Nancy, you know. My husband and I, we went there once."

"So what does it mean, then, nancy boy?"

"Well, I suppose people say that when they think someone's a bit silly. A bit different. People get frightened you know, Spook, if they think someone's not the way he ought to be."

"Like if he's a sort of robber, or he works at night?"

"It's not a thing I really know a lot about, Spook. If my husband was still alive, he could possibly have helped you more."

"It's OK," he says. "I didn't think you'd know."

"Would you like to put the radio on? It's the knob there on the left."

He turns the knob and Mrs Dahlenberg's radio starts to buzz. When it warms up, there's just violins and stuff like that. Mrs Dahlenberg says he can try another button if he likes. He tries a few. Eventually he finds a better station. They're playing Runaway. He hopes Mrs Dahlenberg likes Runaway.

They pull into the car park of a church. This car park is made of stones. Because the church is really high and the sun is going down, the car park is in shadow. He can see a wooden back door to the church. It's painted brown. There's a Morris Minor there already. It's the only other car.

"Mrs Dowsie is always punctual," says Mrs Dahlenberg. "I know it doesn't look great from here, but inside our church is rather pretty. Would you like to come inside? You could give me a hand. You could help save me from Mrs Dowsie."

"I'll stay here," he says.

"You like your radio, don't you?"

"It's OK."

"You could come in just a minute. You might like it. You never know."

"I've been inside a church."

"You haven't been in this one, Spook. There's a lovely reredos. And for our lectern, we have a wonderful brave eagle. He's all carved in wood. He has the most marvellous strong beak."

"I'll stay here," he says.

"Just thought I'd give you the opportunity."

"There isn't any God," he says. "It's all made up."

"That's OK," says Mrs Dahlenberg. "No-one's trying to make you believe in anything."

She gets out. He opens up his door and passes her the bucket.

"I won't be long."

Mrs Dahlenberg crosses the car park and enters the church through the wooden door.

On the radio, they're playing lots of ads before the news. He turns it off and winds his window down. High up in the palm trees, the last glow of the sun is fading, and hundreds of birds are singing out. It's like a riot going on up there. Soon it will be night — cracker night — and he is stuck here in the carpark of a church.

He looks up into the sky. There are no clouds, which

means it will be cold tonight. There are no stars out yet, but they won't be long.

He hears footsteps on the stones. A woman is coming towards the Mercedes, but it isn't Mrs Dahlenberg. It must be the other lady, the crabby one. She must have seen him in the passenger seat, because she is coming straight to his window. She leans in at the opening.

"She didn't tell me your name," the woman says.

"It's Spook," he says.

"Poor little lamb. She'll be down on me like a ton of bricks, if I know anything. I've come out for my other pair of secateurs, you see — and I don't have another pair of secateurs, so fancy that. I will say this, however. A nancy boy, my child, is a homosexual person. A queero. You understand me? A person abhorred by God. A sodomite — and don't you let a single person tell you otherwise. We weren't intended to make babies in our bottoms, lambkin. Filth, that's what's in our bottoms — and filth like that, that's not part of God's plan at all!"

The secateurs pretender turns and hurries back across the stones.

A slant of yellow light spills outward as the church door opens, then shrinks to nothing as it closes. His hand is already feeling for the release.

CHAPTER FIFTEEN

He runs till he is quite puffed out, then walks, then runs again. On and on he goes like this, heading west towards the reddish patch on the horizon, first along side streets, thumping the fences with his fist, and then along the main arterial, Bell Street.

Soon his eyes are bleary, dazzled by the on-coming headlights, wet with sweat and other stuff. This other stuff is plentiful at first, running down his cheeks, but then he is just furious.

Poor little lamb.

Poor little lambkin.

Her low man's voice at his window in the dusk, croaking how his secrets have been betrayed.

A homosexual person, lambkin.

Babies in our bottoms, lambkin.

God's plan is not for filth.

Mrs Dahlenberg must have told old croak-voice everything. Well let the cannibals have Mrs Dahlenberg!

He pushes on. A stitch is burning in his side. A blue bus rumbles past. So what is he supposed to do? Stand on the metal step and blubber out his destination, then sit where all the passengers can stare?

Little lamb.

Fuck croaky voice! Fuck Mrs Dahlenberg! He knows the way. The red sky, that's west, and when he's nearer, he'll find some other way to navigate. He may be just a kid, but he isn't lost.

In public parks, fires are starting up. He sees them from the footpath, flames leaping up through branches stacked like teepees, sparks rising into a jet black sky. Here and there he can hear fireworks going off, though not in earnest yet, more as a rehearsal for the real thing. He hurries past a primary school and hears a rocket whooshing up behind a building. A crimson shower blossoms overhead.

A sook, that's all he is. A sooky girl. As if Mrs Dahlenberg could have done a thing for him. Because her husband caught a fish? Because of chocolate? Because she has a Liberace piano? So what? Her Mercedes with the violins. Then trying to make him go into the church.

She probably knew the whole lot all along. Enrico did ring, Spook. And Enrico too — he would have known. Enrico was in the lane that afternoon when Mrs Grey came hurtling down.

Babies in our bottoms, lambkin.

They all knew. His father, in the shadow of the railway station where the water swirled in eddies. The way he looked away.

Everyone knew of filth and bottoms except him.

They'll all be in the drain park now — the people from the shops and all the streets nearby. The scouts. Enrico, maybe. Tina too, most likely. Tina's mum and dad. Her brother. Thickness and his mum. They'll all be there. The fire brigade. They'll put their ladder up, the big one mounted on the fire truck. Everyone will see his dad in uniform, and at the end, when someone has to go up on the ladder and squirt the fires out, that could be his dad — and he's not even there to see.

Sooky girl!

He has to wait at traffic lights. A tram begins to cross the intersection under a blaze of sparks. Its lights stutter and go off. The tram grinds to a halt, blocking the intersection, and now the traffic lights have changed.

The tram driver is climbing down. Motorists begin to toot. He spots a bike the far side of the intersection, against a milk bar window. He steps onto the road and threads his way between slow-moving cars. The tram driver must have seen him, because suddenly the driver is raising his arm and shouting in his direction. He has no time. He skirts behind the tram and makes a dash for it.

He grabs the bike and runs.

Running with this bike, it's harder in the dark than he expected. The pedal keeps bashing his shin and he's probably bleeding, but he doesn't want to look. He stops a moment to get his breath and glances back. No-one is pursuing, or not yet anyway. He guides the bike around a corner, into a side street.

He's never learned to ride. It just never happened. Now he must figure out how to scoot, at least. He grabs both handlebars, puts one foot on a pedal and shoves off down the side street footpath. The bike shoots forward and wobbles horribly, but then he gets the knack of it. There aren't any

brakes, or no hand brakes at any rate. He jumps off, stagger-
ing. This is how he'll have to stop.

He drags the bike back onto Bell Street and sets off scoot-
ing. It isn't easy in the dark, with all the hidden edges of the footpath, the judder each time he has to cross a side street, and soon
his leg muscles are aching badly. He scoots on all the same,
hoping whoever's bike he's nicked doesn't have a friend who has
a car. He's not exactly hidden on the Bell Street footpath.

Must have grabbed the wrong bike. That'll be his story.
Grabbed the wrong bike, mate. Sorry. Say that real convinc-
ingly, then run.

There's lots of passing traffic, lots of engine noise, but
even above the sound of his own puffing, he can hear fireworks going off. Sometimes he sees rockets now, two or three
together, exploding in the sky. He's missing all of this. He's
missing the way it's meant to be, everyone around the fire, his
dad there in his uniform and helmet, the ladder going up...

Fark!

The car comes out of nowhere. From bloody nowhere,
and he is... Ouch! Straight into a pillar thing, the bike on top
of him, right in his face, and his ankle... Jesus! His poor
bloody ankle.

Backed right out the driveway. What a stupid fucking
way to drive a car! And this man, the driver, is getting out,
coming over, sucking on a cigarette. Big long coat. The man
leans down into his face. Pockmarks on his cheeks.

"You alright, sport?"

"No."

"Give us a look."

The bike is lifted off him, raised by unseen hands.

"You broken anything?"

"Don't know," he says.

"Must have been bloody moving, pal. I never seen a thing. You stand up?"

"Don't know. My ankle hurts."

The glowing tip of a cigarette arcs through the air. He feels his arms gripped. He is being lifted, nearly vertical. He tries to give his feet some weight. Clamps still grip his arms.

"Can you stand up, you think? Give it a go."

The man loosens his hold a little. He finds that he can bear his weight, though better on his right foot than his left.

"Lookin' a bit green around the gills," the man says. "Where's your mum and dad?"

"My dad's in the fire brigade. He's at the fireworks at the park. I'm trying to get there."

"Don't want to miss the fireworks, ay? Where's this park, then?"

"It's just near Glendale shops. Near Blessington Street."

"That's not so far. What about your mum? Is she there too?"

"She's dead," he says.

———

THIS GUY who backed his car out of the drive, his name is Earl, and he's a journalist. Earl explains all this as they are driving. Earl works at The Herald. He rings up people every day and asks if they want to put an ad in the paper. If they want a big enough ad, Earl goes and visits them and writes the news about their business, like if they've been making paper flowers twenty-seven years, or their great-great-grand-father founded the company. Stuff like that.

"Did you ever meet John Ford?" he asks this Earl.

"The Newsbeat tosser?"

"He's really great," he says. "He goes out every Saturday night and interviews the ambo drivers and the cops. If there's a crash and someone's still alive, he makes them wind their window down and tell him everything that happened, like if the other driver was drunk, something like that. One time, he talked to this smashed up guy in the back of his car — this guy was practically crying — and then by Sunday morning, when the program came on, this guy, it turned out, he was dead on arrival, so then John Ford came on and said how probably he was the last person who ever spoke to this guy, real serious like. The last person!"

"So they played this interview, did they?" says Earl. "The interview with the guy?"

"They didn't play it. John Ford said they wouldn't play it out of respect. He just talked about how it was such a privilege, stuff like that."

"Sticking a microphone in front of a dying man?"

"It was really good," he says. "I don't mean how the guy died. That was terrible. I just mean the whole thing. How John Ford said he was crying and everything. It was just that real serious."

"I wouldn't call that journalism," Earl says. "I'd call that running around with a tape recorder. Who, what, when and why, that's journalism."

"It's a good show all the same," he says. "You ought to listen."

This Earl, he's pretty narky about John Ford, but he knows his way around. They get off Bell Street nearly straight away. Earl takes them winding all over the place, and drives pretty fast, too, because he has to get some other place. He's already late. All the same, this Earl does seem to understand he caused the accident, so that's why he's taking him to the park.

He is just thinking how he could introduce Earl to his dad when Earl pulls over and it turns out they are there, except on the far side of the park. They've come round the back way. The fireworks are the other side, near the scout hall. He can see fires burning over there, and people gathered round. The fire truck with its ladder.

"This do you?" Earl says.

"You want to meet my dad?"

"Bit of a hurry, sport."

Earl gets out. They meet around the back of his car. Earl lifts out the bike.

"You got a sheila's bike," Earl says.

"It's my sister's."

"She's going to be pissed with you, mate. Lights and bell next time, OK, or you'll end up on bloody Newsbeat yourself. I gotta make tracks."

Earl gets back in his car, beeps his horn, and takes off. He watches Earl drive away, then drops the busted bike on the nature strip and runs across the park towards the fires.

Is he too late? He can see the scouts have got their stupid flagpole up, and all their stupid tents are there. As he gets nearer, he can see people are already drifting off into the dark, all the mums and dads with their kids running round them, some of the little kids still waving sparklers. The fairy floss lady is packing up. Two scouts drag some leafy branches along the ground and chuck them on a fire. Apart from the scouts, though, there's only a couple of dozen people left standing around. He can see Thickness's mother Lisa talking with the pet shop guy and laughing. He runs up to them, all breathless.

"What happened to you?" asks Lisa Howe.

He follows her gaze and for the first time realises his pants are torn and bloody.

"I fell over," he says. "Where's Thickness?"

"Would that be Theodore?"

"Has he gone home?"

"I thought he was with you. He said you finally got your engine going."

"Gidday little buddy."

He spins around to see Mervyn Reynolds, muffled and helmeted, ready for the fiercest fire.

"Been looking for you everywhere, buddy," Mervyn says. "Figured you wouldn't miss a night like this, regardless. We're going to crank her up any minute. Guess who pulled the lucky straw? You want to watch me put 'em out?"

"Where's Dad?" he says.

"What do you mean?"

"What do you mean what do you mean? Where is he?"

"He's hardly going to be here mate, all things considered."

"Why wouldn't he be here?"

"Jesus, mate. Didn't he tell you? We had to let him go."

"What?"

"Your dad failed his probation, buddy."

"He couldn't have! My dad? He used to be a cowboy! He was rodeo champion of Queensland!"

"A cowboy and a fireman, though, there isn't any comparison, mate," says Mervyn Reynolds. "You gotta see that."

"Did someone say he was a queero?"

Mervyn raises both his hands and starts to back away.

"Ralph...," says Lisa Howe.

"Did they say that?" he asks. "Did someone say that?"

"Mate, I don't know what you're talking about. No-one said a thing like that."

"It isn't true! My dad... my dad can ride a horse! He can ride a proper horse! You're a nancy boy! You should tell Mrs Green! It's you! It's not him! You should tell her!"

"Ralph, there's people everywhere," says Lisa Howe. "Where's your mother? Did she come?"

"She's gone to Aunty Pearl's."

"I knew there was something like that. I thought she might be here, though, all the same."

"Nobody knows anything!" he shouts at Lisa Howe. "Nobody knows anything!"

He starts to back away.

"Ralph, please don't run," says Lisa Howe. "That's the last thing. We always have to talk. We like you, Ralph. We've always liked you. Please..."

Blah blah bloody blah! Lisa Howe and Mervyn Reynolds and the lot of them, they can all go tie themselves in fucking reef knots! He wants no part of any of them, now or ever. If he wants to run, he'll bloody run! He'll run till the bloody cows come home!

———

THE DAMAGED BIKE is where he dropped it on the nature strip. Its frame is bent, but once he rips off the broken spokes, the bike is good enough to scoot on.

He takes his chances in the dark, zooming down back streets in the middle of the road in case there's another Earl waiting to back out a driveway. He can still hear fireworks going off occasionally, but it seems cracker night is all but over, and he's missed it.

So has Thickness really done it, then — told his mother some bullcrap story, and gone down to The Windings with their bombs? Thickness would have to realise it's stupid, the whole idea. Why would Tina go down to a place like that at night, especially with a guy she doesn't even know? But if Thickness wasn't at the fireworks, where else could he be?

He comes out on the main road, near the milk bar. There's still a bit of traffic, so too much noise to hear if anything is going on down at The Windings. He crosses over, then scoots down the last few side streets to the dead end where they usually go. He drops the bike and steps out into knee-high grass.

The moon is high, but only half a moon tonight. He has to feel his way, avoiding boggy patches, waiting for his eyes to adjust now the street lights are behind him. Soon he can see better, but only in black and silver.

The air is getting colder. He stops and listens for any sign of action up the valley. He can hear a distant revving. That could be hoons. Across the far side of the valley, a mile or so away, he can see a flickering yellow light on higher ground. That's probably a bonfire, but there are no rockets going up, no starbursts overhead.

He pushes on to where the shrubs start getting thicker and comes upon a track. There are lots of these down here, criss-crossing every which way, but he knows if he can keep the moon over his left shoulder he'll end up at the bridge. The hard part will be avoiding all the roots, and not getting an eye poked out.

He keeps on going, puffing clouds of mist, then comes around a corner and sees it in the distance, the bridge. The long span glistens in the moonlight, floating on its spidery trestles. Even from here he can see its underparts are lit up with an orange glow.

He hurries on, hands raised to protect his face. Whatever's going on up at the bridge, he wants to see it, but he isn't going to get involved. He'll hang back in the dark. If Turk's up there, and Turk is... well, he doesn't like to think, but if Tina has agreed to come down here from spite and naughtiness, well, even if they are hugging, say, arms around each other, kissing even, he doesn't care. He doesn't. Tina can do what she likes — but if they're doing stuff like that, he wants to see.

And he can almost see now. There's two fires underneath the bridge, or just beyond. The flames are leaping up, and he can see people moving around. Each time they get between the fires and him, he can see their silhouettes. Sparks fly up each time they chuck stuff on the flames, and he can hear them laughing. Actually, there's only two people, he can see now. Each has a bottle in his hand.

Thickness and Wocker.

He steps onto the hard bare earth beneath the bridge. Thickness and Wocker have their backs to him, their outlines dark against the fires. The skinny shape is poking a fire with a long stick. The other swigs from a bottle.

"Where's mine, dickhead?" he calls out.

The boy shapes twist around, each recognisably himself, though he cannot see their faces. The Wocker shape launches a burning stick. Its flaming tip flies past his shoulder.

"Is this your fireworks?" he says. "Is this it?"

"We had a great fuckin' night," Wocker says. "We had a fuckin' cracker night you wouldn't believe."

"Oh yeah. Was there a rumble?"

"Can't you fuckin' hear 'em?"

"Can't hear nothin'."

"Probably up fuckin' Broady by now. Ninny King and Albert Thomas, mate, and half of fuckin' Glendale. You ask old Thicko here. Plus Turk and all the Rockets, mate. Every fuckin' one of 'em. You missed it."

"We made ramps!" Thickness says.

He circles round, keeping his distance from them, but getting nearer to the fires. He wants to see their faces. Thickness does not sound his usual self at all.

"We made these bloody ramps," Thickness says. "And they goes tearin' up 'em, flyin' over the creek."

"Show us these bloody ramps," he says.

"Too dark," Thickness says. "Show yez in the morning."

Wocker sips from his bottle.

"Don't reckon he believes you, Thicko."

"I'm pissed," says Thickness. "It's fuckin' grouse."

"Where'd you get the grog?"

"Got it from his mum's," Wocker says. "From his mumsie's cupboard. Fuckin' muscat."

"Where's your girlfriend?" he says. "Tina. She show up?"

"She had to mind her fuckin' rabbit," Wocker says.

"She what?"

"She got a fuckin' rabbit," Wocker says. "Dipsy, it's called. Fuckin' pet shop guy, he goes Oooo, she's just a little baby, you'll have to look after her on cracker night. They don't like crackers, itty bitty rabbits. She wouldn't come."

"I brought me fuckin' bomb, though" Thickness says.

"Your fuckin' bomb? I paid half. More than half."

"Yeah, but Thicko nicked his mumsie's dosh then," Wocker says. "Got more crackers. Got their gunpowder out."

"D'you bring my bomb?" he asks Thickness. "D'you let it off?"

"We just brought this one. You wasn't even here."

"Yeah, well I had stuff to do. Real stuff, not bloody bullshit stuff. But youse and Turk and all his fuckin' Rockets, and Ninny King and Albert Thomas, all their fuckin' shanghais, they was all here, jumping over the creek in their bomb cars, right? Like that could ever happen, you bloody bullshit artists! You sat here with your fuckin' bomb and camp fires like a couple of boy scouts, didn't you? Did you bring your marshmallows down? Toast 'em by your camp fire? Wiggle all your woggles?"

"You're a wuss," Thickness says. "Didn't even come."

"They show at all, Turk and these other guys?"

"What's it fuckin' look like?" Wocker says.

He grabs Wocker's bottle and swallows down a gulp of the sweet syrupy stuff. He takes a second gulp.

"We ought to let the bomb off," he says.

"I'm saving it," Thickness says. "I want Tina to see it."

"She's in love with a fuckin' rabbit."

"She'll grow up," Thickness says. "She'll get maturer. She's only twelve."

"It's cracker night, Thicko," Wocker says. "It's now or never, mate, I reckon."

Thickness takes another swig from his bottle, then wades out into the long grass. He stoops and begins to walk round in circles, passing his hands to and fro through the vegetation.

"You bring matches this time?"

Thickness straightens, holding up a paint tin.

"You reckon I won't do it, don't you?" Thickness shouts. "Go up there. It wasn't me that shat himself last time!"

Thickness starts stomping off towards the slope that rises up to meet the bridge at the valley's edge.

"Do it down here, mate," Wocker calls. "We just want to see it go off."

Thickness has reached the outer limits of the firelight. He turns to face them.

"Fuckface, he's the gutless one."

Does Wocker grasp who is the target of this barb, or why? It hardly even matters. Thickness is clearly hell-bent on climbing up onto the bridge, and has a good head start.

He chases after Thickness, not to block him, just to see what's going to happen. Wocker joins in the pursuit, and together they scramble up the rocky slope. He happens to glance up as Thickness, nearly at the top, hurls his muscat bottle into space. He hears it smash on the rocks below.

"You're a fuckin' idiot!" Wocker calls. "I'm not gettin' pissed with you again!"

He is the last one onto the rails. By the time he gets there, his head is feeling quite peculiar. Wocker is straddling two sleepers, swigging from his bottle, while Thickness is lighting matches, flicking them towards Wocker with no regard for the bomb at his own feet.

Wocker suggests they wait for the next train and let it run over the bomb. Thickness says there aren't any trains because it's cracker night. He wants to drop his bomb into one of the fires.

"Has it got a proper fuse?" he asks.

"What, you think I'm a moron?" Thickness says. "It's in the tin."

Wocker asks Thickness if he really means to go out on the bridge.

"There's no trains, I'm telling you."

"Fuckin' long way though," Wocker says.

He steps between the two of them, hoping to grab the bomb from Thickness, but Thickness is too fast for him and scoops the tin up, cradling it in his arms.

"Lead the fuckin' way then, Einstein," Wocker says.

They both step back, clearing a path, but Thickness just stands there, opening and closing his eyes like a stunned goldfish.

"I can't see too good," Thickness says at last.

"Fuckin' four eyes!"

"You'd know what it was like if you had glasses," Thickness says.

"Come on," he says. "I'll go."

For possibly the first time in his life, no-one disagrees with him. All it's taken is a bomb, two bottles of muscat and a freight train that probably isn't coming. Fuck the both of them, he thinks. Pissing round, pretending like they're so grown up. He'll show them.

He steps out on the bridge, and for some reason finds it almost easy tonight to tread between the rails without a thought of the drop to either side or what could happen if a train does come. He can move at almost normal walking pace, in fact, just like he's stepping on a footpath, walking down the lane behind Zelda's, although he doesn't dare to stop or look back in case this magic power might suddenly leave him.

He can't hear Thickness or Wocker behind, but he can smell the smoke coming up from the fires now, and from the corners of his eyes can see the glow of firelight reflecting off scrub. Finally he stops and slowly turns.

Thickness and Wocker are eighty yards back, almost

where he left them. It's hard to see by moonlight, but he has the impression Thickness is kneeling.

"You coming?" he yells out.

The valley echoes back his call.

"He's spewing!" Wocker shouts.

Spewing. He finally gets a chance to show them what he's made of, and Thickness has to sabotage it.

He starts the long walk back. He pauses. On the cold night air he can hear the sound of Thickness heaving his guts out.

When he reaches them, Thickness is doubled over, shivering, a puddle of mush between his hands. The bomb is on the stones beside him.

"Chucky Chunder," he says. "Chucky Chucknuckle. That's you, mate."

"Chuckynuckle Choo Choo," Wocker says.

"Chuckbucket! Chucky Chuckbucket. That's who you are now!"

Thickness looks up at them. His glasses are askew. A dribble of goo runs down his chin. It slowly dawns on Thickness what they're doing.

"No!" Thickness says.

"Oh yeah! Chuckybucket Choo Choo Boy!"

Thickness collapses back on his haunches, his eyes wide, blinking. He is like a trembling spaniel at this moment, fallen from his master's favour. The slur of vomit down his jumper glistens in the moonlight. The stink of his stomach contents fills the air.

"We should go home," Wocker says.

"You can't hide, Chuckybucket Choo Choo," he says. "People always find out who you really are."

Wocker mutters something about crook. He isn't listening, though.

"You can't just run and run," he says. "Like what your mumsie wants. Run and run. Hide and hide. You can't go on like that forever. It's just pathetic. You have to make a stand. You have to make a stand and fight."

Thickness sways unsteadily, like he's struggling to come to terms with this unexpected onslaught. Slowly he brings one knee forward, then rises up to his full height. Two pairs of railway lines recede behind him, curving away out of sight.

"Nancy boy."

Thickness's voice is guttural and thick, like something tangled in his vocal chords is coming loose. Wocker is urging them both to move now, but something in Thickness's demeanour has him rooted to the spot.

"Nancy boy," Thickness repeats. "Who said that?"

"No-one ever called you that, mate," Wocker says.

Wocker doesn't know, though. He doesn't know about the afternoon they both came down to make their bombs, and how they both lashed out — but he was the one who started it that afternoon. Now Thickness has smelled it on him, his fear, in some basic, cocker spaniel way.

"No-one's going to call you that, mate," Wocker says. "Never have."

"He did," Thickness says.

"He didn't mean it, mate."

Wocker's out of his depth with all of this. For once, he is the knowing one himself, the one who must take charge.

"You're the one whose father was a missionary!" he says. "Giving bibles to the boogie woogie people. Bibles and their toilet paper."

"Toilet paper?" Thickness says.

"Powdered milk and toilet paper!"

"Where'd you get that from?"

"Only from your mother! She told my mum, then my mum told me."

"He didn't give out toilet paper. He was teaching the word of God."

"Teaching the boogie woogies about nothing! Nothing, nothing, nothing!"

"It isn't nothing," Thickness says. "You have to listen. You have to open up your heart."

Is there nothing so naked, so embarrassing Thickness will not say? He looks about, exasperated. Beyond the fire-light's glow, the farthest reaches of the valley are in darkness, its boundaries picked out in yellow dots, the windows of houses where people are putting their kids to bed right now, or maybe letting them stay up to watch TV this special night. Above, the moon has her own show, and behind the moon, the stars, that maybe are not even there anymore, only the light from these stars still travelling through space, not knowing that the places it came from have disappeared.

He turns towards the frog.

"Blow yourself up, fuckface," he says. "Light your fucking fuse — and don't forget to run!"

"You know God sees everything," Thickness says.

"Yeah, except when it's too dark."

Thickness isn't fazed. Slowly, deliberately, he pulls matches from his pocket, then draws one out and strikes it.

"Let's see you bloody run," Thickness says, and starts to kneel.

He and Wocker don't wait, but scramble onto the bridge, racing from what could be quite a blast. How long is this fuse? Neither has the least idea. When they have run some distance, he grabs Wocker's sleeve and pulls him down onto the track beside him. The two of them lie prone like soldiers, only their faces showing above the ballast.

"Bit harsh mate," Wocker says.

So has the fuse gone out? Did Thickness even light it? In the dark, it's all but impossible to see. His heart is pounding in his chest. Thickness still seems to be kneeling over the paint tin.

"What happened, Thicko?" he yells out. "God run out of matches?"

A sudden flare of light illuminates his friend's neck and trunk, then just as suddenly the clutch of matches Thickness looks to have struck spills from his hand. Indeed, it looks like Thickness is maybe trying to scoop burning matches from the tin when all their childhoods end.

CHAPTER SIXTEEN

Ancient history. He remembers all of it, and it remembers him, that whole six months — was it that long? — when they lived over Zelda's and he changed from being a little narkypants to what? A person who would happily exterminate his friend. That strange, peculiar time when everything seemed to turn for him as on a hinge, no opening door in the end, more like a wild, disorienting tumble from a spinning roundabout that left him physically whole, but in every other sense in pieces. It was years before some semblance of normality could return and he could allow himself to remember earlier phases of that time — to recall the mornings and the afternoons, the corridors in that apartment, the wooden stairs, the lane and then the creek. Now all these places cling to him, whispering a long sentence he can never quite take in. Time flows, but there are moments when he gets caught in eddies and feels the touch of that other world. Then he has to move about, make a coffee, recharge his tools, tie up a rubbish bag and take it out. Sometimes he simply stares at nothing.

You're like a ghost yourself, a woman who came to know him pretty well explained the day she left, more in disappointment than in anger after six years of bumbling and misdirection. This was Claire. I'm not a schematic diagram, you know.

This pattern was repeated several times.

He tried to tell them all of it, immediately, that night, what a bad, bad thing he'd done, but his mother, suddenly returned, seemed to know it all already — had it from Lisa Howe, presumably, who would have had it from Thickness in the ambulance, or whenever he regained consciousness, and anyway she'd been right there with Mervyn Reynolds in the park.

I did a bad, bad thing! Howled this into his mother's lap, over and over, the whole weight of his head on her thighs as she stroked his hair.

I know. I know.

That moment didn't last, of course. She was so fierce after that, so determined he must not accuse himself, that there were factors, reasons.

It's not you, Ralph. It's been all of us. We all of us have had some hand in this.

She saw they moved on swiftly. He hardly even got to say goodbye. Thickness was in St Vincent's, and there could be no question of his visiting. Perhaps later, Ralph, when everything has settled down. There's nothing you can do right now. He'll understand.

Enrico, that was hard. Seeing the Italian trying to meet his eye, but not quite able to. Left the borrowed magazines on his workbench and rushed out. As for Mrs Green, she was simply silent, emptied out of words. How they all knew what he had done, this wasn't clear, but already word had gone around that Thickness would lose his sight. All the faith and hope that anyone had in him, it went up in that blast.

It all happened so fast, the breaking up of every-thing — and then a slow gluing back together of the pieces his mother and Manfred Schlimmicht chose to keep. All this was down in Brighton, only fifty minutes' drive but a world away in every other sense, in the great cream palace with the motherless Schlimmicht twins. Sonya and Sascha — what an education that turned out to be, eating his breakfast and dinner every day across the table from those little princesses. Birthright, privilege, entitlement — they knew it all.

They weren't unkind. That only made it worse in lots of ways. Manfred Schlimmicht might have been a charmless specimen, but he understood his stepson needed help. Four and a half years at Brighton Grammar — that would have cost a few bob, and there would have been more if he hadn't chucked it all. But he was twisting inwards on himself by then, getting bitter and cynical. Sometimes tears would flow after enough shouting and screaming, but Manfred wasn't a fool and it got harder and harder to find relief that way. Right piece, wrong jigsaw puzzle — that was him in Brighton, and no amount of hammering could settle him in place. Out of that, the mishmash that became his life.

The laws of physics, these became his abiding solace — the predictability of a well-made circuit, then his own skills as an electron doctor, diagnosing and fixing faults. A shallow basis for a life, perhaps, but it was something. In the early days, the work was plentiful and he could easily pick and choose, preferring workshops where he didn't have to face the actual customers. Stooped to his work under grey fluorescent lights, his finest achievements anonymous, and a weekly pay packet. It wasn't oblivion, but it was close.

His father's end was grim. The vipers with their tut tut tut, none of them saw the virus coming. An unlucky knot of molecules, and a plague of poofters was wiped away as easily as you might wipe up crumbs with a Wettex.

He was partner in the business by that time with Colin Wise in Thornbury. Colin was the money man, he the tech, but Colin was always trying to draw him out, bring him to the counter, make him say hello at least. That last year, his dad was fifty-seven and a cowboy still, driving that bloody tow truck with the whole adrenaline rush that must have gone with that — the chase each time a smash got called on the two-way. Couldn't even toss a chain or crank his own winch by the end. Dead from an acronym.

People said Why bury him in Karnook? You know he never gave the place a second thought. And that was true — but then who was a cemetery really for? It had always been a lovely place, the cemetery in Karnook, even if his Grandpa Doc's ridiculous pink marble pillar dominated an entire corner by that time — overbearing in life, and just the same in death. He was able to bury his father further off, though, past the cypresses exuding their dark foreverness, in a newer area where the eucalypts grew up tall and airy, fingering the light.

In the blinking of an eye, fifty years passed by.

———

HE'S GOT to stripping all things back now to essentials, simplifying everything. It's not exactly how he thought things might work out — he had a mortgage at one time, and business loan, and three vehicles in his name — but what a man thinks he needs and really needs have a way of converging over time when the little bank clerks set about their work.

He lives out in the thistle country, north, beyond the city's outer fringe. Power lines loop over his caravan. The nearest pylon is a hundred metres off. At night, the air crackles with electricity. By day, a northerly carries the stench of the nearby tip. As the wind blows across the plains, scraps of wrapping paper flatten themselves against the cyclone fencing, catch on thorns, and slowly tear themselves to shreds.

He makes a kind of living now joining cables, sensors and control units into so-called systems to protect against intrusion. The Alarm Guy, he styles himself, implying a certain expertise, though in truth he barely understands the inner workings of the components he connects together these days, and is relieved if they function as intended, all these Chinese units with their instructions in eight languages. The laws of physics have had their day, it seems to him. Everything is digital now — pure logic, a trillion combinations of yes and no.

His caravan sits on a hectare of bare ground behind a farm of shipping containers. Helmut Cransberg owns these iron hulks, all past their use-by date, waiting to be repurposed. His arrangement with Helmut is informal, but in effect he is the caretaker of these iron casings. Helmet lets him camp down back behind them in the caravan and run a power line to the office. In return, he's expected to show common sense, bury his own turds, and open up the gates whenever someone shows up out of hours to deliver or pick up. What each container holds, he never asks. The presumption is that they are empty, but he is not stupid.

One day, a stranger visits. Anthony di Angelo, he calls himself. Some kind of angel, then.

He boils a jug, prepares two instant coffees. The two men sit on milk crates under a flapping canvas awning. He offers condensed milk, but di Angelo declines.

Come to the point, he thinks. Just tell me she is dead.

His mother is not dead, though. Confined to a wheelchair, di Angelo explains, but still a director of the company, still a force. With Manfred gone, the daughters run things day to day. Acquisitions. Mergers. He's seen the signage across town, outside hospitals and clinics. Schlimmicht Diagnostic Imaging. Not too shabby for the identical brats, and not too shabby for his mother, either. But none of this is news.

"So what's the occasion?" he asks di Angelo at last.

"Your mother wishes you would give yourself a life," di Angelo says. "A proper life, where you aren't forever on your knees grovelling, like you still deserve to be punished. I'm paraphrasing. She wishes you would forgive yourself for that whole situation when you were a kid, and she wants to give you money. She thinks it's time for you to rejoin the party of life."

"The party of life? For fuck's sake, spare me."

"I'm just the messenger, Spook."

"I have a life. She can stick her message up her arse."

Di Angelo turns out to be a subtle and gentle man, not easily deterred. He drops his message line and claims to speak now on his own account. He doesn't say so in as many words, but he seems to be suggesting there could be a path to self-forgiveness through a full and honest accounting of a wrong.

"So you're a priest," he says. "She sent a priest."

"I'm not a priest. I help your mother with her finances — taxation, investments — and I consult to the company from time to time. A waste of a good MBA, perhaps, but I find your mother interesting. And she does pay well."

Priest? Gigolo? He quizzes di Angelo on a few financial matters — how would he invest a million dollars? how is the family trust set up? — and di Angelo's answers sound plausible enough, though he is the last person in the world to be a sound judge of that, he realises. Perhaps di Angelo is a psychologist. Perhaps he is a mediator by profession. Whatever, he does seem strangely likeable. He likes the way di Angelo's dark eyes meet his own, quiet and transparent, so different from the troubled opacity he's used to seeing in others.

They argue through the afternoon under the flapping canvas, brushing away flies. He comes to understand di Angelo knows only the barest outline of his own original situation, and he does not care to fill him in. Di Angelo is far better briefed on the arrangement, as they call it in the family — the way his mother has supported Thickness since Lisa Howe's early death.

At one point, Di Angelo asks outright if he's seen Thickness.

"I've seen him."

"And?"

"I've seen him."

"No-one can help you, Spook, if you won't help yourself."

"I don't want help."

The sun goes down and a chill comes on the air. They wee together against the same wire fence, then walk back through the containers in the dusk.

"You're so near, Spook," di Angelo says. "I can feel it. You could get your life back."

"I have my life."

He bids di Angelo farewell, then watches through the thistles as the red tail lights recede, first on one course, then another, until they are lost behind distant warehouses.

Later, in the night, he wakes and finds he is back at Karnook. Somewhere outside, his tadpoles are in their tank, the little creatures oblivious of the tiny legs now starting to descend from their bodies. Some of his tadpoles are swimming, while others simply hang there as if suspended, inanimate. The water in their tank is cold and dark and still.

———

SOME MONTHS LATER, he is working on a construction site in a paddock out the back of Mill Park where the starey-scaries are throwing up an ugly warehouse of a thing to be their brand new praise centre. His job is laying out the comms and AV cables, and the scaries are in raptures, how the Lord in his providence has led him there to wire up their audio-visuals at such a good, low Christian rate. He's up a ladder when the call comes through.

"Spook?"

He can't immediately place the voice, but feels he should be able to.

"Spooking."

"Anthony di Angelo. I came out to see you a few months back. Your mother was wanting to offer you a gift."

"I don't want it."

"It isn't that. There's been a development."

This doesn't sound good. He climbs down from the ladder.

"What?"

"It's Theodore, mate. He's passed."

"Thickness? You mean he's died?"

"Yes."

He hears a metallic crash behind him, and turns to see the head galah has chosen this moment to start sorting through aluminium battens laid out on the concrete floor. He's about to drop the magic word when he sees the eyes of God glaring at him through plastic safety goggles. Half the hard hats on this job are with the scaries, and this foreman's one of the worst.

"This my courtesy call, is it?"

"Your mother feels this changes things, Spook. She really want to see you."

"Yeah. This must end, Ralph. Blah blah blah. I've heard the message."

"The McGillycuddy family trust, that'll all wind up. The Karnook house, that will go to you."

"What does she want?"

"I have suggested to your mother there might be another side to all of this."

"Like what?"

"Spook, I'm not the one you need to have this conversation with. I've found a place where you can meet. Your mother says it used to be a haunt of yours."

"I don't have haunts."

"I'll text you the address. It's not far from you. Tomorrow morning. Ten o'clock."

"I'll think about it."

"I'll be there as well, Spook. Your mother's not so independent now she's in the wheelchair. Just be gentle, Spook. Be gentle with yourself."

———

He heads out to the paddock, grabs his thermos from the HiAce and parks his bum in the sliding doorway. There's still dew on the grass, but the sun is on his skin, at least. He pours a coffee.

So, that's it then. It's all academic now, whatever would have happened if he and Thickness had ever come face to face — not that face to face meant much for Thickness anymore. A voice in a room. A touch of hands, perhaps — but pretty unlikely, that. When he thinks of his own rage at his mother, how much more cause for fury would Thickness have had if he'd ever dared step forward? It's me. It's Spook. I've come to see you.

Yeah, and you can't see me.

Well, that's never going to happen now.

Tina saw him. Met him just the once — or just the once that he has ever heard of. Devastating, Tina said — just the news he wanted, at the time. Tracked him to the shop in Thornbury, not long after Colin Wise had bailed. Debt up to his eyeballs and left to manage all alone, just when the floor was dropping out of the whole game, silicon chips replacing everything — too expensive to repair, so easy to throw away.

"It's just awful," Tina said.

He didn't even recognise her. She'd put on weight —

hadn't they both? — and her hair was blonded. Looked like she'd had some trouble along the way with acne, too, but she was still short, same height she'd always been. No wedding ring. He noticed that.

"You have to go and see him, Spook," she said. "I asked him when he last saw you."

"It's a long way."

"I've been."

"You going back again?"

"You're the one who needs to see him."

"What did he tell you?"

"He doesn't blame you, Spook."

"He ought to."

"Well he doesn't."

"Come up with me. We'll go together."

"You're joking. You know what's in the corner of his living room? First door on the right when you go in. You used to live there, Spook. You can picture it. It would have been nice there once, you can still see that. A stack of cake tins, Spook. Christmas cakes, all the same. Collins brand."

"I send him Christmas cakes."

"They're all unopened, Spook."

"I can't spoon feed him."

"He's waiting for you, Spook."

She wouldn't leave a card, a number, anything. She'd said her piece, she said, and that was it. The rest was up to him.

He doesn't blame you, Spook.

Well good for fucking Thickness. Good for all of them. Talk about a way to gut a person's childhood — install a blind man right where you grew up, inside the very house, then set him wandering through your memories, bumping into furniture and walls. He doesn't blame you. Yeah. Everybody has their view. Move on. Say sorry. Let it pass. But which of them has any idea what it's like to be the actual twisted snail, curled up in his shell, each time the heat of fire approaches?

At the dinner after Grandpa Doc had passed, his mother left a photo underneath his plate. Rabbit stew, and then he found it. The photo showed the latest flesh-like plastic hood, the fabric straps, the toupee glued on top. Theodore's going-out outfit, his mother said. It would hide the scarring, help people feel more comfortable in his presence. She laid it all out then, with Manfred furiously nodding — Parkinson's or actual agreement, it was hard to tell — the arrangement, now that Lisa Howe had lost her battle and Grandpa Doc had so conveniently passed soon after. Karnook people were good people, his mother said. They were country people. They would understand. A nurse and physio, part-time cook, help with housekeeping — it would all be courtesy of SDI, and all he had to do was visit now and then. He didn't have to make a big deal out of anything. They were hardly children anymore, Theodore and he. He should just think of it as common courtesy, she said.

He did. He sent the cakes.

Just once he visited, saw Thickness in the actual flesh. Stopped by the Karnook bakery to buy an apple pie to take on to the house, and there he was across the way, a kind of broken hobo in sandshoes, tapping his way past Cantwell's with a basket on his arm, the mask thing on his face. No-one was laughing at his limp or claw. No-one sneered. The street was almost deserted, and that may have helped. The unearthly tap and sweep, tap and shuffle, tap and sweep. He set the pie down on the curb right then and there and drove on home.

He doesn't blame you, Spook.

Yeah, maybe. But then old Thickness always was in a club all on his own.

———

THE NEXT MORNING, he locks the caravan, climbs into the HiAce and sets off up the track past the containers.

The front gate is already open, the Dutchman's car parked outside his office. Through the window he can see Helmut's profile against a computer screen. He gives a wave, gets nothing back. Nothing too unusual there.

He turns onto the bitumen and accelerates, a burning feeling in his gut. The coffee, probably. The coffee, and a few other things.

A blessing, that's what people always say at times like this. A blessing in disguise — but if there's any blessing here, it's not for him to share.

He sees the sign ahead for Mahoney's Road and thinks of Wocker up there in the wrecking yard. Bloody moron, that's as far as Wocker's ever gone, and on Wocker's lips the terms has always seemed to embrace both Thickness and himself in equal measure. He has never been judgemental, though, beyond that, and if Wocker's always been cynical as a rusty nail, still, to hear him talking of the old days, you'd think they were some kind of paradise. Wocker would want to know, of course. One day, when he's passing, he'll drop in and let him know — but not right now.

How long since he last went back? Four years? Seven? He can't remember things like this anymore. There have been so few distinct markers in his life since his antenna business went bottom up and he took up Helmut's offer with the caravan. He couldn't even describe the way back anymore, and yet the route seems to have a way of announcing itself. Something in him obviously knows the way, and yet it doesn't feel like that. It feels like he is guided.

It's always so strange and disillusioning, going back. It's awful what has happened to the old place, yet after each return, within a month or so, the real Blessington Street comes back to him, as vivid it's always been.

So he returns.

The high red brick facades confront each other across an all but empty thoroughfare. He pulls up where the chemist used to be and sees it's now dispensing parts for pumps. The bank's become a Chinese loan shark since he last came by, though the old Zelda's still lives on as Zelda's Mannequins, the naked shapes of ladies staring out through glass oblivious to all dictates of modesty. Above the awning, his parents' old bedroom has acquired venetians, but already a few slats have separated from their tapes. The ladder that he climbed to get up on the roof that day has fallen down or been removed. Enrico's old place is still a nail emporium, but they have a sideline now in pain-free permanent hair reduction. Up towards the newsagent's there's a pizza joint and Korean takeaway he doesn't remember seeing before. The mangy carpet of a double shop front opposite bears the impressions of dismembered workstations, with empty cartons scattered here and there. Proudly serving your financial needs no longer, Moorhouse Featherstone have moved to a unit address in Moonee Ponds, a texta note in the window suggests. He spots the Coffee'n'Chat where the pet shop used to be.

At ten, di Angelo said. A coffee and a chat. A bit optimistic of di Angelo there, but that's probably his angelic nature showing through.

He's early. In all the times he's come back, he's never once gone down to see what used to be the wilderness, that secret place of promise and of threat. If anywhere should be obliterated from his memory, that would be the place, and yet it's always seemed like sacrilege to him to go encroaching on that last ground where he experienced magic, however dreadful the ultimate price.

He glances at this watch. He has twenty minutes. Twenty-five. It is enough. He takes a left on Wallace Street and heads west, down the hill. They never had a fixed route back when they were kids, they made it up each time, but they always came out on the main road at more or less the same place, in sight of the old milk bar, just as he does now.

The traffic is bad, tempting patience. He makes the most of a narrow break and zips across, provoking hideous hooting — stupid, really, taking this risk today, of all days — then takes the next side street and zig-zags down till he can go no further.

It's all gone. Of course it has. In each direction, a council mowing strip extends as far as he can see. A concrete bike path divides swathes of lawn. Specimen trees are dotted across the grass like raisins in a fruit loaf, each with its own watering tube protruding above the mowing level. Metal rubbish bins appear at intervals along the concrete track, and by the nearest entrance, adjacent to the sign, there's a doggy poo receptacle. The Windings have become the J.C. Pendlebury Reserve.

He gets out and heads across the grass to see what they have left of the old creek. As he crosses, the railway bridge comes into sight, and this at least is just as he remembers it — the great majestic span, floating on its narrow stilts, reaching across the valley.

He pauses for a moment, taking in this sight, then steels himself and steps up to where the creek must be.

Or not.

Two sloping concrete sides. A narrow concrete tray, rippling and wet. Their creek is now a drain.

What can you do? You can do nothing. Night follows day, and you are powerless.

He changes course, heading across the grass towards the bridge, picking up the concrete path. It isn't pain he feels, exactly. It's more an ache — an ache he's known so long, like an old familiar friend. Is it grief, this pull inside that's always with him, or a longing for what can never be? All he really knows is that they are one, now, his ache and he, and probably always will be.

The bridge looms large as he draws nearer. On certain patches of bare earth the council's seed has failed to take, he is relieved to see, and even in these modern, cleanly times he can see fragments of broken glass scattered here and there. He finds some comfort in these symptoms of unparkliness. Even the graffiti on the pylons does not raise his ire — but the former aura of this place is gone.

He stands beneath the bridge, and looking up, he is surprised to see the moon above, not quite half full, pale against the blue — no centre of attention at this early hour, just slipping by, going about her business. Old secret keeper, silent one.

Soon his mother and di Angelo will be arriving at the Coffee'n'Chat. His mother will be dressed in that peacock cape of hers, rings aglitter, pearls of advice dripping from her lips. Advice for the waitress. Advice for owner. Advice for anyone within earshot. Ludicrous, preposterous woman — yet she gave birth to him.

He leans back against a bridge pylon just as a young mother is passing by, wheeling a covered pusher, avoiding his eye. A little girl on a pink bike with training wheels pursues her mother, riding erratically for the sheer fun of it, for the sheer daredevil excitement the careering movement brings her.

They pass. He puts his hands up to his face. The sheer ridiculousness of everything! He was an innocent kid when they came here. He could be petulant and petty, he could harbour a grudge, but there was a sweetness in him, and a vulnerability. Then something changed. A wilfulness grew up in him, a capacity for spite, a preparedness to wound. All that sweetness in him grew sour and bitter, and eventually was acid.

The human lot? Perhaps — but it isn't everyone who taunts his friend without mercy, intending actual harm, and then when that harm is done allows his mother to swirl her magic cape and pretend it can all go away. Even that day when all he had to do was cross a street and whisper Thickness, it's me, he could not do it. Even that little fragment of humanity he could not manage.

"Maddie! Maddie, leave him. Leave the man."

He parts his hands. Five metres off, the little girl has stopped before him on her bike, her yellow gumboots planted on the asphalt, her blues eyes on him.

"The man is sad, Maddie. Leave him."

He does not dare to look round. He's heard the apprehension in the mother's voice, how any moment that could shift into rebuke for this public exhibitionism. He eyes the ground, and they are quickly gone.

Sad. Of course he's sad. It's been so long since his feelings were appropriate to his actual situation, but he's getting near there now. Sad. Moonstruck. Guilty. Afraid. All of the above.

He looks up into the bridge, its mighty span. It's all still there, exactly as it was when he was a boy. All those struts and beams and crossbars, put together by some great, invisible mechanic — that was how he thought of it back then, though the men who built this structure were probably just men like himself, not especially well-educated, but quietly chuffed to be part of something larger than themselves.

Even now, as it used to do, the steel sings out from time to time as some creak in the taut framework sets off a cascade of vibrations, and just as they did when he was little, the swallows fly in and out through the highest reaches, emerging from the shadows into sunlight, then darting back again.

He glances at his watch. The Coffee'n'Chat. It's time. Even now, there are still a few things he needs to say.

ACKNOWLEDGMENTS

I would like to thank Tom Flood for his warm encouragement and practical tips on how I might bring this work to the wider world.

I am very grateful to Lyn Tranter, of Australian Literary Management, for invaluable advice she gave me on improving the draft she first sighted, and for her unwavering support as she sought a commercial publisher for this work.

It was a real delight working with Josh Durham, from Design by Committee, who created the cover.

For the love and support Marilyn, my wife, has given me as I have pursued my writing dream, no words can ever express my full thankfulness.

ABOUT THE AUTHOR

Peter Dann has written for stage and television, and has worked for a long time as a technical writer. Peter has read many works (including many of Joseph Conrad's novels and stories) for Librivox, a publisher of free audiobooks. Peter lives in Melbourne, Australia. This is his first novel.

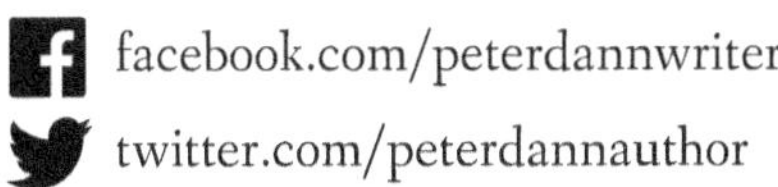

facebook.com/peterdannwriter
twitter.com/peterdannauthor